W9-AUG-250

O Sacred Head

ALSO BY NICHOLAS KILMER

From the Fred Taylor mystery series

Harmony in Flesh and Black

Man with a Squirrel

Nonfiction

A Place in Normandy

O SACRED HEAD

Nicholas Kilmer

Henry Holt and Company

New York

Henry Holt and Company, Inc.
Publishers since 1866
115 West 18th Street
New York, New York 10011

Henry Holt® is a registered trademark
of Henry Holt and Company, Inc.

Published in Canada by Fitzhenry & Whiteside Ltd.,
195 Allstate Parkway, Markham, Ontario L3R 4T8.

Library of Congress Cataloging-in-Publication Data
Kilmer, Nicholas.
O sacred head / Nicholas Kilmer.—1st ed.

p.   cm.
I. Title.
PS3561.I3902   1997   96-44301
813´.54—dc20   CIP

ISBN 0-8050-5033-7

First Edition—1997

Designed by Michelle McMillian

Printed in the United States of America
All first editions are printed on acid-free paper. ∞

1   3   5   7   9   10   8   6   4   2

for Julia

O Sacred Head

1

The pounding was downstairs, on the front door: authoritative. It made the wind rise and snow batter the windows—the snow that had threatened before sleep.

"Jesus," Molly said, sitting up naked and trembling for her children and her life. The bedroom's darkness was confused by light glancing off the whirling flakes outside, tearing away; and by the house shaking, with the storm and the knocking. Fred, already awake, was pulling his pants on.

"It's three in the morning," Molly said. The knocker pounded again.

Terry, in the hall, rubbing sleep into her eyes with one hand and into the narrow chest of her Red Sox pajamas with the other, said, "No school, right?" as Fred pushed past her.

"Stay up here, Terry, all right?" Fred said. "Get in with your mom while I see what this is." He left the house dark while he felt for the stairs and went down. Sam, Molly's elder child, fell in silently behind him. Fred hadn't noticed he was there.

"I think it's cops," Sam whispered. "I looked out my window. It looks like an unmarked cop car."

Another knock as they reached the end of the hall carpet, cold from the draft under the door. Sam was too close, breathing hard with fear, excitement, and the chemistry of combat. "Give me room," Fred said, "in case I have to move."

"Fred?" came Molly's voice at the top of the stairs, as Fred snapped on the overhead porch light so he could see through the glass panes in the door. The snow was rocketing as if it had a lot of gunpowder behind it. A dark space huddled on itself on the stoop, looking up at the light.

"Cops," Sam said. "I knew it."

"One cop. Look, there's not even a driver in his car," Fred said, opening the door to a blast of cold air, a scurry of white, and the gnarled, lanky body that Molly said looked like it needed a shave twice a day.

"It's Bookrajian," Fred called upstairs.

Bookrajian, a stork, shivering and dropping drifts, made no move to take his black coat off. He was wearing street shoes, with the snow already over three inches on the ground. Terry, escaping her mother and running downstairs, was panting, "No school, right?"

"Idiot, you think they send a messenger?" Sam sneered. "From the police? To tell you there's no school?"

"Mom's in the committee," Terry argued.

Bookrajian's face was gray, but he grinned and said, "I can almost promise no school, kids." He hesitated then and twitched with discomfort.

"Upstairs," Molly told her children, pulling her tatty blue wrapper tight around her. She was always prettier when alarmed, her dark curls bristling, color appearing in patches on her face like clouds. The children, hearing something in her voice that did not invite argument, retreated to the top of the stairs and hovered there, more or less out of sight.

"What's up?" Fred asked.

"A mess," Bookrajian said. He was embarrassed, or distraught. He wore no gloves. He rubbed his knuckly fingers while he talked. "I'd appreciate it if you could come for a ride with me, Fred. Can you do that?"

"You got a warrant?" Molly demanded. Snow, acting for her, tapped impatiently at the house. Molly had never cottoned to Bookrajian.

"I shouldn't be here, and I don't have time," Bookrajian said. "Warrant? What for? Something came up, Fred, and I thought of you. If you've got nothing better to do."

"I'll put some shoes on," Fred said, turning for the stairs. He didn't really know Bookrajian, a Cambridge cop who was over the border and out of his jurisdiction at Molly's house in Arlington. They'd met in the course of business, and each had quickly realized the other was a hard man to get around.

When Fred came down, wearing his Korean knockoffs of L. L. Bean half-treads and enough clothes to keep him warm, Molly and Bookrajian were facing each other in the hall like boxers who hate each other anyway but are not being paid enough to get hurt.

"One thing I know," Bookrajian said, "it looks like snow." He opened the door. "You want to ride with me?"

Fred looked at the weather and thought about captivity. "I'll follow you," he said. "Give me thirty seconds to warm up old Betsy." Bookrajian started wading down Molly's walk toward his car. The snow was up to his shoe tops. Molly's car being in the garage, Fred had left his in the drive. He knocked snow off the windows while the engine warmed. He took his time. The engine needed two minutes at least.

"Just for fun, where are you going?" Molly called.

"Cambridge," Bookrajian shouted before his door thwocked closed.

The storm was a phenomenon, filled with beauty, mystery, action, and snowplows that were not making much headway. Aside from the plows, almost nothing was on the road other than drifts and broken branches. Bookrajian drove too fast along Massachusetts Avenue, through the center of Arlington, disregarding traffic lights and natural hazards. He turned right along the parkway toward Fresh Pond and Cambridge. Fred, following, tried his radio for a hint of what was happening, but the radio hadn't worked in six years, except once in a long while, if you fiddled with it just right. Driving with one hand in these conditions wasn't bright. Their speed, the packed silence under the wheels, and the turbulence outdoors made nothing real, until they reached the pack of frolicking blue lights in the horseshoe driveway at 1001 Memorial Drive, the apartment building with the Gucci and Godiva reputation, next to the river. Enough cops were gathered around the bastion of the gown to fend off all the townie rabble of Cambridge.

Fred found a place to park away from the snarl of strobes packed against the building. When he joined him at the entrance, under the canopy, Ernie—Fred suddenly remembered Bookrajian's first name—was bawling out a knot of uniformed officers. "Cut off those lights and keep it down. What's the matter, you don't have enough excitement in your lives, you got to start a circus every time the phone rings? Are the medics and techies here yet?"

"In the hall upstairs," someone said. "Waiting on you. You said no one goes in—no one went in."

A crowd of wakeful sleepers from the building stood in the lobby in varied dishabille, worried, talking among themselves like strangers at a bomb site. The crowd made Fred feel strangely nervous until he realized why: he saw no one under the age of thirty. Back of the desk, the uniformed night watchperson was tearing her hair and crying, saying something Fred couldn't catch about "the manager." A cop stood over her, in back of the counter.

"They don't look like much," Bookrajian muttered, leading Fred through the chunky slop that was building up in ridges on the plate-glass lobby's upscale neutral carpeting, "especially in their nightshirts, but there's more Nobel Prizes and Pulitzers and would-be Dershowitzes and whatnot-have-you per pound in that gang than there is peanuts in a Snickers. That means enough potential interference to derail Amtrak's finest, once they get past their shock and start shoving in their two centses—so let's move."

A cop in uniform stood at the bank of elevators. Nobody was getting back upstairs, not even residents. They were not getting outside, either, and they were not making phone calls. Bookrajian had this thing, whatever it was, sealed off.

Closed into the elevator, which smelled of the canned hope they spray into used cars, Fred listened to the whisk of packaged speed upward and asked, "You want to fill me in, Ernie?"

"Anything I could say would only get in your way," Bookrajian said, shrugging out of his coat. "I took one look around and thought of you. You're sneaky and you're tricky and you put something over on me on that Cover-Hoover thing. But so what? The IRS is gonna get her. The IRS is like pneumonia—the old cop's friend."

The elevator stopped on the seventh floor, and the door opened. About twenty cops jostled in the hallway, watching each other, dripping on the carpet, some, in plain clothes and lab coats, unpacking the instruments appropriate to a crime scene. One youngster with a spool of yellow crime-scene tape stood wondering how to use it in a corridor.

"Also," Bookrajian said, heading along the hallway, "I can talk to you. I go to an expert at that college down the river, I spend all my time worrying how much he has to pay to have his undies washed in French Champagne. So if you can help, you save me some aggravation, OK?"

At the end of the hall, a female linebacker in uniform faced them from the place where she was planted, blocking entrance to 710. She and Bookrajian exchanged nods. Nature had intended her to be black, but she was mostly greenish-gray. "No one's been in?" Bookrajian questioned.

"Sweet mother of Jesus, no," the officer said. She took a deep breath. "Nobody got past Gus, either. He's on the fire exit."

Bookrajian dropped his coat on the carpet and knelt to take his wet shoes off. He motioned Fred to follow suit. "Don't want to complicate things, tracking stuff inside," he said. "We've got plenty to keep my techies happy as it is."

"Sweet Jesus knows that's true," the guard affirmed, handing over two pairs of latex gloves. Fred, standing in his socks, pulled his on.

"Give me six minutes," Bookrajian announced to the hall. "After, I want the photo people first, then the medics and techies. I am going to say this once: if one photograph gets to the press, you are all going to wish you had it as easy as this guy did." He opened the door with the key the guard handed him, telling Fred over his shoulder, "Did I mention it's not pretty?"

The look of the woman at the door had prepared Fred for the stench of decay, but the air that met them in the dark apartment was bland and recycled, like airplane air after a long trip. Beige, Molly would call it. Fred followed Bookrajian into the dark and heard the door close while his eyes adjusted to the gloom, enlivened by light cast into the distant rooms by snow thrashing big windows that must overlook the river. They passed through a niggly entranceway with closets. The kitchenette off it hummed from an exhaust fan. It smelled like breakfast. Then quickly they were in a big dark space that should be the living room: silhouette of a couch next to the window filled with the glancing storm, and the river lighted by streetlights on either side, and plows working the far side, along Storrow Drive; silhouettes of end tables and oversized lamps with big stupid shades on the right, either end of the couch. On the left, a naked body leaned out oddly from the wall—correction: mantelpiece—whiter than the darkness in the room, but darker than the snow behind it, in the window. Bookrajian fumbled at the wall. The body gestured a welcome. It looked very wrong.

"Don't touch anything," Bookrajian warned. "I can't find the switch." Fred waited until the lamps at either end of the couch came on. The corpse was headless, adult, male, in that order— propped strangely, the arms splayed out along the mantelpiece. Bookrajian, saying, "Got it," found another light, a spot, that fell above the headless corpse, where its head should be, illuminating a brown painting that gave Fred a little jolt, its being the head of Christ, crowned with thorns, pop-eyed with meretricious agony. A matched set of china dogs pointed in eager attendance, one on each side.

"Jesus," Fred said.

The wrists of the headless corpse were nailed to the mantelpiece, and the nails checked his aborted looping-forward, swan-dive arc. The ringed neck was ragged but almost bloodless. The bunched mess at the man's genitals resolved itself into pink ribbon tied in a florist's flourish around the penis.

"So much decoration makes me uneasy," Fred said.

"Artistic but not pretty," Bookrajian agreed.

"Therefore you thought of me," Fred answered, swallowing bile, still taking in the scene. The corpse's feet—not nailed—were splayed to either side like those of da Vinci's perfect gentleman. The object appearing between them, behind the Easter ribbon, looked like a foot and a half of broom handle; so the rest of it was stored inside.

"Incidentally," Bookrajian said, "anybody asks you, you were never here, you got that? What are those, about twelve-penny nails? Fourteens?"

"Twenties," Fred said. "Common. Galvanized. They won't rust. He'll be fine." The palms of the man's hands, pulled into weak grasping gestures by the weight of his body against the nails, were black, crusty. Bookrajian, noticing the direction of Fred's gaze, said, "They're burned. Frying pan in the kitchen. All I want you for is the artwork."

Fred looked again at the painting of Jesus in agony. A nimbus of coincidental holiness lit the brown sky in back of him. Drops of blood leaked from the forehead where the thorns had pierced the skin. The thorns cast shadows on his face. The painting had quality: Fred's original instinct had been to write it off as a holy card turned out before lithography could do it cheaper.

"So tell me about the artwork," Bookrajian demanded. "I gotta get moving."

The gilded frame looked like about two hundred dollars' worth to Fred. As for the painting itself—Fred moved in closer, aware of the intimate scents of the man's opened neck, and the sharp char of the hands. The fireplace had not been used. Dried flowers hunched in it, in a vase in back of the hanging broomstick. Fred noted the remarkable length of the corpse's foreskin, from which the bow was a distraction. Once past all that, the painting was not badly done for what it was, putting aside the subject matter, which, gruesome and sentimental, was not Fred's cup of tea.

"Oil on canvas," Fred said. "You'll want to put a tape on it, but I'd say about twenty-four by twenty inches, and it's old, maybe—let's see the back, Ernie."

"Someone went to a lot of trouble to make this look right," Bookrajian said, "let's not mess it up. If you want, we'll lean it forward. We can do that without moving anything. I'll hold it. You look."

The china dogs wobbled and chattered when the painting was tipped to expose its backside. The canvas was brown and stiff, mended in one place with silver duct tape, a do-it-yourself repair Fred hadn't noticed the need for from the front—there was too much information coming in at once. They had to handle the painting and examine it without rubbing against the naked, wounded body.

"I'm noticing this blackened area," Fred said. The center of the canvas, behind the victim's face, was dark. It smelled like ironing. The stretcher was old but not remarkable. Fred was not that familiar with the materials of the Old Masters; he was more comfortable from the early nineteenth century on. "Nothing written on it anywhere," Fred said, "unless there's something under the tape."

"Don't touch that," Bookrajian barked.

"Of course not."

They leaned the painting back into place, where it more or less served as the missing portion of the corpse. A jostle and knocking at the door made Bookrajian shout, "Hold it!" He looked at Fred. "Well?"

"Italian," Fred said, deciding. "The image and the execution are seventeenth-century. I can't place the object with an exact date. Say sixteen fifty, give or take thirty years. It could be a good copy made later. It's by someone who repents of Mannerism, who's concluded Caravaggio is full of shit. Or, as I say, it's a good copy. I don't need to mention that the subject is not original: just in seventeenth-century Italy, there must have been maybe three hundred painters—"

"Look," Bookrajian interrupted, "in five minutes I am going to have the Staties in here, and the Fibbies, and for all I know the fucking CI and A, and besides them I am up to the ass in my own experts. We are in a building where next thing I know, they say the king of Thailand keeps his pad here, for him and his thirteen snow-bunnies, and he would appreciate it if we don't make trouble. Everyone is going to read this their own way and fight to make their version true. All I want is to keep it simple. What I need from you is, so I know if it's an issue, tell me what that painting is worth."

"There's no blood," Fred observed.

"Plenty in the bathroom. What do you say, Fred? Are we looking at real money here?"

"Depending on who it's by and if anyone cares and if it's not a copy, between five thousand and a quarter of a million bucks," Fred said, "for a seat-of-the-pants guess. The market for a holy picture is real soft, even if it were a Van Dyke or a Rubens— which it ain't, if it's Italian."

Bookrajian grunted with disgust. "As long as you're here, look around and see if there's other artwork you can tell me is worth something. Stay out of the bathroom." He shouted at the door, or maybe at Fred, "One minute." Snow was beating against the big window. Fred had lost track of the storm, what with the corpse and the painting.

There was nothing more in this room but travel posters in

9

Nielsen frames showing bikinied women at peace, or exercising, in luscious and exotic places. Fred followed Bookrajian through the entry passage again, and through the kitchenette, whose fan still worked to exhaust the odor of fried fingerprints, and into a master bedroom as bland and beige as the rest of the place. The bedroom enjoyed its own luxurious spread of window over the river, opposite a wall of mirror against which leaned an overearnest still-life painting of zinnias, over-the-sofa size, in an appropriate frame.

Fred told Bookrajian, "That big Jane Peterson set somebody back about twenty grand if they were fool enough to buy it on Newbury Street. Peterson's a false market—but then what market isn't?"

"I've gotta let my people in," Bookrajian said, moving himself and Fred toward the door.

"I'd guess the flowers used to be over the mantelpiece," Fred said, "until this recent decorator got more avant-garde ideas."

"You can't help me with the Jesus picture, that's what you're saying?" Bookrajian asked, standing inside the door and almost pleading.

"Get me a good photo. I'll see what I can do."

2

M y theory is the heater and the radio are connected," Fred told Molly, shedding cold air from his clothes into a kitchen warm with the scents of coffee and bacon. It had taken him about two hours to fight the elements back to Arlington. He'd expected to find Molly's house asleep.

Molly, at her kitchen table, was in jeans and a big green sweater of Fred's, under the blue wrapper she'd put on again after she dressed. She had coffee in front of her, and she looked furtive, like someone who had just hidden a smoldering cigarette butt on her person. She'd been worrying.

"You're not going out in this?" Fred said.

"What did Bookrajian want?" Molly asked. "And what took you so long? An hour ago I started hearing the wolves of Arlington ripping the frozen flesh off your bones."

"They're coyotes," Fred said. "And they're supposed to be in Brookline. The roads were bad."

"I have a question on the table," Molly insisted.

Fred, pouring coffee, started describing the drive home.

"I can look out the window and see that," said Molly. She could sense the drag of trouble on him.

"Also, I stopped on the way home, just to stop. This thing was pretty awful. A murder Bookrajian had." Fred stopped. A silence lengthened between them.

"No, I am not going in to the library today," Molly said. "Walter called early. He said if they do open, the Cambridge contingent will handle it. Sit down and tell me about Bookrajian's murder, or else tell me you aren't going to tell me. You want bacon?"

"I'll wait," Fred said. He sat across the table from Molly and drew thorns with his index finger, extending outward from a spill of coffee on the flowered oilcloth. "The reason he wanted me was to help him understand a picture. It was at One-oh-oh-one Mem Drive, the murder. In one of those apartments."

"My God!" Molly said. "Who died? Fred, everyone lives there except Dershowitz and Julia Child and Kenneth Galbraith."

"Look," Fred said. "I feel like I'm coming into your house covered with dog shit. I almost didn't come back, thinking—Molly, it was ugly. It still *is* ugly. It makes a scum of prurient violence that I can't shake. If *I'm* here, *it's* here. I almost drove to Charlestown. I've got a right to my bed there, even if Teddy's in it. Then I thought . . ."

"Tell me about the picture."

"It's part of such an elaborate mess—I feel as if I'd been given a thirty-second look at the Sistine Chapel during an earthquake, then been asked to testify, on oath, what happened."

"So," Molly said, "what happened?" Snow howled around the backyard and rattled the branches of the pear tree against the window over the sink.

"I can't get loose from it," Fred said. "The tableau clouds my judgment, like a phrase you can't get rid of from a song, or the stomping you experience from a powerful scene in a play that, whether it's good or bad, you've been so kicked around by that you can't tell what happened, or what you think about it, or what, if anything, it means."

"So what's the picture?"

The bacon smelled like the burned hands of a headless corpse with a ribbon on its dick and twenty-penny galvanized common nails hammered through its wrists—from which only a small quantity of liquid, blood and lymph, had leaked, despite that provocation.

"God knows Bookrajian doesn't want me interfering with the larger picture—but he hauled me into a whole triple crosstick. I'm not capable of limiting my attention to line seventeen down— two words, eight letters, meaning 'Look at that guy.' "

Molly said, "Snow makes me hungry. If you don't want that bacon, I'll have it." She reached over to the stove and got the plate she'd been keeping warm there.

"On the theory that appearance is or is not reality," Fred said, "pretend you are Erwin Panofsky looking at a really complex Baroque painting that I will now describe to you. Tell me how you'd read the iconography, or the symbolism, of this scene."

Molly wrapped soft white bread around a sheaf of bacon strips and took a bite. "I am prepared for ugly. Go on."

"To quote Bookrajian, 'artistic but not pretty.' " Fred described the scene as accurately as he could, while trying to avoid terms that demanded sympathetic suffering from the audience. The nudity, the nails, the broom handle, the ribbon, and the lack of a head made this hard, even though he had had plenty of time to rehearse during the cold drive from Cambridge. Molly listened solemnly to the catalog of grief and orchestrated mayhem, until Fred felt he'd fleshed out the horrible icon sufficiently. Molly took the last bite of her bacon roll and polished her fingers on a scrap of paper towel printed with tulips, studying the image Fred had painted between them in the air. She stared at it until Fred concluded that her mind was wandering or overloaded.

"What do you think?" he prompted. "How would you read that?"

"Maybe the man owed someone a good deal of money," Molly suggested.

"And all this other nonsense?"

"It could be nonsense," Molly said. "Especially if our starting point is the proposition that appearance is reality." She readied her fingers to count as she made suggestions. "Aside from accidents and suicide, which it sounds like we can rule out, either someone hated the guy, or he owed someone money, or someone owed *him* money, or he was part of a domestic arrangement that got crowded, or he had something somebody wanted, or . . ."

"Or he was unlucky in love," Fred said. He was hungry now that the bacon was gone.

Terry came in, calling, "Fred, will you take us sledding?" She was in her pajamas, her fine tan hair matted with a combination of sleep and her defiantly independent efforts to brush it. She looked him over and added, "Or do you have to shave first?"

"Now we change the subject, but 'unlucky in love' sounds good," Molly said. "I'm sure that's how Panofsky would have viewed it."

"We'll see how the snow builds, then go out," Fred told Terry. "There's not much we can do while it's coming down. But it's already deep—you won't be going to school tomorrow, either. Why should I shave if you don't have to go to school?"

"I know: grow a beard, Fred. It's so deep already, if we had a dog, we couldn't see him," Terry said. "We need a dog. Sam's only going to sleep and waste the whole entire day off."

Fred got up and stretched. Molly, saying, "Let's see what the weather people say," crossed the kitchen and turned on the radio she kept over the sink. She found a station that made a point of turning every storm into an orgy of anxious information. Traffic was said to be at a zero, ships were being battered in the Atlantic, two feet of snow were reported to be paralyzing Logan Airport, and there was no end in sight because the storm was stalled, comfortable where it was. "Meanwhile," the glutinous male voice went on, "this just in: word of a bizarre sex killing in Cambridge, apparently the work of a bizarre religious cult . . ."

Molly killed the radio. Terry shrieked, "You guys ate all the bacon! I smell bacon."

• • •

When Fred stretched out on Molly's bed upstairs, he felt restless. He'd already called Clayton Reed. They'd agreed they had nothing stirring that was of enough consequence to justify Fred's mushing in to Boston. Clay could spend his day happily enough reading or prowling around his house on Beacon Hill, gloating over his pictures.

Fred's plan had been to lie down for ten minutes and then to try to wash off some of the grime of death by standing under the shower of the new bathroom he had caused to be built off Molly's bedroom. He would not shave. Then he'd sleep for a few hours. But the business Bookrajian had brought him into in Cambridge shrieked for his attention, even though the painting Bookrajian wanted Fred to think about was nothing that either Fred or Clay would normally take an interest in.

Fred got up from the bed. The holy picture, because of the circumstances of its discovery, would not let him rest. He stood next to Molly's window. Twisting armfuls of whiteness howled and thrashed against the glass like Jupiter disguised as a snowstorm. "I'm screwed," Fred said, and he went to take a shower. Under the hot splash of water, he worried at the retinal image of the painting, all the while cursing at himself, "Who cares? It's not that good a picture. It's about right for the mortician's calendar Molly's mother gets for free and gives Molly for Christmas every year."

When Molly came into the bedroom, Fred was standing next to the bed, naked and wet, saying, "Shit! This isn't going to let me alone. I've got to get to a library."

"You're not going far unless you put on at least a ribbon, Fred."

Fred started pulling his clothes on again, then stopped and went for a towel. He'd been distracted, suddenly recalling a Rembrandt at the Fogg of almost the same subject, and the same period as well—a small painting, tender, modest, with a Flemish tact that showed the painting at 1001 Memorial Drive for the vulgar thing it was: worse than the Peterson.

"Ecce homo," Fred said. "Those were Pilate's words, introducing the condemned criminal to the people, right?"

Molly said, "Speaking of *ecce homo*, who was the guy?"

"What guy?"

"The guy you dropped in on this morning with our friend Bookrajian. You neglected to mention. The one without a head? Nailed to the mantelpiece? Maybe his mother's looking for him."

"The subject didn't come up," Fred said. He started dressing.

"Curious. Maybe the mother in me made me wonder."

Fred heard an ominous crackle in Molly's maternal reference. She and her kids were having the grand windfall of a snow day, and Fred, the stranger in their midst, was reading the signs wrong, preparing to abandon the homestead for research.

"I thought I'd roust Sam out," Fred said, "before I go into Cambridge. We'll shovel some of this snow. Then I want to hit the library at Harvard—a little snow won't close them down. Maybe I can help Bookrajian interpret this business."

"The only way to *interpret* all that hoorah, in my view," Molly said, "is to get so tied up in sex and religion, you don't know which is which. Skip the interpretation, is my advice. Sex and religion, those are opposite ends of the same snake."

"Which snake is that?"

"Don't ask me—talk to Saint Theresa."

3

Sam wouldn't wake up, and if he did wake up, he said from under his faded red blanket, he wouldn't go outside but would only play Genesis with his friends. His room was smelling like the onset of adolescence, and Fred, exasperated with him, thought of opening a window and letting the blizzard try to roust the fug.

Coming downstairs, he heard the rattle of dried peas into a saucepan. Fred could avoid shaving; Molly's way of declaring a snow day was to make her mom's pea soup. Fred saw Terry sitting expectantly on the couch in the living room, dressed for the outdoors, in front of a TV she had not turned on. With the exception of the boots, which matched, each article of outdoor clothing was a different color: red knitted hat, green scarf, black and white striped mitten, pink glove, yellow parka, blue jeans.

"You want to help me shovel?" Fred asked her.

Terry jumped up. "Mom said you were going to be busy."

"We have to keep ahead of the weather. Besides, you look like tutti-frutti ice cream."

"Thank you, Fred."

Between the descending snow and the wind blowing, there

17

was not much progress to be made. They took turns with the shovel, Terry, during her turns, moving with a concentration of abandon that made up for the small size of her limbs. They did the stairs and the cement path to the sidewalk. Here and there up and down Molly's street of small clapboard houses were others who could not wait for the snow to be finished doing what it was doing. A block away, an old man with a snowblower was putting his drifts back into circulation.

Terry leaned on her shovel and surveyed the new pile building over Fred's car at the foot of the driveway. She brushed the melted fog of snow and effort off her brow and said judiciously, "Your car looks better this way, Fred. It's good white. Maybe you should paint it. I never noticed. Mom's is named a Colt—what's the name of your car, Fred?"

Fred studied the heap of snow under the skeleton of the neighbor's maple tree. "I call it an Impulsa," he said. "It was an impulse purchase one time when I was in Mexico."

"You were in Mexico?"

"Not everybody knows that," Fred cautioned. "If you want, bang on the door and tell your mom we're going for a walk to see what things are like in all this snow."

Arlington didn't salt. The roads in the neighborhood had been plowed a couple of times since the snow had got heavy, but the DPW couldn't keep up. Terry skittered and prattled while they made their way through the suburban drifts and windfalls toward Spy Pond. Fred, haunted by the events of the early morning, tried to let the scour of snow and wind blow through his eyes and brain, to clean them. While walking with Terry, he had wanted not to be thinking about death. Also he wanted to think about the project Bookrajian had given him.

"And so, see, if we had a dog," Terry was insisting as they forged through one windrow under which there should be a side-walk, "he'd go in front and make a tunnel for me. He'd be making it with his nose and sweeping it with his tail."

They talked about dogs until they reached Spy Pond, which lay out black and crusting with the press of falling snow that the wind whipped into sullen heaves. Soon it was going to freeze into a porous cheese that would tempt kids to skate and drown here. The wind seemed almost strong enough to take Terry out over the water. She struggled with it, excited, filled with a traveler's optimism, like a leaf on a stem.

"If you had a dog, what would you call it?" Fred asked, turning them away from the water and starting home, past drifts that hid upended modest pleasure craft like skiffs and rowboats and canoes.

"He might already have a name," Terry said, as if she had long been considering this problem. "But if I had to name him, or if I got to, I think Grace."

"That's a good name for a dog."

"You can't call a dog the same as something to ride in," Terry said, forgiving Fred for the dorky name he'd given his old brown car.

Sam met them at the door, angry at not having been included. "We went everywhere," Terry told him.

Molly came in from the kitchen wiping her hands on her rump, still in the blue wrapper. She was having a day off. "You aren't going to try to get into Cambridge in this?" she asked.

"Mom says you were at a murder," Sam said. "But I bet she was just trying to wake me up. Were you?"

Fred hesitated. What kids had to know these days was bad enough without adding things they could do without; also, he wasn't used to telling people his business. But evidently Molly figured this was a part of their common life, as long as Fred was living here. Since it had scared them all awake that morning, and since the kids had seen Fred being led off into the storm, that seemed fair.

"It was a pretty bad one," Fred admitted. "They wanted me to see a painting in the apartment where it happened."

"We thought they thought you did it," Sam said.

"With your gun," Terry added. "But you didn't."

19

"Right," Fred said. He and Terry were kicking off their wet boots and letting Molly whisk them into the kitchen.

"Who was killed?" Sam asked.

"A good guy or a bad guy?" Terry asked.

Fred started, realizing how his own instinct had simply begged that question. You see a man nailed up like that, you naturally assume it's a bad guy. Given the scars he himself carried, Fred should know better than that, since he considered himself one of the good guys.

"I don't have the answer to either question, but give me five minutes in the living room, and I'll fill you in," Fred said.

"I'm going in the kitchen," Molly said. Fred followed the kids into the living room, where Sam began to rearrange the TV so as to accommodate the components of his Genesis. Fred couldn't tell them enough to satisfy them, and he wouldn't even if he could, but he gave them as much as they could see they were going to get before he joined Molly in the kitchen. Molly, leaning against the sink, was on the phone.

"It's Dee," she told Fred, sotto voce. Fred noodled around the kitchen and made coffee while Molly talked. Dee was Molly's inside line to the City of Cambridge police force. An old friend, and married to Walter, Molly's boss at the public library, Dee kept track of what was interesting in Cambridge gossip and law enforcement from her vantage point in the Department of Traffic and Parking.

"Hold on, tell Fred," Molly said, offering him the phone. Fred took it, and he and Dee established contact. You wouldn't know to hear her talk that Dee was almost pure Italian.

"I was reading Molly the list of items the folks in homicide apparently do not know," Dee said. "You saw the headless wonder? A trainee dropped his notes, and I picked them up. You want to hear?"

"I wouldn't mind."

"Give you some idea of what we're training."

"Should I get a pencil?"

"You decide. I'll go real slow. This trainee is the pinkest person ever made, and you have to imagine his handwriting, which has not evolved since Sister Mary Guernica stood over him in fourth grade." Dee coughed and began. " 'One: Who is the alleged victim? Two: Who owns the condo? Three: Where is the alleged victim's head?' "

"*Alleged* head," Fred interrupted. "No one has proved there ever *was* a head."

"Point noted. 'Four: When was he killed? Five'—"

"Are you serious?" Fred asked.

"I swear, the guy dropped it next to my desk. He's going to be looking for it later, for the test. They were all coming out of a big brainstorming session. Shall I go on?" Fred took a sip of coffee and let Dee have her fun. " 'Five: Did someone hear hammering? Six'—remember, this guy has been to law-enforcement junior college—'six: Is it, like, a symbolism thing, with the nails and the crown of thorns? Seven: What did the guy die of?' "

"That's the first good question," Fred said. "What *did* the guy die of?"

"We don't know yet. Then he asks, 'Where are his clothes? Why was he killed?' and finally—the one I like best, Fred—'Who did it?' "

"And that's the inside dope from Homicide?"

"That, and there's blood in the bathroom," Dee said.

"How are your roads?"

"Impossible," Dee said. "We're towing as fast as we can, but it's slow work. Honest, Fred, if you come in, don't drive. If you get stuck in town, we'll put you up. It's really hell, and I don't believe the buses are running. It's like the blizzard of 'seventy-eight all déjà vued again. The part of this whole thing I like is that there're so many police and reporters all around One-oh-oh-one Mem Drive, those people all look like they're under house arrest. Maybe they're under quarantine."

Fred handed the phone back to Molly, who talked into it for a few more minutes while she stirred her soup. "You're going in, aren't you?" Molly said, after hanging up. "You're crazy."

21

"I'll walk over to Mass Ave and see if there's a bus," Fred said. "If not, I'll walk in, or hitchhike."

"What I'm going to do," Molly said, "is get back into bed with about six *National Geographics*. I won't go sledding until this calms down."

Fred followed her upstairs. They were in her bedroom when Sam called, "Fred! Clayton is on call waiting. I mean Mr. Reed. Can you be quick? Because Arjun is giving me directions on how to get to Level Three."

"The most remarkable thing," Clay exclaimed.

"Yes?"

"That awful woman called."

"What awful woman?" Fred asked.

"From New York," Clay said. He could not bring himself to say her name. Fred watched Molly settle herself under the covers, next to the thrashing white window and its moving white diaphanous curtains. She opened the first *Geographic* from the pile she had heaped on Fred's side of her bed. "Mrs. Whitman," Clay admitted. "It happens she's in Boston, at the Four Seasons Hotel. That is where persons stay who haven't the imagination for the Ritz."

"Lavinia Randall Whitman?" Fred said. "The dealer?"

"Be careful on the telephone, Fred," Clay begged. He would not be convinced that an international conspiracy of rival art collectors was not tapping his phone. "Because of this anomaly of nature, she is forced to remain in Boston and hence thought to offer me an exclusive option of a limited time—"

"Option on what?" Fred cut in. Clay had more sense than to do business with Lavinia Whitman.

"Please, not on the phone," Clay pleaded. "Is there any way you can get in?"

"You know you can't trust her, Clay! She can't tell the truth, she wouldn't walk a straight line if she could, and she's been known to try to sell you your own picture!"

Clay entertained silent pain on his end of the line. "I know, but she gets good things," he said. "Admittedly, the Watteau she offered to sell me was already on my wall, but she did not know that. She showed good judgment, believing I'd like it."

"And wanting two hundred times what we paid for it."

Clay harrumphed, came up with nothing reasonable to say, and instead offered, "Not on the telephone. Fred, I can say no more. The opportunity is one I must not miss. Can you come? I gather the precipitation continues unabated?"

Clay had windows, but he was too upset by the scent of some wonderful quarry to use them. He was on the brink of making trouble for himself—and therefore for Fred. "I'll get there," Fred said. Bookrajian's head of Christ would have to wait.

4

Fred found Clay in Fred's office on the ground floor of the Mountjoy Street townhouse. Wearing one of two identical blue suits he had bought the fall before from Brooks Brothers, he was nevertheless almost transparent with agonized anticipation.

"I have been waiting for three hours," Clay announced when Fred thumped in, shaking the snow off as best he could before it got onto books and papers.

"It's snowing," Fred pointed out. Almost nothing had been moving. It was as if Boston were being bombed, to skew Goldwater's mot juste, back into the Stone Age. All bus transport was down. Those who fared best were skiers, who were celebrating God's gift of the perfect conditions to go adventuring in search of Starbucks coffee. Fred had walked and hitched his way from Molly's house to Alewife Station in Cambridge, from which, after a lengthy delay, he had taken the subway, which had then stalled underground between Central and Kendall. Once they reached Kendall, he had walked across the river in conditions that recalled an Eisenstein movie in fast forward. So it was now almost three o'clock.

"Come upstairs if you want," Clay offered, so nervy he was dancing like a spider on a griddle. But he did not forget his manners. "I can make cocoa to revive you after your journey. Something stronger? I have sherry and crème de menthe...." Clay's shock of white hair, which he normally kept awry, like Warhol's wig, expressed an attitude of almost Learlike frenzy.

Fred shook his head.

"It's Velázquez," Clay blurted. "That woman let it slip she has a Velázquez. And solely because she is pinioned by this act of God, she will allow me first refusal."

Fred flung his frayed brown parka over the back of his chair and sat down. His office was crowded, as always, with paintings he and Clay were thinking about. His desk bristled with Clayton's notes, lettered in Clay's Linear C hand on three-by-five index cards that only he and Clay and Michael Ventris could pretend to read. ("Check Boston Athenaeum exhibition, 1884, Ritter. Currier connection?")

"Velázquez, huh?" Fred said, sitting at his desk, trying to slow Clay down. Some influx of hope, abetted by self-congratulation, was persuading Clayton to jettison his normally wary posture when a snake offered him something juicy. "Tell me about it, Clay. It's not the problem one that was finally bought in at Christie's?"

"No, no," Clay said, pacing in a jerky pattern next to the desk. "No, she swears it is not a holy picture. Beyond that I don't know. I forced out of her only that she's got a Velázquez that's in private hands. I must see it. The thing is, I don't want to seem too eager," he stammered, almost peeing down his leg. "She had intended this for another collector for whom it would be perfect; but I persuaded her that what with Logan snowed in, I should have the first chance."

"They don't give her a phone at the Four Seasons?" Fred asked. "Or access to a fax machine?"

"I am reporting what she said," Clay answered, petulance crowding his good manners.

"What else can you tell me?"

"It sounds like an important picture," Clay said.

"You got dimensions? A date? Description? Price?"

"Of course not, not on the telephone! Neither of us would be so foolish—she, like myself, knows how to breast her cards. Fred, I must see that painting."

Fred interrupted, "And who does she represent this time? A disadvantaged Irish nobleman? Or a cardinal who's having doubts and maybe something female on the side? An ex–Soviet diplomat on the lam, or—"

"I've told you what I know." Clay stopped his pacing and reached over to Fred's desk to pick up a catalog of flotsam and jetsam that Doyle's was offering for sale next week. "I am to visit her this afternoon, in her suite at the Four Seasons. She will do nothing until then. I have her word."

Clay smiled proudly, but unless he had fallen into his second infancy, he knew as well as Fred did that Lavinia Randall Whitman's word was worth its weight in play money.

"So," Fred said. "The program for the afternoon is to trek to the Four Seasons for a Velázquez and maybe a small pink elephant she's got to sell."

"I felt it would be good to have you along," Clay said. "In case the encounter results in a purchase that needs to be carried. My back, as you know—"

Fred interposed, "I'll go alone. We need elbow room on our side. I'll look the thing over, hum and haw. You'll stay in the background, mysterious, hard to convince. If it looks like Lavinia Randall Whitman has something for you, I'll say—did she even intimate whether she's talking sketch or finished painting?" Clay shook his head. "If a Velázquez were available in the area, we'd know it. And if there was one we *didn't* know about, we couldn't afford it. Knowing Lavinia, it's a scam or a con. But anyway, I'll see what's on her mind, then I'll say, 'I'll have to consult with my principal.' You know the drill as well as I do, Clay. It's a matter of tactics. Don't let our own weight work against us."

Clay weaseled and worried until his native caution returned. "Very well," he said. "I shall stay here until I get word from you."

"Right," Fred said. "Tell me the room number. Don't let her know I'm coming in your place. I haven't met the lady, and I'm looking forward to this."

Clay cautioned, "Don't allow lack of faith to cloud your judgment. If, for instance, the owner should need cash instantaneously for some reason—who knows?—the price should be . . . well, I told her four o'clock, never imagining how long you would take to come in. I wanted you to refresh your memory of Velázquez's oeuvre—but you must leave right away. There's just time—Fred, forgive me, but I notice that in your haste, you neglected to shave."

"An experiment," Fred said.

"Unfortunate. You brought your car?"

"Impossible," Fred said. "I'll walk."

When Fred stepped outside again, the snow was letting up. Almost three feet lay on the ground, though it was hard to gauge the precise amount on account of the wind. Fred plunged along the almost vacant roadways, thinking, This must be a bitch for those poor cops in Cambridge: your killer drops the head in front of 1001, you won't find it until spring. Or it's been plowed and scooped and bucket-loaded into a DPW truck and it's already on its way to Woburn or wherever Cambridge dumps snow. Then he thought, This act of God could also put a glitch in the killers' plans. "Killers plural," he said aloud, "unless the alleged victim"—he snorted at the trainee's self-protective dodge—"unless the *victim* was unusually cooperative. If I tried to do that to someone with a broom handle, I'd want four men to help. None of the rest looked like fun for the victim, either. There was no bruising on the body. Apart from the obvious, he was unmarked as this new snow, his skin waxen and perfect, with fine dark hairs standing out against it in the appropriate places."

Fred marched through drifts, dodged snowplows, and kept

musing. "Suppose the killers intended to drive back to Hartford or New York after the job was done; or, better, take a plane home to, say, Miami? Didn't it look like a drug thing? The scene had such a heavy public-relations component. It was designed to strike terror, with so much decoration you almost missed the murder. And now the public-relations department of the Miami brotherhood, four or five men wearing black suits, are sitting in a row on a bench at socked-in Logan, watching for cops while they stare at the flickering columns of 'Canceled' signals on all departure and arrival monitors."

Fred reached the Boston Common and started cutting across it. Once pasture land for this rural town, its rolling hills had long ago been gentrified with ponds, gazebos, flower beds, and fountains, none of which was now visible, beyond hints of the gazebos. The statuary glorified opulence or heroism, both of which looked better, like Fred's car, under a good dose of snow.

The management of the Four Seasons was doing its best to offer the distraction of creature comforts to its marooned guests, who were buying more time than they wanted. A pianist in the lobby played popularized Scarlatti. The guests had comfortable chairs, and tables to drink tea and coffee at. A padded bar in a corner was doing a roaring trade with folks of middle age who had left their outer clothes upstairs. It might have been festive and Christmasy had this not been February.

Fred finessed his way around the management and courtesy personnel and slipped up to the fourth floor using the fire stairs. He preferred, when he could, to arrive unannounced. A perfumed "Yes" answered his knock.

"Clayton Reed," Fred called, kicking the last snow off his boots and onto a runner. The door opened on a slightly plump and middle-aged woman in a bright-pink velvet suit. She was a mouse-blonde, with hair lacquered into a shell-like puff. The quizzical expression on her face suggested fun undertaken only on behalf of a worthy cause. They'd never met, but Fred had seen her before, whispering into the ears of closely guarded clients at the big New York sales.

"You are not Clayton Reed," she said, raising her eyebrows.

Fred said, "The weather. He sends regrets, and me. My name is Fred."

Lavinia Randall Whitman pursed her lips and whispered, "One moment," as she closed the door. Clay was prepared for her to telephone. Fred cooled his heels until she threw the door open and crooned, "Come in," managing to sound as if she were saying both, "Isn't this fun?" and "Quick, they'll hear us."

Fred stepped into the suite's drawing room. The far end was windows overlooking the Common. Lavinia Randall Whitman was getting a good view of what was keeping her in Boston. The setup was disquietingly like that of the condominium on Memorial Drive where he'd been that morning, except that it was missing a body and a fireplace, and a painting. But yes, there was the big couch and the end tables supporting huge lamps with huge shades; a big Louis XV TV set, and occasional armchairs. Here the prevailing shade was not off-beige but unwashed gold.

"After we have tea and get acquainted, we will talk," Lavinia Randall Whitman confided, while Fred looked around the room. "I depend on the nice people downstairs." She picked up a telephone and ordered, "Tea for two people. With those lovely scones, and strawberry jam." When she hung up the phone, she started whispering, "Fred, I have such respect for Clayton Reed. He has an excellent eye. Delicious!" She clasped her hands together. "Please call me Lavinia," she went on, leading Fred toward the couch. She was between, or she was either/or, forty and/or sixty.

"I do apologize for keeping you in the hall," she said, winking. "Naturally I recognize you, Fred, since you stand out at the sales." She shivered as if a tree threatened to fall upon her, lush with ripe peaches. "One cannot be too careful in this business, the art world's being so small."

Her laugh was an unnerving whisper. Fred had automatically taken off his parka, which now rested across his knees. Lavinia reached for it, saying, "I'll throw it across my bed—goodness, it's heavy!" She licked her lips and took up its male burden. When she opened the door into her bedroom, Fred saw the backs of at least three sizable framed canvases that faced the wall in there. Lavinia Randall Whitman came out again, closed the door, and stood against it, her hand poised in back of her on the doorknob, looking smug, coy, and expectant, like someone who'd just slept with the governor and now, betrayed, knew she was at the brink of either fame or large amounts of hush money—maybe both!

Behold the apotheosis of ambivalence, Fred did not say. Then he did not add, You are wasting my time.

"Maybe I won't wait for tea," Fred said. Not knowing what climax impended, he was impatient with all this foreplay. "Tell me about the Velázquez."

"Oh, goodness," Lavinia whispered. She sat down next to Fred on the couch. "First you must know the confidential background."

"I'll get my coat," Fred said, standing.

Lavinia reached to restrain him with a pink left arm. "Forgive me, Fred. My client demands absolute secrecy. As I told Mr. Reed—"

"I may as well see the picture," Fred said. "Since I'm here."

They were interrupted by the arrival of tea on a rolling tray pushed by a waiter as exotic as he was insolent. "So civilized," Lavinia enthused after he left. Fred hoiked a chair toward the couch where she sat pouring, and gave in to the ritual. Snow beat against the window next to his face. If he hadn't seen the backs of paintings in her bedroom, he would have left by now. She'd intended him to see them. His job was to direct himself into her trap; it was how she wanted it to work. He'd leave, but the fact was, she sometimes handled excellent things, transferring them quietly from one important collection to another, bailing out Lloyds "names" who were desperate for both cash and anonymity, helping furnish film stars' apartments on short notice with credible

Cézannes and Renoirs. She'd had her hands on a Goya . . . well, so what? It was also true that her reputation was like that once enjoyed by Swifty Lazar, who'd arrange to sell B the services of A for X amount of money before he'd ever met or spoken to either A or B.

"You control the picture?" Fred asked. He'd automatically accepted the white china cup with flowers that she'd handed him. He put it down.

"Pictures. Plural," she said. "As in more than one."

5

Lavinia Randall Whitman sipped from her cup, said, "Lapsang souchong—they remembered," and sipped again. "Mr. Reed could not understand the situation in his excitement. I notice that he, like Berenson, is shy of the telephone."

She maneuvered cream and jam onto the scone she controlled. She was determined to govern the pace of this interview.

Fred said, "As far as other paintings go, I have no instructions. For now I'll just see the Velázquez, so I can report back to my principal."

Lavinia regretted, "Sadly, the Velázquez cannot be sold separately. The situation is this—if you have time?"

Fred said, "If it's too complex—"

"It's absurdly simple," Lavinia objected. "The collection is ninety paintings, Old Masters, European."

"In Boston?" Fred asked. He knew of no such collection.

"The collection is nowhere," Lavinia said, and winked. "These paintings are not in this country, nor legally in any country. They are in transit at present—under no country's jurisdiction, and therefore carrying no tax or export implications. The opportunity is ideal for the discerning investor."

Fred winced. Clay would cavil at the word *investor*. That was not what he was. He was a collector who loved pictures.

"And so . . . ," Fred prompted.

"The paintings are in Switzerland, in a bank vault. The collection is simply fabulous. It includes a Velázquez, yes, but to give you an idea—what do you say to Rembrandt, Rubens, Lucas Cranach, Brueghel—" she paused and smiled.

"Go on," Fred said. "The other eighty-some?"

"Before I describe them further, I should know if Mr. Reed is interested, given the way the deal must be constructed. He— or she—my client—is adamant. I shall sell the entire collection only as a unit, not piece by piece." Her voice had suddenly turned clear and hard, brilliant with reasonableness. "The owner, through me, insists upon the following conditions. One: the price for the collection is forty-five million American dollars, which will be placed in escrow before the collection may be examined. Two: the potential buyer pays an initial fee of sixty thousand dollars in order to see the paintings. This fee is not refundable, though it will be subtracted from the purchase price. Three: my client guarantees that there is no prohibition governing the transfer of these paintings to any place in the world. As I say, they are in transit."

"Who *is* the owner, Ollie North?" Fred asked.

"Given the works in the collection, the price is most attractive," Lavinia said.

"You have a list I can show Clay?" Fred asked. "You have a sample with you? The Velázquez maybe?"

Lavinia said, "I shall describe the works in the collection when I feel there is sufficient reason to do so. As to the Velázquez—I know that interested Reed—this painting by itself is valued at three million. He'll let me know if he wants to chat about this further?" She stood abruptly and made for her bedroom to get Fred's coat. The blank backs of the paintings in there sneered at him.

Clay's first reaction was to hit the roof. Fred hadn't telephoned him but had instead walked back over, wanting to let white space develop between himself and Lavinia Randall Whitman before he tried to make a judgment about the situation. The big trick—a surprise—was that Fred had enjoyed her. She was funny and able, absolutely expert at what she was doing; and dangerous. Fred liked that.

Thunder boomed and lightning crackled as he crossed the Common again—rare phenomena during a snowstorm. The night had come down, hidden behind the lighted clouds of snow that transformed Boston. The wind was so strong it was impossible to tell whether it was still snowing. It was so hard to see at all that Fred almost bumped into trees, as well as the few pedestrians he encountered.

"She's played me right," Fred muttered, realizing he'd reached an edge of the Common he hadn't been aiming for. He'd got turned around. "I don't believe a word of it. Clay wouldn't spend forty-five million on paintings if he had it. And what would he want with ninety at a time? She should know this ain't Clay's league." Clay was cheap anyway, but part of his pleasure in collecting lay in what he called getting hold of a picture for its real, not its commercial, value. Fred hadn't trusted a single thing said or implied during his whole encounter with Lavinia Whitman. Even so, and despite all the reservations of his better judgment, he was dying to find out what she had for sale. For God's sake, Rembrandt? Lucas Cranach?

"It's like that thing at charity auctions," Fred said after Clay had calmed down somewhat. "Where people bid against each other for the chance to be the one to open the paper bag and see what's inside—which, whatever it is, they now own."

Clayton had called him upstairs. They were sitting in the living room that Clay called his parlor, where Clay, in a deep armchair covered with blue leather, faced Copley's painting of a young man with a squirrel. Now beautifully mended and cleaned, it presided over a room located only a stone's throw from the place Copley had lived when he painted it. Clay had removed his suit coat in favor of the red satin dressing gown he sported when at rest. He was drinking crème de menthe. Fred had found beer in the refrigerator.

"Sixty thousand dollars to see what's in a bank vault in Switzerland!" Clay exclaimed. "I never heard of such a thing!"

"It would discourage window shoppers," Fred pointed out. "They use a routine like it in some kinds of businesses, such as arms sales, where the opposing parties don't love one another. Sometimes people who want to bid against each other for a commodity—say, a ton of heroin—are forced to put up a non-refundable fee up front just for the chance to bid. Still, in the art business . . ."

Clay said, "That woman intends to make fools of us."

"She already has made fools of us," Fred said. "We knew it was a trap. It's what she does. We took her bait. Do we complain now if the bait turns out not to be edible?"

"What are these paintings?" Clay marveled. "Great God! Lucas Cranach! Rembrandt! Brueghel! Which Brueghel? What else does she have?"

"You mean, what will she *say* she has?"

"Yes, yes," Clay said. "I am simply speaking in shorthand. Drat this weather. I would love to get to the Museum library to see what paintings by Velázquez remain in private hands." Clay took a last sip of his green liquor.

"Whatever the circumstances, I must see that list," Clay said. He fretted and tapped his fingers on a side table that might be Chippendale. Fred did not care about furniture. His passion was for paintings, because a good one caught and held the human soul, taking its print like the shed skin of a snake.

"They're not going to open Logan tomorrow, either, are they?" Clay said. Fred shook his head, looking at the commotion out the window. "In that case, Nature, at least, is on our side," Clay concluded. "We are allowed the opportunity to develop a stratagem by which we can outwit this woman?"

Fred said, "I ought to call Molly." Clay gestured with his head to where a telephone sat on the Kashmir shawl that draped his grand piano. He looked the question of whether he should let Fred be alone. Fred gestured, Stay where you are. Halfway across the room, he recalled something Lavinia Randall Whitman had said in passing, and asked Clay, "Do you remember reading anything about Bernard Berenson and telephones?"

Clay shook his head. "Curious juxtaposition, but why not? The man was alive until almost nineteen sixty, dispensing cultured pearls of wisdom from on high. I suppose he had a telephone at I Tatti. Why?"

Fred said, "An irrelevant exercise in name-dropping I ran into recently."

"A day on which I do not think about Berenson is a happier day for me," Clayton chided. Clay wished he had *been* Berenson; he was angry at Berenson for having thought of it first.

Molly said, after they swapped news, "Honestly, Fred, you'd be a fool to come home." She hesitated, noticing what she'd said. She had never before referred to her house as Fred's home. Fred's own habit was to equate the concepts "home" and "trap."

They both knew they must quickly say the next thing, but neither could think what that was until Sam's voice interfered on an extension, "Mom? I have to call Arjun. I'm stuck."

"You're going to be stuck worse if you break in again when your mother's on the phone," Molly threatened.

"He's been at that Genesis all day?" Fred asked.

"Since you left. We didn't feel like going out. The snow's too heavy."

"I don't know about coming back to Arlington."

"According to my sources, everybody's getting nowhere. You're better off in Boston than halfway between Mountjoy Street and my place." She didn't say "home" again. It was Molly's home; Fred was a guest.

"I suppose I can get to Charlestown on foot," Fred said.

"Bookrajian called, looking for you. I didn't tell him where you were," Molly continued.

Next to the telephone was a photograph of Clay's wife, Prudence Lucy Stillton, who had died suddenly, shortly after their marriage, years ago, of a cruelly wasting illness that Fred speculated partly accounted for Clay's eccentricity. He hadn't known what had hit him in the first place, and had not lived with her long enough to find out. She had left him many relatives on the North Shore and a place in Boston society if he wanted it, as well as the piano and the shawl and all those spindly gilt chairs lining the walls.

"I'll call him. Why don't you let up on Bookrajian, Molly?"

"Why should I like a man who practically accused me of lying and stealing?" Molly exclaimed. As it happened, she *had* been lying and stealing at the time in question—smuggling a painting away from a crime scene, hidden against her skin. But never mind.

Molly continued briskly, "And he scares us all to death coming to my house at three in the morning? I do not like Bookrajian, and I do not want his business in my house. I am surprised at how well *you* seem to get along with him."

"You all right out there?" Fred asked. "The road's clear for fire trucks to get to you? The hydrants dug out?"

"I'll take a look."

"And you have provisions for a couple of days?"

"We're fine," Molly said. "Until the power cuts out. Ophelia's lost hers, in Lincoln."

"Did Bookrajian give you a number where I can reach him? Home number?"

Molly read a number while Fred took it down. He checked his

watch, Bookrajian's interest dragging him back toward the morning's errand, which he had not mentioned to Clayton. It was after six-thirty, so he'd missed the local news, which would have been dominated in any case by pictures of newscasters standing in the snow, their coats romantically open, and traffic messed up behind them with a background noise of spinning wheels. Whatever coverage the event at 1001 might merit, it was someone else's project; still, as a fellow human, Fred wondered if they'd learned the identity of the alleged owner of the missing head. The corpse looked too young for a Nobel Prize, but you could never be too young for a Pulitzer.

"You listened to the evening news?" Fred asked Molly, but she said she was taking the day off. She'd get the *Globe* tomorrow if it came. It'd give the story all the play it could. Hoping to stanch subscriber hemorrhage, the *Globe* liked to get sex on the front page, thinking of it—correctly—as human-interest.

"Tomorrow is soon enough for chapter two of that story," Molly said. "Right now, I'm going back to Bhutan." She signed off.

"You will sleep here, of course," Clay said. "As my guest, in the guest bedroom. I will hear of nothing else. I shall not sleep myself for speculating about the collection Mrs. Whitman is representing. I must decide on my next move."

The old leather couch in his office downstairs would be more Fred's speed, once cleared of books, magazines, and sales catalogs; but Clayton's guest room was being offered, and it would be churlish of him to refuse.

"You know the room," Clay pushed on. "On the third floor, across the hall from mine. Maria keeps it ready, and you should be comfortable. I fear you will be unable to squeeze into my pajamas."

"I'll be fine. As a matter of fact, there's a piece of research I need to do—a painting neither of us would ever give two hoots about, but a fellow asked me to look into it as a favor. As long as I'm here, I'll spend some time on it in our office library. I'll go out and grab a sandwich later. As far as Lavinia's paintings go, my advice—"

"I have food," Clay said. "Maria left a pot-au-feu yesterday. There will be plenty."

"That's all right," Fred said. "I'm itching to start, and there's a time factor."

Though Clay cared little about Italian painting of the seventeenth century, his art library was extensive, and he never threw away a sales catalog. A large portion of the library was in Fred's office, so Fred went down there to poke around, but not with much hope. A million Italian churches might have wanted, ordered, and obtained that head of Christ in agony during the seventeenth century, when there were crowds of people who could churn such pictures out, from Alessandro Allori to Zaccaria Zaninelli.

These guys liked black, and dark, and blood, and gaudy torture anyway, and tended to justify their taste for kinky mayhem by concealing it behind religious themes, or motifs from classical mythology. Fred flipped through various sources, the gloomy images rolling along like photos from a perverted civil war. Here in a sale catalog were two women, their scanty clothing disturbed by the effort, trying to pull arrows out of a still-living Saint Sebastian. The painting had lost its author, being identified vaguely as "Northern Italian, seventeenth century, 52 × 73 inches." That could dominate a hospital waiting room! It had been offered at Sotheby's, London, a few years back, estimated at a mere thousand pounds. Try getting that operation in the States for such a price! Or here was Cain beating Abel to death in apparent resolution of an incestuous tiff; or the god Apollo skinning the satyr Marsyas alive—a popular theme beloved of many. Reni had liked to portray the event at its inception, with the satyr tied to a tree by his raised arms, and the god of music and poetry enjoying the foreplay, his flaying knife poised at his victim's armpit. Or switching from the classical to the Christian theme, but keeping the story, torture, skin, and blood, in place of Marsyas, some artists portrayed Saint Bartholomew being skinned. Martyrdoms were big with the Italians: Saint Andrew pounded with sticks; Saint Catherine broken on the wheel; Peter crucified upside down; Laurence on the grill. It was an unpleasant school of prurient fads and gratuitous, lurid violence: artistic but not pretty. Bookrajian had summed it up quite well, and more quickly than Berenson ever did.

6

At ten o'clock Fred was at the bar of the BarOK on Charles Street, at the foot of Mountjoy, where they would serve him a plate of beans with a side of bourbon and let him overhear the news and hearsay while gilded cowboys, angels, and mermaids kibitzed from the walls. It was still snowing, but everyone had said as much as they had to say about the storm long before Fred came in. The murder in Cambridge was the topic now being elaborated in a lively conversation among the bartender and four patrons on stools down the bar from Fred. The bartender, Gustav, was decked out in black pants and white shirt; the four customers at the bar, one female and three male, wore almost identical lumberjack outfits from L. L. Bean.

It seemed that the main details had been rolled in, on news shows and talk radio, for most of the day. One of the drinkers claimed to have a friend who had a friend close to the investigation, and so they even knew about the painting Fred was supposed to be working on.

As Fred, sitting at his end of the counter, got around his beans, the woman said, "Look, we're talking this to death. I'm getting confused." She was the same age as the others—between twenty and thirty. She hadn't taken off her plaid cap, which she wore backward. She looked cute in it. "What we'll do is, each of us'll put ten dollars in a pool, which Gustav will keep under the bar—"

Gustav interrupted, "Only if I can play, too."

"Sure. Then each person'll say what they think happened—the reason, the motive. Then, when we know, whoever came closest will get the pot, which, with Gustav being in, is fifty bucks."

They gave themselves three minutes by Gustav's outsize Mickey Mouse wristwatch. The bar's seven or eight other customers, at tables, alone or in close couples, pricked up their ears.

They drew straws to see who would start, and a patron called Francesco won. The order was crucial, since one of the rules established was that whoever spoke a theory first owned it.

"OK," Francesco said. "You will all shit. This covers everything. Ready? The killer is a former altar boy, the victim is the priest who abused him, and he had it coming. Heck, let's make it twenty bucks apiece." The room would have applauded except for the uncomfortable interface of sex and religion.

Bill, next in line, took a swig of his dark draft and said, "I can't believe they don't know who owns the condo. I mean—anyway, it's not politically correct, but how about Christians killing a Jew, or vice versa? Or Moslem, Hindu—some religious thing."

So the lengthy foreskin was not common knowledge; if Bill had known about that, he could've narrowed it down.

Next was Gustav. Gustav swept the bar with a rag until he had the room's attention, then he spoke deliberately. "This right-wing Christian cult worshiped at One-oh-oh-one Memorial Drive. It's a secret cult, or they'd know who owns the condo. The dead guy tried to leave the cult, or, no, gave away, no, *sold* its secrets. He told the cops where the members' hideout was—their, like, temple. By the time the cops got there, this guy had told his last secret."

"How come they left the painting behind?" someone asked from one of the tables.

"No questions," everyone agreed. Let the free-for-all wait till all theories had been entered.

Randy, next to speak, had been the quietest of the group. Now, put on the spot, he trembled with stage fright. His glass stuttered against the bar until he gripped it with both hands. "It's about sex," he said. "And it isn't funny. It's jealousy and homophobic, homoerotic hatred. The key is the broomstick, which they won't mention on TV or in the family newspapers. But we know about it from my friend, and that's enough to kill a person, driving it in. Read *Edward the Second*."

He spoke with such passion that the room was silent. People shifted uneasily in their seats. Nevertheless the woman, Wanda, had to follow his act. She began, "They towed my car five hours ago. I don't know where I'm going to sleep tonight, and save your suggestions. I've gotta start making phone calls to my girlfriends. Here's my theory. The painting is stolen from a church, maybe in Mexico. The dead guy was a detective. The picture is worth a million dollars, right? You forget, these old paintings are worth *mucho, mucho dinero*. He's—the dead guy is—the detective they sent to find the painting. He tracked it down. Then the guy who stole it, a rich international guy, makes his goons torture the detective to find out who sent him. One thing leads to another, since whenever a bunch of men starts having fun . . ."

She was drowned out by general clamor. Fred finished his whiskey, and everyone looked at him expectantly. "You're next, buddy," Wanda said.

"I'm not playing," Fred told them. But the game had its own momentum. "Come on, guy, just for fun," was the general demand, as if they'd fallen into a TV show about some bar in Boston.

"None of these theories takes the weather into account," Fred said. "You're all yapping after false clues and missing the main thing. An act of God changes everybody's plans—like Wanda's suddenly not having a car, so who knows where she's going to sleep? Everyone assumes it's murder, but why not look at this in a positive light instead? The evidence suggests that a committee was working to construct the perfect man. Before they could finish, and get the head in place, they got interrupted by inclement weather."

"Yeah, like the Tower of Babel," someone helped. "The old boy knocks out the competition."

Fred, having registered his bona fides, went to grab the pay phone before Wanda could start using it to canvas her friends.

Bookrajian's home number raised a female voice. "Ernie," Blanche Bookrajian blurted into her end of the line. "Oh, Ernie, I'm sorry." Her voice immediately brought back the memory of a startlingly developed naked female body, displayed in some glossy photos Bookrajian had accidentally let Fred see one day, shortly before he took the young lady to Atlantic City and the altar, in that order. So when the woman's breathless voice came on the line, despite her message, Fred's mind filled with the luscious playfulness of her nudity.

"It's bad news. I'm so sorry, Ernie," she went on. "There's good news too, but mostly not so good. I'm sorry, Ernie."

Fred had to tell her who he was. It was like finding himself in a stranger's bedroom.

"Fred Taylor?" she asked. "I don't know that name. What happened? What happened to my husband?"

Fred told her, "I'm looking for him, is all. He'll be home. Things are slow, on account of the weather. I'll call later."

"Do you know where he is?"

"Sorry," Fred said.

"Please, if you see him, tell him to call."

"I will," Fred promised. "I'll try again in the morning. What time's too early?"

There was silence before Mrs. Bookrajian said, "We probably won't be asleep."

Fred went back through the BarOK and out onto Charles Street. It was beautiful and wild outside. Boston, blasted into somnolence, had found a compromise between wilderness and architecture. Each streetlight or traffic light was haunted by its own swirl of action. The sidewalks were deep in snow, and the street as well. Fred put up his hood and walked the flat couple of blocks of land-fill crowned with apartment buildings, until he reached the river. Bookrajian was going home to bad news. When you had a home, bad news could always find you. Molly, for instance, lived in con-stant dread of what might happen to one of her children, through accident or illness or inattention.

Fred stood in the field of drifts next to a river helplessly clotted with snow. He could see to the Cambridge side but could not make out, except by using his memory, how far away it was. Too much was going on in the air. It seemed colder, which sug-gested that the precipitation was going to give over to a solid freeze that would keep all this around for a while. And under the surface, out of sight, who knew what might be moving?

A home with children in it—that was a hostage situation. Bad news would find it every time. She had bad news and good news both, Ernie's wife had said—confiding that fact to Ernie, not to Fred, but Fred had been between them. Standing in Ernie's way, he'd overheard a sad part of their pillow talk.

"I should be in Arlington," Fred told the snow. He started pushing along the bank, heading downstream. The texture of the falling snow was now finer and glassier; underfoot, it squeaked more than it had. There wasn't any sign of traffic on the parkways on either side of the river. Everyone had given up. Lights burned in the apartment buildings on Fred's right, where people cele-brated the strangeness breaking their routine. Fred, pushing against that strangeness, was going on with his routine—as Ernie Bookrajian was doing also, no doubt, caught up in a big case.

Fred made it up the windy iron stairs to the Charles Street sta-tion entrance, suspended at the end of the Longfellow Bridge, which at the moment resembled a tramway hung between Alps. Aside from an old lady in black and two drunken teenage boys throwing snowballs at the posters on the inbound side, Fred was the only passenger in the open shed waiting for the train to Cambridge.

45

If they had all been thinner, including Fred himself—given the snow, and the lights, and the sense of the theatrical—they might be in a pastel painting by Everett Shinn, and fallen through a time warp into 1928.

The train, when it came, was too noisy, too hot, too drafty, and too crowded. The people on it talked too loudly about how long they had waited, but Fred couldn't hear most of what they said on account of the noise. When they pulled into the Central Square station, Fred, on his way out of the car, realized what part of his plan had been when he decided to make for Arlington again. He hadn't reached Bookrajian. It was not midnight yet, and the headquarters of the Cambridge Police Department was right here on Western Avenue, just two blocks from the MBTA stop. He'd put his nose in, then finish the run to Alewife, then find a way to Arlington from there.

The uniform at the desk wanted a lot more information than Fred had to give him, but eventually he admitted that no, Bookrajian was not in his office. It was late, buddy, and it was not Fred's business where Bookrajian was, if there even was such a person. A couple more uniforms gathered as the conversation went on. Fred was a change from accident reports and massive towing operations.

"Did Bookrajian by any chance leave a photograph for me?" Fred asked. "Of the picture, the painting from that crime scene at Ten-oh-one Mem Drive?"

"This is Ernie's art dude," one of the uniforms said. "You tried his house?"

"His wife didn't know where he was," Fred said.

"We try to give the guys a little peace," a uniform said. By now there were about six uniforms of various sizes, various degrees of cynical exhaustion, and various racial and sexual preferences, all making up one complex uniformhood. They were confused, sensing that Fred was either a member of the team or a similar type from the opposing team. After they took his name and checked it against his ID (with its address in Charlestown), they started wanting more.

Fred said, "Bookrajian seems to have a time consideration." He shrugged and waited.

One of the six made a decision, crossed the thin blue line, and said, "After the day he's had, and the days he's gonna have, if I was you, I'd try the G Spot." The officers shuffled and made room for their spokesman to extend an arm. "G for Green Street. Down Green Street three–four blocks."

Central Square, unlike the streets he'd come from in Boston, was not deserted. Being arguably the true heart of the City of Cambridge, it was always lively. Poor people lived here, though many of them—students, mostly—were poor only for the time being. Only one subway stop farther toward Arlington, at Harvard, the austere institutional blight caused by the university's predatory real-estate policies had pretty much blasted children out of the picture. But here in Central Square, at midnight, kids thronged on the occluded streets and sidewalks, working the snow into missiles around rocks and throwing them at each other, at street signs, and at the windows of affordable housing.

Green Street, a block behind the main drag, Mass Ave, where snack stores, restaurants, and convenience and grocery stores were still alive, was mostly dark. It boasted large garages and parking lots, as well as establishments depending less on random street traffic. The falling snow had become sparser, and the wind was dying down. They'd got well over three feet of snow in a brief time here. Arlington, over a snow line, higher and farther west, should have even more.

Past Pearl Street, on the left, Fred found the G Spot, which he would not have noticed unless he'd been looking for it, and would not have known was a bar until he went in and was surrounded by the aura of distressed male. It was the direction Sam's bedroom wanted to go in, unless civilization went well for him, pulled him through adolescence. And Sam had once been so orderly a person.

Fred found Bookrajian in one of the six booths, drinking beer with a man Fred had seen in the lobby at 1001, who'd now exchanged his uniform for plain clothes—a gray sport jacket and a tie with ducks on it. All the booths were filled. At each end of the long, empty bar, a color TV projected a sports program—two opposing programs, one of them being bowling. Back of the bar, an old man in an apron scratched his ear and encouraged the show Fred could not see, "Come on. Kill 'em."

Bookrajian looked up when Fred reached him, not recognizing him at first. Bookrajian was still wearing the shiny black suit he'd had on that morning, but he'd removed the yellow necktie that he must have put on during the day; most of it flapped from the breast pocket of his suit coat.

"I don't want anything," Fred told the man behind the bar, as Bookrajian, finally recognizing him, motioned him to sit.

"I've gotta go anyhow," the other man said, rising.

7

Got that photograph for you," Bookrajian said. "You're not drinking? Coke or something?" He took an envelope out of his inside jacket pocket and handed it to Fred, who transferred it into his own. The bartender stared meaningfully past them. Fred should have opened the envelope and let anyone who cared see that it was only a photograph, not hundred-dollar bills; but it was too late now. "When can you give me something on the picture?" Bookrajian asked.

"There's this snow, and a couple other projects," Fred said. "I'll get on it. You'll save me some time if you can help with the painting's provenance."

"Provenance?" Bookrajian was drinking Rolling Rock. He tipped an empty bottle over his glass, squeezing out a few drops.

"Where it's been, who it belongs to," Fred said, "who it *used* to belong to—like the title search on a house."

"Ask what you want," Bookrajian said. Fred took his parka off and laid it on the table. It was hot in here. The noise from the two opposing TV sets created an illusion of hectic activity in the air above men who seemed to be slowly drowning.

"For example," Fred said, "do you know yet who the dead guy is?"

"We do not," Bookrajian said.

"Did he live in that place?"

"We don't know. During the last week, people saw a man on that floor who sounds like the right size, give or take a head. People at that level of society don't talk to one another unless they are introduced. They are all too important."

"Who owns the condo?"

Bookrajian squirmed. "We've only had one day. But normally in one day you get more. Talk to one person, get a lead to the next, they say look under this rock, you turn it over, by the end of the day you've gone the whole six degrees of separation and then some. This here, once you're inside One-double-oh-one, who knows? Nobody talks. You understand, this is a current investigation, and you are not hearing this. Not that it's anything. The owner of that condo is a company in the Bahamas. Don't you love it? Blind corporation. All correspondence with the building management comes out of a lawyer for a bank in Freeport, which represents a company we so far cannot find. I say a company in the Bahamas, but we don't know even that." Bookrajian looked ready to punch the first nose that swam into his ken. "So," he went on, "if you want to think like our friends the lawyers, who make more in a minute than I do in a week, the inference is there's a laundry operation between the condo and whoever owns it. The inference is that it's organized crime or organized rich people, which maybe you can tell the difference, but damned if I know what it is. Someone took as much trouble to hide the condo's owner as they did to hide the identity of the dead John Doe.

"Everyone says there was a girl living in the place until last summer, a woman, what have you, blond, but they change that when they want. The people in that building do not talk to townies, which includes police officers. The girl on the desk said maybe a student, college. She'd be the right age. She didn't get mail, she didn't talk to the other people—who hate it if you call them 'tenants.' I learned that much. I still don't know what they want to be called. Because they don't want to be called. We're already getting complaints from the mayor's office. Not that they notice local politics, but one of their lawyers found out that Cambridge has a mayor, and how to get her ear. The people on the desk say they think she was Spanish, or South American, and sometimes she'd come in with a man. Different men. She didn't keep a car in their garage, or we'd have its make and tags. We've advised them to try a new security system."

Bookrajian raised a finger toward the man behind the bar, who bent out of sight, rose again, and placed a bottle of Rolling Rock on the slick wood. He began scratching his ear again, admiring his reflection in the bar.

"Pardon me," Bookrajian said. He stood, walked over to the bar, slapped money down, and came back with his beer.

"With half our forensic people stuck out in the sticks, we don't know shit about the body. To make a long story short," Bookrajian said, "we know zip. If the art is part of it, anything you tell us puts us ahead."

"You might run a photo of the picture in the papers," Fred suggested. "Ask anyone who's seen it since sixteen fifty to get in touch."

"It's evidence in a crime," Bookrajian said.

"Like the Shroud of Turin," Fred said. "You're already asking local churches if they're missing a sad picture from a side chapel."

"We do not publish evidence in a crime. That's for your personal use, that photo, to tell me what the painting is and what it's worth. Anything else to do with it, you keep out of. We do not run the picture in the paper. You do not run around showing it to this or that art gallery, this or that professor, or the rest of it. I've got enough trouble in my life already. Half the people in that building are related to God, and the rest of them, God owes them money. I appreciate your help, Fred, if you can help, but do not fuck this up. Don't try to do my work. Keep out of my way."

Fred stood. "I'll be off." He'd almost reached the door before he remembered he had made a promise to Ernie's wife. Book-rajian had a trap waiting for him at home. Bookrajian, pouring beer, looked a question at him.

"I tried to get you at home earlier. Mrs. B.—maybe you talked to her since?" Bookrajian shook his head. "She wants you to call home."

Bookrajian lurched upright, the color draining from his face. "Christ, I forgot," he said. "This is Tuesday. I haven't been—it hasn't—God, the trouble the world dishes out already, who needs murder?" Tears burst out on his face, which looked as if it had been carved out of gristle with a hatchet. The tears were blue, reflecting blue light from above the bar. "How did she sound?" Bookrajian asked, struggling with his coat.

"Like she could use some company," Fred said. "She was upset, I have to say."

Bookrajian beat a fist against the table. "It was today. I thought it was tomorrow. Not sleeping, I lost track." He ran out suddenly, like a released mechanical toy. The intensity of his distress was so immediate that Fred half thought to go with him—the way you keep next to a person who's been shot, forcing him to resist the urge to run, because at times like that it is the rare head that gives the wounded body good advice. But Bookrajian knew what he was doing.

Fred put on his coat, told the bartender and the bar good night, and slogged back to the subway station, which was now closed. It wasn't one in the morning yet; they'd closed it on account of the weather. Other than a few pedestrians like himself, nothing moved on the streets, which were deep and silent. The sky was all cloud, out of which snow continued falling in a fitful way. If Fred had to, he could walk to Arlington. It might take him six hours. But once there, how could he work? It was too much. He had Clay's wild-goose chase after ninety pictures to worry about. Since the subways were down, his plan to go to Arlington had been preempted. He must put his work—no, Clay's work, and Bookrajian's—ahead of his family—correction, Molly's family. It was Molly's home. Fred was a guest.

Fred made a map in his head, deliberated, and followed Main Street out of Central Square, through closed or vacant commercial wilderness, until he hit the river at the Longfellow Bridge, where he was the only pedestrian, indeed the only traveler. It was hard going, but the effort was a good balance for the murder and worry in his mind. It was almost five by the time he reached his bed in Clayton's guest room and found Clay's note on the index card perched on the pillow: "I shall lunch tomorrow with that woman. Therefore her room will not be occupied between one and, I should guess, two-thirty. Verbum sap. C."

Fred rolled under the blankets and stared, for thirty seconds, at the moral wreck Lavinia Randall Whitman had made of his host's New England ethics. "Clay will use his sex to entrap her while I break into her room?" Fred mused in wonder. "That's the plan?"

"In this you are on your own," Fred told Clayton the next day, finding him dressing deliberately, and apprehensively, for the great outdoors. "Your plan, if there is one, is a pig in a poke, though it is billed on the menu as Beef Wellington. I will not break into her suite, however hard you lunch her. Do what you want. I am out of this one."

Fred had wakened himself at eleven and then taken his time making an appearance. He'd talked to Molly a while on the room's extension, and then taken a long shower. It was still snowing, and Molly told him travel had been forbidden in the greater Boston area for all but emergency vehicles. Not only were the planes not flying; the subway system was out, and buses and trains were stopped. "So if you're coming to Arlington in the near future," Molly said, "you'll have to make like Louisa May Alcott and walk."

"From Concord, wasn't she?"

"Walking between Boston and Concord, she'd pass through

Arlington. Many a time and oft have I pictured her pausing in Arlington to take advantage of a passing bush."

Fred needed coffee, and he wanted to see the papers. Clay's papers either had not arrived or had been buried under drifts. So Fred went out into the beleaguered city and, coming back with both newspapers and portable coffee, found Clay in the front hall, winding a red silk scarf around his neck and tucking it under the astrakhan collar of his camel-hair coat.

"We walk, I gather," Clay complained, to which Fred answered, "In this you are on your own."

Clay's mouth fell open. "It's all arranged," he said.

"Your part is arranged. Not mine."

Clay looked through the windows of the heavy street door, the only one either of them would use for now, since the stairwell down to Fred's office floor was filled with snow. Clay flicked black leather gloves from his coat pocket and began putting them on. He'd pulled Tote boots over his shoes. Nothing would make him wear a hat, but he'd propped an umbrella ready.

"There are no taxis," Clay said. "I am surprised at you, Fred, when the game includes Rembrandt, Lucas Cranach, Velázquez."

Fred peeled the lid from his coffee and took a drink. "I am surprised myself, Clay, that the conditions appeal to you."

" 'Appeal'? The conditions are insupportable!" Clay said. "That woman doesn't own the pictures. She doesn't own anything. I shall bypass her. But first I must discover what they are. Among ninety paintings, there has to be something perfect for me—something the owner does not understand or undervalues. You know how I work, Fred. It is a matter of outwitting Mrs. Whitman at her own devious game. Once I learn what the pictures are, I learn who the owner is—and then we talk to them, or him, or her—the owner. Mrs. Whitman's rigmarole about banks and Switzerland and secret passwords and forty-five million dollars in escrow—sixty thousand down—that's all window dressing to make her look indispensable, and to daunt us. Sixty thousand, tchah! Only as a last resort would I hazard any sum on mere chance. I am not daunted, Fred. Nay, I am intrigued. I am disappointed in you. But never mind. I shall proceed. Alone. And in this weather! On foot."

Clay approached the front door, doing his impersonation of Nathan Hale climbing the ladder. Fred left him to his dramatic exit and took the newspapers downstairs, along with his coffee. He pushed the accumulated materials from the couch onto the floor and settled down.

As far as the *Globe* was concerned, the snow had been eclipsed by the "Grisly Slaying in Luxury Condo." The paper had got all it could from a situation in which the only name it could use for quotation was that of the police spokesman, who would reveal no more than what everyone knew already. The two teams of reporters assigned to the story had nevertheless filled two articles and two earnest sidebars. They'd relied heavily on old stories of Harvard-related murders, and pronouncements from experts about the phenomenon called overkill, in which a corpse is mutilated after the fact. The people they'd found to talk to at 1001 refused to be quoted by name. But there was much gratuitous parading of the names and makes of glitterati living at this address: the hostesses, prizewinners, poets with additional sources of revenue, and recovering kings and queens. It was the first recorded murder at 1001, where all such previous distasteful events had instead been passed off as unhappy accidents. The newspapers delighted in their access to the scandal, sweet mystery and sex and murder all in the shadow of privilege. Fred counted the word *bizarre* five times—three times on page 1 and twice on page 26. *Gruesome* figured prominently, too, and *grisly* a second time, and *horrifying*—all more than justified. A professor of criminal justice professed that the arrangements at the crime scene were impulsive, and suggested a killer who was confused and disorganized, rather than someone who was carrying out a well-considered plan.

Fred mumbled quickly through the articles, looking without success for real information. Speculation, yes—there was that. The possible religious aspect was reported, though the word *cult*

55

was not used. They'd got a description of the painting and its placement; only the broomstick and the ribbon were reserved. This was an unusually grim and ghastly killing for the Boston area, everyone agreed, and particularly for 1001 Mem Drive.

Fred called Harvard, and learned its libraries were open; but they were a hard half day's trek away. The Boston Public Library was closed. He took out the three-by-five glossy black-and-white picture the police photographer had taken for Bookrajian and studied it, bringing back to his retinal memory the textures of the paint, the age of varnish, the evidence of crackle and possible old inpaint, as if he and Clay planned to add the dismal thing to Clay's collection.

The head was beautiful and masculine in that misleading Italian way that dares you to risk a knife fight by underestimating its owner. The subject/victim wore about a three-day growth of beard—about the same length as Fred's own new growth, though Fred's was heavier, on a face that deserved more conceal-ment than Jesus' did. The man's hair was shoulder-length, his chest bare but for a few drizzles of blood, with the suggestion of Pilate's purple cloak over his shoulders. (Was it Pilate's? Some-body's purple cloak.) The head was well modeled and, like the thorns, excessively three-dimensional.

"The question is, whatever the picture purports to be," Fred muttered, "and if it's even relevant, is it authentic?" He was not happy with the limit Bookrajian had imposed on a task that was already next to impossible. Starting with so little, he'd be more likely to get the dope on Ernie's picture by looking for something else entirely.

Fred called Molly's again and had to get past Terry's "Listen, Fred, we need a dog. One bigger than Sam, that's mine. Sam hogs the TV. Also, Fred, I made up a riddle."

"Shoot," Fred said. "Then let me talk to your mom."

"You're never gonna guess it."

"Try me."

"And I'm not gonna tell you the answer."

"Terry, ask me the riddle."

"Why is Roger Clemens like a TV set?"

Fred studied it a moment, and nothing, in great quantities, occurred to him. He said, "I give up. Because he went to Toronto? No? Why is Roger like a TV set?"

"You have to guess. I'm not telling the answer."

Fred tried, "They both do better when they've got their stuff?"

Terry snorted.

"Let me think about it," Fred said. "Meanwhile, put Sam on while you get your mother."

Fred and Sam talked for six seconds about the weather in Arlington and Boston. "Are you all making out all right? Can you and Terry keep the stairs shoveled?" Fred asked.

"Your car's in the driveway," Sam said. "What if Mom needs to get out?"

"She has keys to my car."

"OK," Sam said. "I'm on pause."

"We're all on pause," Molly said, taking over. "Except you, Fred."

Fred said, "I'll get there when I can."

Fred paced the small space available for that activity in his office, and worried at Clay's being on his own. But he knew he had done the right thing in hanging back. It was Clay's money. If the man was determined to make a bad deal, Fred couldn't help; and if Clay wanted to outwit Lavinia Randall Whitman, probably Fred couldn't help with that, either.

"Forty-five million!" Fred exclaimed. It was so much money, and so far from the amount Clay could imagine spending, that Fred had not focused on the fact that huge amount though it might be, it was peanuts for bona-fide paintings by Rembrandt, Lucas Cranach, and Velázquez alone, regardless of whatever else might be in the group of ninety they were part of. Given the presence of those names, the whole deal was as unlikely as a seventeen-cent gallon of gasoline.

The phone rang. Fred checked his watch: 1:10. This should be Clayton, excusing himself from the luncheon table and leaving Lavinia alone with the hors d'oeuvres in order to give Fred one last chance to relent and break into her room.

"Mr. Reed?" a male voice asked, scratchy with nerves or bronchitis.

"May I take a message?" Fred asked. The voice was familiar: Hillegass. It was Burton Hillegass, whom he had last run into in the parking lot at Doolan's, where Hillegass had been flogging old paintings out of the trunk of his car.

"This is Burton Hillegass," the voice said, trying to sound as if that were good news. Hillegass was only recently out of the penitentiary, after five years of thinking up better ways to deal in stolen goods.

"Fred," Fred said.

"I'm in town," Hillegass went on. "Fred, like everyone else, I'm stuck and I'm stir-crazy. So. Mr. Reed at home?"

"I'll tell him you called," Fred said.

"Ask him does he want to buy a Rembrandt," Hillegass said. "Small, but cherce." He chuckled.

8

This kind of thing didn't happen. It didn't happen anyway, but *if* it happened, *when* it happened, it didn't happen this way. People did not appear out of the blue with Rembrandt and Velázquez. The likelihood of two such people appearing with two such paintings and within two days of each other, was truly a stretch.

"What kind of Rembrandt?" Fred asked evenly.

"Mr. Reed at home?"

Hillegass was, as everyone knew, on parole in the state of New Jersey, with all the usual conditions (such as not leaving the state of New Jersey). To this, also as everyone knew, the judge granting parole had added the proviso that Hillegass was not under any circumstances to occupy himself again with dealing in works of art.

Fred said, "Clay's out. He's taking the snow."

"When can I reach him?" Hillegass tried.

"I'll meet you somewhere," Fred offered.

Ten years ago, Hillegass had presided over a shop on Newbury Street, furnished in English antiques, from which he had done a roaring trade in old paintings, prints, and furniture and objets d'art, many of which, as it developed, were being trucked in from Cape Cod during the off season. When his New England supply dwindled, he set up in New York, where one day he responded incautiously to an invitation made by an FBI sting operation in New Jersey. Then, from the penitentiary, he'd been active on the telephone, calling owners and buyers and doing business, weaseling out sales and storing information for later use. He had charm, and none of that instinctive consciousness of human guilt that evokes distrust in other people.

"Tell me about the Rembrandt," Fred said. "Or not. Where are you in Boston?"

Hillegass finally understood that this was as close as he would get to Clay. "I'm not in a convenient place," he said. They waffled and dodged until Hillegass agreed to come to the BarOK on Charles Street, where Fred had eaten beans the night before. "Give me an hour," Hillegass said.

Gustav had been replaced today by a woman who looked better than he did in the house uniform of black pants and white shirt. She and Fred acknowledged that it was snowing before Fred asked her to call through the square opening behind her and get him a grilled steak to go with his Lime Rickey.

If this was the BarOK, why not go for broke and infect the menu with baroque indulgence? Cash in on all that dismal mayhem. Redo the menu, naming all the entrees after the appropriate motifs. Instead of a grilled steak rare, offer Beef St. Laurence. Lamb shishkebab could be Lamb Joan of Arc. If he were desperate for company, Fred could try his idea on the woman behind the bar, who would say to him, as she did anyway with less provocation, "Sit down. I'll bring it over."

Fred was the only customer in the bar. "Give me something to do," the woman went on. She had a cynical look about her, like the Mona Lisa's younger sister. Fred had arrived early, wanting to be well established before Hillegass got there. In all transactions, turf was an important consideration. If the issue was buying or selling, best to put your opponent at a disadvantage by making him come to your stamping ground: if he had something to sell and had to pull it out of a satchel on your turf, whatever it was would already have lost a chunk of its value to him.

So Fred was spread out in the booth, reading his paper, his lunch already eaten, and ready for coffee, when Hillegass came in, carrying nothing. Hillegass looked through the gloom to find him, recognized Fred's as a familiar face (though slightly bearded), waved, and took off a stained yellow coat that he hung by the door.

In the old Boston days, Hillegass had flaunted English tailoring, side vents and all, but now he'd devolved to a more multicultural, indeed almost derelict, look, closer to Fred's own working rig of khakis and sport jacket, except that Fred's brown tweed was from Keezer's, and Burton Hillegass must have poisoned some Italian count with balletic tastes in order to get his baby-blue cashmere with piping on its pockets instead of flaps. His white dress shirt was dirty. The paisleys on his tie were being fed a mixture of ketchup and egg yolk. The man was tall and gaunt; every limb and digit seemed double-jointed. When he smiled, which he remembered he should do right after he waved, his teeth looked as if they were in backward or upside down. He came over and gave Fred the glad eye and the glad hand, and asked the woman at the bar to give him coffee to go with Fred's.

Fred cleared a place for him, making him seem both late and accidental. "What's that you had there, steak?" Hillegass asked. "How was it?"

"I recommend the beans," Fred said. Hillegass raised a hand, and the attendant glanced over. "You got a hamburger?" Hillegass called.

"If you've got the Rembrandt on you, it's small, all right," Fred said. "Oh, shit! Don't tell me you walked across town with an etching."

61

Hillegass performed a grin that would enrapture any shark and handed Fred a folded sheet, a Xeroxed page, a copy of a photo of a painted portrait head, male, balding, bearded, looking worried about all the darkness around him, which extended to his clothing. Fred could make out a collar probably as white as Hillegass's, and a light earlobe—the subject's right ear. There wasn't much more detail. The image was a Xerox copy of a Xerox. Fred couldn't tell whether the original was a photograph or a print in a book. He'd guess the latter if he had to guess.

Fred fiddled with the image and looked over at Hillegass, who was hanging his lengthy upper lip into the surface of his coffee. Fred said, "This is the Rembrandt? It's hard to see much on a Xerox copy. I do notice it's a portrait of a guy. You want to talk about it?"

Hillegass reached across the table and flipped the page over for Fred to read the penciled notation: *Rembrandt van Rijn. 72.5 × 58. Court Preacher Johannes Uytenbogaert.*

"How d'you like them apples?" Hillegass bragged. "Great-great-grandpa of Humphrey Uytenbogaert, don't you guess?" He chuckled in an "aren't we smart" way that made the woman in back of the bar look over apprehensively, as if the next thing might be paper airplanes.

"How much are you asking for this here man of God?" Fred asked lazily, studying the smudged picture.

Hillegass started the spiel. "It's a hell of a picture and a hell of an opportunity," he said. "The situation's delicate and confidential, but this much I can say. There's real pressure to sell. The way I read the situation, it's almost a buyer's market. The owner of the Rembrandt wants about three million, but maybe I can do better."

Fred stood, pocketing the image as Hillegass, taken completely off balance, reached for it. "How do I get in touch?" Fred asked.

"Hold it. That's mine!" Hillegass said, half standing himself. "You haven't heard the rest of the story."

Fred dug a dime out of the tip he'd left on the table and

flicked it toward Hillegass. "That's for the copy. How do we reach you if my guy's interested?"

Whatever Hillegass's pitch was going to be, Fred had interrupted it so badly that the man didn't know what to play next. Meanwhile, the woman from behind the bar arrived with the plate of burger and fries and made a fuss of laying it out and scooping in her tip while Fred went to the rack next to the door for his parka.

"Give me a call tomorrow," Fred called. "Or the next day. There's no rush."

The restaurant in the Four Seasons was not crowded: but it was well filled with guests, and others waited. Fred jumped the line, telling the maître d' he was joining people for coffee, and entered the dining area. He spotted Clay and Lavinia Randall Whitman on the far side, against the window and the sidewalk. They looked as if they were in a temporary truce while negotiating a complex divorce over scallops accompanied by labor-intensive vegetables (Clay) and (Lavinia) white meat beaten flat, which the BarOK under Fred's new management would entitle Veal St. Andrew. Clayton wore his most fawning gray flannel, Lavinia the blue version of yesterday's pink velvet suit. Clay glanced up, startled, with a wild, unspoken question that Fred answered quickly, shaking his head while taking off his parka and hanging it over the back of a chair that he then pulled over from a neighboring setting just being vacated.

"Ah, Fred," Lavinia said. Then silence descended. Love did not brood at this table. Lavinia and Clay had been sparring, pretending to get along, until Fred came along and ruined it, and now the bubble of illusion, pricked, was letting out a bad smell. Not far away, behind Lavinia, an elderly couple ogled the dessert menu and discussed the arterial implications. The man, refusing to consider sorbet, said, "If I'm paying this much for dessert, they're gonna damned well work for my money. I won't eat a popsicle in a bowl."

Fred dismissed the waiter who had tried to interfere when he rearranged the furniture. "I'll have coffee when my friends do," he said.

Clay had had enough time to let his manners overcome his surprise and disappointed hope. "Mrs. Whitman—Lavinia—and I are enjoying the luxury of becoming better acquainted." Lavinia Whitman pursed her lips. Clay offered, "Fred, I am having an excellent Coquilles Saint Jacques. Have you lunched?"

"Thanks, I ate a Beef Saint Laurence, followed, as I walked over, by a Banana Saint Bartholomew from Store Twenty-four."

"Banana Saint Bartholomew?" Lavinia asked. "How is that prepared?"

"Peel the banana," Fred said. "In the old days B.C., they called it a Banana Marsyas."

"Fred jokes about food," Clay explained. It sounded like a greater failing even than refusing to break into Lavinia's hotel room.

"I was telling Clayton how much I would love to view his collection," Lavinia said. "I am so disappointed that he is redecorating. Everything in storage! How can you stand it? All your precious things hidden away!" Clay had the grace to blush at having his bald lie exposed so coldly by its victim. Lavinia pushed on, "Still, there's a silver lining to this cloud. When the decks are clear, you can consider new purchases."

"The next step is to make plans for Switzerland," Clay said hastily as he attacked a scallop with his knife and fork.

Lavinia bridled. "After certain financial formalities have been satisfied," she purred.

They were drinking Liebfraumilch, Fred noticed when Lavinia directed a waiter to remove the bottle from the ice bucket and pour for her and Clay. She raised her eyebrows toward Fred, who shook his head. "We will compare schedules after lunch," Clay finished. He consumed a third of a scallop for emphasis.

"Not wishing to confuse business with pleasure," Lavinia said,

"I left my calendar in my room. Suppose we take coffee upstairs, Clayton, and get down to brass tacks?"

"About the Swiss collection," Fred said.

Lavinia interrupted, "Not Swiss—*in transit*. An important distinction." She simpered and drank virgin's milk, as jaundiced and clear as virgin's lymph but with more nose.

"There may be a time factor," Clay told Fred.

"Crucial," Lavinia said. She took a fork to the last bite of her meat.

"But it is an exclusive option you offer, correct?" Fred pressed on. "Your being the exclusive agent?"

Lavinia nodded, chewing. She glanced toward a waiter who was passing with a loaded pastry tray and lifted a hand to flag him. Fred asked, "Has either of you heard about a Rembrandt portrait that's being shopped around?" He pulled Hillegass's Xerox copy out of his jacket pocket and began unfolding it into a space he'd cleared for it between Clay and Lavinia. Lavinia sucked air as he continued, "The guy who offered it to me says it's a portrait of Johannes Uytenbogaert, which I may not be pronouncing correctly."

Lavinia, gaping at the reproduction, tried to appear unruffled. Clay, catching on, twitched the paper so he could look at it right side up before turning it to face a still-speechless Lavinia Randall Whitman, who smiled, thought for twenty seconds more, and then said smoothly, "The collection is not meant to be offered piecemeal."

Fred said, "I'm puzzled."

Dessert was either marred or made more interesting by Lavinia's unsuccessful attempt to learn, without asking directly, who had offered Fred the Rembrandt, and by Clayton's ignorant effort to press what he saw must be their tactical advantage. It did not help Lavinia's state of mind when Fred pointed out, "I did not say that the Rembrandt had been presented to me by itself."

Lavinia was shaken. Her invitation to adjourn to her suite for coffee was not repeated. Instead, she remembered some long-distance calls she must make. Clay stood as she excused herself, saying, "If it is convenient, then, I shall come up with you and just get that list. An image of the Velázquez, also, would be most—"

"My client, I must tell you, is naive. Wisdom does not invariably accompany great wealth. Let me find out what's going on," Lavinia said sharply. "Fred, could you not make it simpler for me—I will respect your confidence in this—by telling me who offered you the picture?"

Fred shrugged and spread his hands. He seized the moment and took the Xeroxed page back, not wanting to wrestle it from her in the dining room of the Four Seasons.

"Local dealer?" Lavinia persisted, though she knew better. If Fred wasn't going to tell her outright, he wouldn't be stupid enough to drop hints.

"Who knows in this fax age?" Fred asked. "In this business, we could get a telephone call out of the blue, the three of us sitting here, from a Japanese dealer traveling in Uganda who wants to sell you Clayton's apricot flan. Or, better—such things can happen—wanting to sell Clayton himself the very flan he's almost finished eating."

Lavinia was not certain this was a joke. They'd never bothered to explain to her why Clay had not expressed an interest in his own picture when she'd tried to sell it to him that time. Never give information to the opposition, was Clayton's first rule of engagement, closely followed by, and almost indistinguishable from, the second rule: Consider everyone the opposition.

Lavinia saw she'd lost this round. She displaced her anger and confusion onto the invisible authority of superior secret knowledge. "I will have a few words with my client," she said. "Then I shall be in touch. Clayton, I am known for my integrity, and I stand by it. When I am promised an exclusive, I expect no less. Thank you for the lunch, Clayton. It was delightful."

"Just to be fair," Fred told her back, "I did not say it was a dealer who had offered me the Rembrandt. It may have been your client."

Lavinia turned back toward them briefly, her smile belying the tempest of riled Chanel she left behind her when she swept out. Clay waited until he was sure she was beyond hearing. "Fred, I congratulate you," he said. "What an extraordinary guess, or—how did you figure the Rembrandt to be on her list? It looks magnificent!"

9

At three-thirty they acknowledged the increasing obsequious-ness of the waiters. Darkness had already lowered across the plate glass next to Clayton's table, with the almost virgin street and Public Garden laid out under a new down comforter, like the Garden of Eden before the concept of transcendental wilderness got into the act. Clay had held the table by ordering a snifter of kirsch and sipping it as if it were the only thing standing between him and death by hanging.

"Something is going on," Clay had observed after Fred told him of the Hillegass encounter, a few minutes after Lavinia left them. "Who is the owner of the Rembrandt? I should have purchased that Stichting Foundation *Rembrandt Corpus*. But listening to your advice, I did not."

"All the libraries have it," Fred said. "A set like that, the defini-tive last word on Rembrandt's paintings, they *have* to buy it. As you kept mentioning, it's expensive."

Clay gestured operatically out the window, toward a city forced on pause. "In fifteen minutes we could know everything about this picture—if only we had purchased the set," he said. "As it is, we are impeded by mere weather."

Fred told him, "I'll get to a library tomorrow. Harvard's open. Acts of God don't faze Harvard. Or you could call Ann Mendelsohn right now."

"You jest! Ann Mendelsohn may be a friend, but she is first of all a curator for the most aggressively acquisitive museum in the land! You can't be suggesting we should alert her to this opportunity."

Fred reminded him, "So far we haven't even seen the smoke and mirrors we've been promised. There's nothing to buy, and if there were, we couldn't even come near speculating what it might be."

Clay said, "My interest is aroused, and my instinct is that an opportunity is being offered that, once I get past that woman . . . I am convinced there is a secret cache of important Old Master paintings here in Boston. Lavinia Randall Whitman should be ashamed. The proper function of a dealer is to facilitate, not to obstruct. So you conclude that Hillegass offers us a better approach to the same prize?"

"Hillegass is a crook," Fred objected. "And he consorts with crooks. He's a dealer in stolen goods, you remember. We might as well start back to Mountjoy Street. It's going to be slow going."

"No," Clay said. "I shall stay here, letting the Four Seasons be my base of operations. Not on account of the weather, Fred. I wish to press my present advantage."

" 'Advantage'?"

"My proximity to Mrs. Whitman. I shall keep her under my nose." They moved into a lobby that was cranking up for the snow-emergency cocktail hour.

"She's a dreadful liar," Fred insisted. "All that crap about Switzerland, and an unbreakable collection? And meanwhile, here's Hillegass with one of the same pictures under his arm?"

Clay waved the observation off. "Exactly. Knowing her, we know to accept the opposite of what she says." They stood in the lobby, Clay impatient to book a room with a view, and Fred to do whatever it was he was going to do—which was not, this late, going to include a library search, either for the Hillegass Rembrandt or for Bookrajian's crime-scene painting. On an impulse, Fred pulled Bookrajian's envelope out of his pocket and showed the police photograph to Clayton, whispering loudly, "Feelthy pictures?"

Clay held the photograph at arm's length, his face a grimace of disgust. "Please, Fred. I am a Unitarian! The sadomasochistic phantasms of the Italian Seicento . . ."

"That's where I placed it, too," Fred said.

"Hillegass offered you this picture also?" Clay asked. "And you gave it a moment's notice?"

"No, no, it's unconnected," Fred assured him. "This is the painting that's caught up in that murder in Cambridge." Clay looked inquiringly blank. "Surely you've read about the murder in the news?"

"I focus on international developments, if any," Clay said, handing the photograph back. "I disregard pornography. There has been a murder, I take it? And you are involved?"

Fred drew Clay into a corner and laid out the situation quickly, though Clay didn't want to hear about it any more than he would want to watch home videos of gang rapes. Fred finished, "They asked me, as a favor, to help identify the painting and give them a handle on its value, if it has any."

Clay said, "Indeed. The image is all too familiar as a generic type. As you know, Fred, I am concentrating on another project."

After five minutes' trudging through a city that had been transubstantiated into bulging white light, it was evident to Fred that snow was no longer falling. The total was just shy of four feet, but it had come down so relentlessly, and blown with such determination, that everything had been knocked crosswise. The sidewalks meandered with narrow six-inch paths that pedestrians had broken between high walls of tight pack. Cars tipped across smaller streets, foundered, blocking them, their drivers having run away screaming into the ice floes. Bucket loaders manned by desperation had picked up chunks of snow bristling with garbage cans and heaped them on top of parked cars from which tickets streamed forlornly. The place looked like Pompeii on the morning after: plum pudding under clotted cream. "Spotted Dick," Fred said, tapping nostalgia.

Fred chose a route that took him through the dignified brick residential quarters near the State House, expecting that the combined forces of old money and government might produce walkable streets. But the snow had been too fast, the old money too forgetful, and government too disorganized. The magnolia trees shuddered and dropped clumps of snow as indifferently copious as the leavings of cows that had made free of green apples. The sidewalks of Beacon Hill were impassable, the streets too deep for anything but all-terrain vehicles equipped with plows. Although nothing had been shoveled anywhere, some citizen had got the idea of marking a fire hydrant with a broom, to which a colored scarf was tied—and the whole region had then been decked out this way by volunteers.

Fred made a detour to buy provisions but balked at the lines of panicked hoarders needing large amounts of chips and beer and candles to see them through this event. It was almost seven when, empty-handed, he kicked off his boots in the Mountjoy Street entranceway. He hesitated, unsure whether he, as Clay's guest, was headed into the kitchen on this floor or downstairs to his office and the task he'd hardly started for Bookrajian.

Clay would permit neither answering nor fax machines in his house because of his conviction that these devices allowed the opposition to "know what we are doing." Clay's eccentricity offered protection from responsibility. Molly could have been calling for hours with an emergency in Arlington, and Fred would not know she wanted him. Fred balanced his parka on the newel post and walked in his socks into Clay's kitchen, where he started

71

water to make tea or coffee and, uneasily recalling the last place and time he'd walked around in his socks, phoned Molly.

"Yes? Shut up! Leave me alone! Hello?" came Terry's passionate cry, before Molly's voice joined in on another extension.

"How's your snow?" Fred asked. Terry launched into a babble of excitement that Molly trumped by stating, "Yes, the newspapers are right: snow is general all over Arlington."

"I want to talk," Terry demanded.

"You have been talking all day," Molly said.

"There's nothing to do, and Sam's a big poo head. If I had a dog . . . I have to ask Fred something."

"Two minutes. Then I want you to hang up," Molly said.

"It's going to take more than two minutes. It's my best riddle," Terry said.

"One minute."

"OK. Fred, did you think of the answer?"

" 'Why is Roger Clemens like a TV set?' "

"Right. You will never guess."

"Let me think," Fred said, deciding on tea and looking among Clay's things, the horribly neat lineup in the cabinets, until he came to the space reserved for tea bags—all of them herbal. Damn the man. He did not hold with stimulants.

"They both have iron in them," Fred guessed. He did not require Terry's snort of contempt to tell him how lame the guess was.

"OK, Mom," Terry said. "He's so cold, he's an iceberg."

Fred poured boiling water over a bag of leaves that claimed to have lemon in it. "You getting on all right?" he asked.

"As long as I don't kill the children. We're snowed back to about eighteen-oh-two, and the TV is on the fritz. The kids won't say what happened to it."

"Hold it. Did the TV conk out before Terry formulated her riddle?"

"On the subject of Terry's joke I say nothing, since she will construe anything I say as a hint. She plans to get into Ripley's with the most unguessable riddle since the Sphinx. Listen, Fred? Ophelia's frantic to talk to you."

"She got her power back?"

"I don't know. She says it's an emergency. But you know my sister. Call her, would you?"

"Maybe a glitch in her TV program," Fred said. "But aren't they done shooting until next month sometime?"

Molly's sister, Ophelia, was a glamorous whiz kid who had taken to the medium of TV like a roller-derby queen to the tilted track. Her elbows and her ruthless good looks, with her genius for tactics, kept her ahead of the closest competition in her chosen field, which was pop culture. She could sense the fads before they came, and she never ditched one until six minutes before it peaked.

This year's late-night series was entitled *Be Your Own* . . . It was designed to be the cherry on top of the self-help froth of Reddi-wip that graced the prurient interests of those afflicted with middle age and middle class. Each night she presented a different self-proclaimed self-made Realtor, prophet, model, boxer, cosmetic merchandiser, or inventor who, gazing with either lust or envy down Ophelia's cleavage, confessed personal intimacies and at the same time hinted how the audience could also make it to the top in the field of, for example, training horses for ex-Princess Di. With the pump primed by the grubstake from her early marriages, and thanks to her relentless optimism and past successes, the advancing crest of Ophelia's wave was sweeping in pots of money.

"Oh, thank God," Ophelia exclaimed when she understood it was Fred on the invisible end of her line. "You big beautiful ugly man. I am saved. I was almost—listen, Fred, in five minutes I was going to have to give up. I can't get in from Lincoln. Nobody can."

"There's nothing moving but emergency vehicles," Fred confirmed.

"And you are the only person I can call on," Ophelia said. Fred

73

took a sip of his Lemon Fraud, which tasted like the memory of some discontinued product such as Airwick. His instinct was to drop the phone and run.

"I had some cash to hide," Ophelia said, "or invest, or whatever—and I decided on art!"

"What!!?" Fred blurted. "Ophelia, you know nothing about art, not even what you like! You might as well set out to buy real estate in Cambodia, by mail."

"Now don't go on," Ophelia said.

"Ophelia, honey, tell me you haven't bought anything."

"I know my limits, Fred," Ophelia reassured him. "I have engaged an expert. To be my curator."

"Oh, Jesus," Fred said.

"His advice is to start with the Old Masters and move forward. To the New Masters," Ophelia explained.

A sinking feeling broad enough to swallow cars yawned crookedly in front of Fred. "Who is your expert?"

"I am getting to that," Ophelia said. "First—Fred, let me get my notes—are you familiar with a Mexican painter called Veelaqueese?" She spelled the name for him while he stared at the widening sinkhole.

"Oh, shit," Fred said. "Velázquez. Spanish."

"Mexican, Spanish—well, anyway, good, you've heard of him. My curator said he knows a hundred collectors who would sell their grandmother for the chance I am getting. Which I know you will not tell Clay about, but will keep just between us. He says, my curator, that you can't be too careful because of fakes and all, but this one's in the book. The Velázquez book. Number One-sixteen. Where you come in is, because of the snow, I am stuck here and he is stuck there, in Boston."

"That may be just as well," Fred said. "Tell me about the picture."

"It's three men at a table," Ophelia said. "They're eating or drinking, like at an inn, an Old World theme. There's one just like it in Russia, in the Hermitage Museum, he says. By the same artist."

"Oh, good." Fred threw the rest of the tea in the sink.

"Maybe you saw that program on TV? About the Hermitage? I missed it, not being interested in art—I mean, not at that time. Anyway," Ophelia went on, "my curator left a message on my machine yesterday telling me to meet him at his hotel this evening so he could give me more information and show me photographs, and then I would make a down payment to keep my option—he is holding the painting for me, keeping the owner from showing it to anyone else. . . ."

"Ophelia, you haven't spent money on this, have you?"

"He's at the Hotel Brittannee," Ophelia said. "Which is not a great hotel but is convenient for him, being next to South Station. Burton Hillegass. Maybe you've heard of him?"

"I know him," Fred said.

"I'm supposed to meet him there at nine o'clock, but I've been calling, and he isn't in his room," Ophelia said. "I'm afraid he's going to give someone else the chance. So Fred, can you act for me?"

Fred said, imagining the feel of Burton Hillegass's scrawny neck between his hands. "I'll trot right over. Tell me, just for fun, how much is Hillegass asking for this picture?"

"About four million dollars," Ophelia said. "Maybe a little more. What's the matter, Fred? Is that too much?"

10

When Amtrak decided to stay alive by throwing money at its East Coast terminals, it made of Boston's South Station a commuter's dream of yogurt shops, but it didn't do much for the Hotel Brittannee across the way. It still was, as it always had been, a sleazebag, waiting for the area of Boston contiguous to South Station to catch the drift and cause it to be imploded in favor of, maybe, some nice yogurt shops.

But sleazebag or not, the hotel was now booming because the snow had killed the trains. Its bars and grills spilled over with men who had thought themselves temporarily in transit and must reckon with that as a prolonged condition. The Hotel Brittannee was filled with male existentialists, along with a few females who were angling to take advantage of that fact. Outside, the world howled and made its scurryings of intemperate weather; inside, all was bonhomie that would be paid for later.

Fred cased the public area inside the big street doors but saw no sign of Hillegass. It was shortly after nine. He might have got impatient and come down, but his angular, ill-dressed frame was not among the stymied travelers sheltered here. Fred made himself look like a well-wrapped, hurrying guest, certain of his destination (if out of reach of his razor for a few days), and took the fire stairs to the tenth floor, where he broached the corridor and started looking for Hillegass's room. The place was honestly threadbare, with a frank ambience of anxious depression. Ten fourteen, which Ophelia had told him housed Hillegass, sported a DO NOT DISTURB cardboard sign draped from its doorknob. The sign, like everything else in the hotel, looked as if it had been disturbed frequently for a long, long time.

Fred knocked, and nothing responded but the TV voice inside, telling him loudly what he should spray on himself so as to encourage closeness. He knocked again, waited, and, finding the door locked, was forced to fiddle with it before he could let himself in. The room was brightly lit. As he entered, the TV screen flipped from the confident embrace of a well-sprayed couple to a show about men in uniforms, which Hillegass, stretched across his rumpled yellow bedspread, watched with protruding eyes. His purple tongue expressed distaste, but that was involuntary, since he had been strangled with that paisley necktie.

Fred caught the room's drift in a second and slid the door closed behind him. "Do not disturb," he muttered, looking around quickly. He shuddered. Hillegass was dressed, his yellow coat, like the blue frizzy jacket, tossed across a chairback next to the dirty window that overlooked Atlantic Avenue. Trying to breathe, the man had flopped and fouled himself, and his pants were darkened with the mess. Fred didn't see any luggage: no suitcase, portfolio, or knapsack—nothing of the kind. "What's going on?" Fred said aloud. He slid his hands into the empty jacket pockets of the coats on the chair before moving to the bathroom, where he found a toothbrush (dry), a plastic comb, and a container of green dental floss. But that mess in the toilet—Fred gulped with dismay—within the flush of much diluted blood, suspended in a rosy glow, a man's genitals bobbed sluggishly.

Shots from the next room came from the TV. Shooting and screaming. There was nothing here. Hillegass had been cleaned out. Fred went back into the bedroom and gingerly slid his hands under the corpse to find its wallet—missing. Yes, that was blood mixed with the mangle of other byproducts that had been inside Hillegass not long ago. Fred shuddered and swallowed hard. Fortunately, the hip pocket had stayed dry. A lot of blood pooled and scabbed into the various fabrics.

"Lovely business, the art business," Fred said, "when you add a little overkill. Wasn't that what the professor called it?"

The first flash of anything like logic or reason had brought back the scene on Memorial Drive: lugubrious excess in conjunction with real (or expected) paintings purporting to be from the opulent brushes of the seventeenth century. The Jesus picture from Mem Drive—that would have looked exactly as good as part of Hillegass's decor. The room needed something, any explanatory object, beyond the tormented body; but there was nothing. Beyond a creeping global revulsion that he'd be certain to take with him, there was nothing for Fred here: no papers, no paintings, not even faint dents in the ratty orange carpet where the lower edges of frames had rested. He slipped out the door again, ready to raise the alarm if anyone saw him, but the corridor was as empty, seedy, and nondescript as it had been when he went in. Saying, "Sorry, Louisa, or Mabel, or Sophronia," he flipped the Do Not Disturb sign over to read Please Make Up Room. Should he have been noticed downstairs, he wanted Hillegass found in short order, obviously several hours dead.

He took the fire stairs down two flights and boarded the elevator with a party descending from the eighth floor.

Atlantic Avenue was a broad snowfield blowing smoke and drifts. South Station could not decide how to handle the fact that it was open but no trains were running. Must sushi and books therefore remain available? Must stranded travelers be allowed to sleep there, and if so, how could one tell them from the homeless? The guards milled about, itching with consternation and the desire to roust someone they were sure was getting away with something, taking advantage. Fred shouldn't be in a lighted crowd this near to Hillegass, but he needed a quick phone. He called the Four Seasons, found Clayton in his room, and told him, "Do not mention the Rembrandt man to anyone."

"Uytenbogaert?" Clay asked.

"The seller. You understand me? Not a word. Not a hint."

"Of course. Of course not," Clay assured him. The advantage of working with a paranoid was that he demanded no further explanation. Fred could explain later, when they were face to face. While he stood at the bank of phones, one of a frantic crowd, Fred listened for sirens, watched for the throbbing lights that should start screaming if the maids were quick. Ophelia was trickier. Fred didn't know her well enough to guess how to protect her interests, and his. She was expecting his call anyway, though, and he had to report. He telephoned her next and limited himself to the bare minimum: "I couldn't reach him."

"I called to tell him you were coming," Ophelia said. "The desk didn't get an answer, either. God, I hope I haven't missed my chance."

"Listen, Ophelia," Fred said. "Don't feel crowded if I tell you the man's reputation does not put him among the blue chips."

"All the art dealers are jealous of him," Ophelia said.

"That will pass," Fred answered. "Leave it until we talk again. I'll call tomorrow." Neither he nor Ophelia could afford to know that Hillegass was seriously indisposed. He'd check with Molly before he decided how much to tell her sister.

Inside South Station, all the mechanical notice boards were blank, as if Boston had lost a war. Fred had been sweating while talking on the telephone, hating to be in so public a place, so near a crime that would soon be much more public. Outside, the wind whistled down his neck and dried the sweat on his body into a pall of ice. He put a dozen blocks between himself and the Brittannee before he allowed revulsion and dismay to make him puke into the drifts of an alley. That done, Fred ducked and bobbed toward

Mountjoy Street again, reluctantly. He was almost as close to his place in Charlestown. If he wanted to disappear, the guys living there would help him do it. But he had work, two killings in two places that connected, and the end of a string that led to paintings he had not seen. The work must keep him circulating.

The trek back to Beacon Hill would give him time to arrange the scene and the situation in his mind. Part of what he must do first was to see through the fog of his revulsion. This might touch him so closely he was obliged to act.

Tossing the guy's genitals like that, with contempt, into the toilet, Fred's instinctive prejudice was saying to him, displayed a Latin flourish: you're Italian or South American or Mexican. But Fred had been around enough in the world to know that wherever men were enemies, the gesture of castration was common, as likely in Morocco or Korea as in Mexico. As far as the toilet went—if the shoe fits, wear it. The impulse would occur easily to the killer or—if that was the situation—the questioner. Hillegass was alive and aware when his organs were hacked off. That gesture was to give him a jump start of despair. He'd catch the hint he wasn't going to get out of this alive, but still he'd work to go for the quick finish.

Hillegass had life left in him to pump out so much blood. The butchery was part of a campaign of persuasion while Hillegass was incapacitated by the choking, not a mark of triumph after the fact. Then, as the heart was doing its last work, someone had cleared out everything Burton Hillegass had in his room. If there'd been a Rembrandt with him, or a Velázquez, it or they were gone.

Orange trucks in chains, with snowplows attached, traveling in pairs, were working the main arteries and making it possible to walk more quickly. As Fred got closer to Beacon Hill, more and more people were leading their dogs outside to make steaming punctuation marks in the new snow. Not being that sort of person, Clay did not own a shovel, so Fred had no way of clearing the stairway leading down to his office entrance. He climbed the stoop, let himself in, and was asleep by midnight, hungry.

Molly woke him. "Fred?" after the ring. The air outside his third-floor window was clear and threatened sun. He sat up. The room was cold on his skin since he'd turned down the thermostat. It was six-thirty.

"What's wrong?" Fred asked. He sounded like Molly, afraid in that same intimate, familial way—when you panic about what you love in a world where nothing can be controlled, not even what you love, not even the love itself.

"Bookrajian called just now."

"Bookrajian woke you?"

"Worse than that: he woke Terry. No, Terry, you are not talking to Fred, not before breakfast. Fred, Bookrajian won't believe you're not here."

"What's up?"

"Something in the paper. I don't know. He's coming over here. Do I let him in?"

"Why is he coming?"

"He doesn't believe me. Do I let him in, Fred?"

"Why not?"

"Do I give him your number at Clay's?"

"Let's hold off on that. Did he say which paper?"

"No. Of course, I don't have mine. Randy Fibonacci came by on his dad's snowmobile about two o'clock yesterday and threw my *Globe* at the living-room window, but not hard enough to break it."

"Molly, I'll call you back. If you don't mind, let him in and give him coffee. I wish goddamned Clayton Reed stocked coffee. I'll go out for the papers and call you."

"Get back to me before he gets here," Molly demanded.

"I'm already putting on my socks," Fred said.

"Bookrajian sounds awful," Molly said.

"Things could *be* awful."

"Fred," Molly went on, zapping suspicion across the trackless wastes, "what's the matter? What's happened?"

"You know how paranoid Clay is about the phone?"

"Yes."

"It's catching," Fred said.

"The fish takes on the flavor of the water," Molly told him.

"I'll call you as soon as I can. The sooner I'm off, the sooner I'll be able to call."

Fred hung up, rammed his fist into the mattress, and said, "Shoot!" He was nervy. There was no way he'd been seen, much less identified, outside the Brittanee or, worse, on its tenth floor, was there? Clay, the secretive paranoid, set the prevailing tone in this place, and Fred must factor it out if he was to use his own intelligence. Not likely. Still, stepping onto Mountjoy Street, he half looked for the pair of squad cars parked out front, their windows furred by steam from Dunkin' Donuts coffee, and crumbs pattering down inside, escaping the large bites of the law only to land upon its lap. Mountjoy Street was old brick and new snow, empty and placid. The voice of Mr. Currier whispered to the ghost of Mr. Ives, "It's too goddamned cute. They'll never believe it. It won't sell. You gotta put in a dog, some horseshit, something!"

MIRACLE PICTURE AT SLAY SCENE triumphed the *Herald*'s headline. But what first caught Fred's eye was the grainy, retouched horror of the head of Jesus leering and grieving for mankind on the front page, his agony resembling that of a press hero trying to decide whether to run for national office and maybe lose. The *Herald* had it as a scoop; there was no mention of it in the *Globe*.

He'd picked the newspapers up in a convenience store on Charles Street and changed his mind about adding a takeout coffee to carry back to Mountjoy. Instead he took the papers to a coffee shop next door, sat at a red-checked tablecloth, and let a waitress bring him a bagel with his coffee. Now that he knew what was eating Bookrajian, he skimmed the papers quickly to see if there was anything about the Brittannee. Hillegass's murder had missed this edition of the *Herald* entirely, but the *Globe* had it, though in only a few last-minute lines. The body had not been discovered until almost midnight, when a guest noticed that the door was ajar (though Fred had locked it as he left). Hillegass was not named, pending positive identification of the body and notification of his next of kin.

So Bookrajian's beef was only with the release of that photograph, the SLAY PICTURE. "Not guilty," Fred told the waitress when she poured him more coffee. She was the human version of the red-checked tablecloth, a woman in her late forties, round and honest as Wonder Bread, who snorted at him and answered, "If you're not guilty, you're the only one."

"Thinking about something else," Fred told her. The waitress looked at the film-star image on the *Herald*'s front page, asked, "Brad Pitt?" and had more to say, but just then a couple of Boston cops came in looking for breakfast and a warmer place to be. "Nobody in here's guilty," the waitress told them. "Relax. What'll it be?"

Fred took a few more minutes with his coffee, reading the MIRACLE PICTURE article, most of which was buried deep inside. According to the paper, the painting was well known—in fact, notorious. It was associated, among those who followed such things, with a recent outbreak of miraculous cures. The painting was said to work miracles. It wept blood. On tour.

"The grateful head," Fred said aloud, folding his paper and looking around the shop. No wonder Bookrajian was having a fit. That was all they needed at 1001 Mem Drive, to go along with sex and murder: the scandal of religion. Fred carried change to the coffee shop's pay phone and called Molly. "He there yet?"

"Not yet."

"I'll be quick. That photo Ernie gave me, someone sold the same one to the *Herald*—you can see the shadow of the frame down the right side. So Ernie's pissed. He thinks I did it. You don't have to let him in the house. Give him Clay's number; I'll talk to him."

"So if I get a *Herald*, I'll see this famous picture? There's the door," Molly said. "You got anything else?"

"To fill you in, a Spanish priest, Father Ernesto Gigante—Spanish or Mexican or Colombian or Puerto Rican, who knows?—was recently on tour with this thing, working cures, collecting money, I would guess, and letting the people worship the picture until it bled tears. Tell Ernie to call me, but give me twenty minutes."

11

You son of a bitch! You happy?" were Bookrajian's first coherent words. Molly's voice was in the background, talking to Terry: she'd let him in out of the cold.

Fred waited for the outraged spluttering to dwindle, then answered, "Ernie, I won't waste your time or mine denying anything. You know your own people. Instead, let's look at this new information. Where are we? Who is Father Ernesto Gigante? *Where* is he?"

Ernie was hard to deflect, but he had to admit that the damage, if any, was done—and that the benefits of publicity might even outweigh whatever damage there was. Grudgingly, he released his grip on his outrage and accepted coffee from Molly, as Fred gathered from the bits of conversation he overheard

"Thanks," said Bookrajian. "I haven't been sleeping much. Sorry to blow my stack in your kitchen, Ms. Riley."

"I'll get dressed," said Molly.

Bookrajian told Fred, "Who Father Ernesto Gigante is, we will learn. Where he is, or where most of him is, we have a guess. Fucking miracle worker. We think somebody was saying to him,

85

'You're so good at mystic cures, try fixing *this*.' Logic tells us he's the headless one. But you know and I know better than to rely on logic in a mess like this, where nothing looks like what it is. You maybe did us a favor, Fred."

"For the record, and to be fair, I can't take credit for the *Herald* leak," Fred said.

"Shit, it's done," Bookrajian said. "Water over the damned whatever. This is good coffee. What are you doing in town?"

"I work here. Ernie, don't try the gambit of the friendly voice, not over the phone, and as exhausted as you're sounding. We should make some progress on that picture now that it's gone public. What else can you tell me, about the circumstances or anything?"

"The boys in Worcester have been tracking this Gigante, or trying to, it looks like, in a kind of half-assed way, since about a month ago, which is when he turned up there. But they got other things on their mind, and like everyone else, they're being cut back. Tax base out there is shot to hell. People don't think. They give everything to the goddamned School Department to run rehab programs that send the youth offenders back out into the streets stronger and wiser."

"Father Gigante worked out of Worcester?" Fred prompted. The Worcester tax-base situation he'd just as soon not get into at eight o'clock in the morning. Bookrajian's voice was more than just exhausted; it was strained, and sad, and—other. That made it harder to measure what he said.

Bookrajian said, "He did a gig in Worcester a month ago, is all we know. Worcester Fraud ran him out of town on a technicality, with a warning. They went easy on him and didn't push it. He was traveling with a gorgeous girl, they said. They don't want to tangle with the issues, they can't afford to: Jesus and nuns and bleeding pictures and manifestations in the clouds and the rest of it, miracle cures, stumped so-called experts, and a bishop who was sympathetic, in a state where the legislators are about ninety percent

Catholic? How could law enforcement go up against all that? So they told the guy to take his bleeding head of Jesus and his miracle cures and his blonde and his goddamned collection bushel basket, and get lost."

"Where'd he go?"

"He did what they said: he got lost. I've been on the horn since five this morning with Worcester. They called after they saw the paper. They're trying to round up witnesses, maybe get hold of some curees. None of which is your business. I've gotta go. Thanks, Ms. Riley. You want to talk to Fred?"

"I'll call you later," Molly told Fred.

"Whooee!" Fred exclaimed, putting the receiver down with all deliberate speed. "Cross whatever Pandora had in her box with a can of worms, let them breed under a rock, and you get a swarm of what Ernie's up to his eyes in."

There was no answer when he tried Clay's room at the Four Seasons. But he knew he could rely on Clay to keep his mouth shut about Hillegass; that was the advantage of working with a paranoid monophrenic. The Hillegass thing was bad, and what was more, it was pertinent to Clay's interests. Hillegass, before he died, had betrayed the particulars of two paintings in the big collection: the Rembrandt and the Velázquez. If Fred could find them in the published record, he could follow them and thereby learn more of the cache Lavinia held so close to her chest.

Fred had put together some notes on the three pictures he was tracking: the Rembrandt, the Velázquez, and the miracle slay-scene picture. All three shared one peculiarity at least: proximity to the blasphemy of death by violence. Coincidence or not, he'd let that go until later. For now he'd go after the paintings.

Fred called the Four Seasons again and left a message so Clay would know where he'd gone. He added, as a postscript, "Do and say nothing." He gathered his notes together and started walking into Cambridge, through a world shocked into paralysis by cold and snow, and sun glare on snow. Snow, Fred figured as he plunged along, had doubled the bulk of matter in the city.

The residential institution does not shudder to a halt simply because the rest of the world does. Harvard was sparsely populated since commuting students and many professors could not get in to their appointments, but the place was grinding along anyway, a juggernaut of learning. The Fogg Art Museum was closed, but its Fine Arts Library was awake and aware, if understaffed. Fred blundered out of the howling wilderness and into the jungle of the museum where Harvard keeps captive its endangered paintings. Clay kept Fred's membership green so that he need only stow his coat in the rack provided, bow, show his pass to the lady sitting next to the umbrella stand, and save his five bucks for lunch.

Rembrandt's *Bust of Christ* had been haunting Fred ever since the spectacle of butchery at 1001 Mem Drive, and he wanted to remind himself of the flesh of the painting itself: its real paint, its red-blond wood showing through from scratches made by the end of the painter's brush, in order to subtract lighted hair into the young man's beard. The portrait had been done from life. Especially if events led him, in the coming few days, to lay his hands on what Hillegass had been offering as by Rembrandt, Fred wanted the three-dimensional fact of a work from Rembrandt's hands fresh in his mind.

But the Rembrandt was not on the wall among the feral presences of other paintings hanged like predators around the Fogg's small rooms. These were old friends and enemies of Fred's, some of which, like Dirck Bouts's *Virgin and Child*, he'd known since it first took him hostage during his flaming, almost instantaneous passage through Harvard. Midwestern mud up to his eyes, he'd wandered into the Fogg one day, in search of a cafeteria, and been appalled by the sudden revelation of robust, sneaky, vicious, and benevolent human souls, flayed and framed to dry. He'd never seen paintings before, not like this. The start of fear that had visited him then in front of Bouts and Botticelli had burned a track in his nerves that still shivered when he was alone with a painting of substance.

He walked through the Fogg like a person on night patrol. Things had been turned inside out since his last visit. A third of one room was filled by a painting he'd never seen or heard of— eight feet by five of heaving orange cloud made of cement: a leering, toppling huddle of crusted paint declared the triumph of the illusion of human joy. This resolved itself, after the first shock, into a picture that could be interpreted like a story—the only way most people read a picture.

A man made of bewildered optimism, masquerading as fat, was the old Greek god Silenus, drunk but still game, and gamey, all five hundred pounds of him. He was supported by a pair of satyrs vicious-looking enough to serve as his chief of staff and his press secretary. Behind them lurked a woman mostly in shadow. A two-year-old boy, naked, a hundred pounds worth, sat cheerfully in a bucket of grapes, and peed. The thing was bloated with hope.

"Francesco Fracanzano," Fred read, glancing at the words on the wall. "Never heard of him. Sixteen forty? It's the same age group as the paintings I'm playing with—Velázquez, Rembrandt, and whoever made the head at One-oh-oh-one Mem Drive."

The truth of Fracanzano's painting burned away and left mere work and architecture. Fred studied the skin of the monster as safely and impertinently as if it were a Mongolian tiger behind bars. He nodded across the room at the trap where Joseph struggled with Potiphar's wife, and toward Ribera's *Saint Bartholomew* waiting naked, holding the knife they'd use to skin him. The wrinkles under the old man's arms were brutally tender slashes of gray paint.

Then he grabbed his parka again and crossed past the trinket store into the adjacent Fine Arts Library.

Frankie Wong watched the library entrance, its being his

excruciating job to put down the sports section from time to time and check the IDs of persons seeking entrance to the library, or search their belongings as they left. "Gee, Fred, I didn't recognize you," he said. "What's the beard for? You going Hollywood?"

"Understudy for Brad Pitt," Fred said.

"I hate a knife," Fred muttered to himself as he descended the dark staircase to the stacks. A knife in a very adept hand had done that damage to Hillegass: a big knife in a quick, skilled hand belonging to someone who'd done that job, or jobs like it, often enough to know how not to get covered with blood himself at the same time. "I really hate a knife," Fred said, moving through the underground stacks toward Spain and Velázquez. "The killer who looks for the thrill of feeling the resistance of the flesh—I hate a knife."

The three men in the reproduction of the painting had a knife—quite a big one, too. They clustered around a table that also supported a round loaf of bread to use the knife on, as well as a lemon and a bowl of cherries. The youngest of them held a clear glass carafe of red wine. This was the picture Hillegass had offered to Ophelia, number 116 in the Velázquez book, all right: Lopez-Ray's 1963 catalogue raisonné. It was in the book, listed, even reproduced. The problem was that it was not by Velázquez.

Fred sat at the vacant desk he'd found along the stacks in the musty cement basement, and he looked over the evidence. Anyone could have told Ophelia after looking at it for ten minutes, "Stay away from that picture." It wasn't a field Ophelia understood, so she was as vulnerable to her chosen expert as Fred would be if he hired himself a lawyer from the TV ads. Clay would never have fallen for this picture. He'd be relieved and tickled to know what it was, though. Fred started pulling the evidence together in a way that would educate Ophelia and also convince her not to make the same mistake again. She had to be made to understand that only the weather had saved her from a big loss, of both face and money—especially since so many people, once they lose face, in order to cover that loss, keep throwing more money into the same hole after it. There would be plenty more like Hillegass to take his place.

Fred put it together in a note, with Xerox copies of a few relevant pages.

Ophelia:

The picture you were offered is *like* Velázquez, but not *by* him. Yes, it's in the book—number 116, as you said. But it's listed in small capitals, which means the scholar, Lopez-Ray, doesn't want to swear Velázquez painted it, or touched it, or even saw it. He thinks maybe a person could argue that Velázquez may have had something to do with it, but you can't prove it because the picture is in such bad shape. Think of it as an old copy that's badly damaged, that someone made look better by painting over the worst parts, like a car with lots of body putty and a cracked engine block. It might be worth a few thousand as a decoration, in my opinion. For fun, here're copies of the real one at the Hermitage (which Catherine II of Russia bought) as well as a couple of the other duds. Don't feel bad. There are six *Three Men at a Table* wannabe's, and some belong to snazzy collections. If you had bought this ringer, you would be in the same league as the Marques da Casa-Torres, Lord Iveagh, and Lord Moyne.

Cheers,
Fred

For himself and Clayton, Fred took note of the fact that Ophelia's Velázquez number 116, had last been recorded, as of 1963, in the Zurich collection of one Z. Goldberg. "So much for Clay's Velázquez," Fred said, and he moved along the stacks toward the ponderous organ music of the seventy-pound Rembrandt canon, three volumes so far, complete up to 1642, with twenty-five years of the painter's productive life yet to go.

If you elect to be a committee of scholars, Fred thought, dragging the volumes to the desk he'd commandeered, it's nice to have a government behind you; and the government of the Netherlands, since it lost its empire, doesn't have much going for it beyond Rembrandt and Shell Oil. He pulled out his Xerox copy of the ancient masculine head and settled down comfortably for a long, satisfactory perusal of the detective techniques of J. Bruyn, B. Haak, S. H. Levie, P. J. J. van Thiel, and E. van de Wetering, with the collaboration of L. Peese Binkhorst-Hoffscholte and J. Vis.

It went so depressingly quickly that he barely had time to get spread out amid the collected research materials of the desk's regular occupant, who seemed to be committed to an exhaustive study of classical Greek erotica on red-figured pottery. In no less than three minutes, surrounded by all those athletic Greeks, there was Fred's quarry, the man of God, Johannes Uytenbogaert. As of 1986, he was number A 80 in volume 2, in the collection of the Earl of Roseberry. Page 392. In ruff and haunted-looking impasto, poised before a luminous gray background, the preacher stared out from the reproduction on the page, vivid and right as rain. The committee had written pages on it, including reports of X-ray and other photographic examinations. Rembrandt had painted the portrait in 1633, and the committee had documented its history all the way back to October 20, 1664, when it was listed in the inventory of the estate of one Abraham Anthoniensz of Amsterdam, who had commissioned the portrait of the preacher and used it to decorate the main hall of his country house in the Waatergraafsmeer. Unfortunately, this was not the painting of which Hillegass had handed Fred the photocopy. Rembrandt's man had a ruff, two hands, and a waist, while the Hillegass attempt had no ruff and one hand, and was cut off at the bottom of his rib cage. If it was even mentioned in the canon, it would be in one of the footnotes, under "copies." Yes, this must be it: the second copy mentioned, said to be a wood panel measuring 72 × 57 centimeters. The dimensions matched, or close enough. Hillegass's source had added a half centimeter to the recorded vertical dimension, and a centimeter to the horizontal; enough for the lip of the frame to cover.

Following the Stichting Foundation's lead, Fred paced back to the Dutch section of the stacks and pulled out the definitive work by von Moltke, which added, in black and white, an illustration. Yes, there was the same painting of which Hillegass had given Fred a Xerox copy. Since 1965, the "Rembrandt" Hillegass had wanted to sell had been in the record as being by another painter altogether: Govaert Flinck, a decent craftsman but never a household word. Von Moltke was confident in his attribution of the unsigned portrait, which the Stichting scholars did not question. So for well over a generation, anyone who cared to could have found out what this painting was. You wouldn't say the Flinck was a fake, any more than you could say it was a Rembrandt. It had been an honest picture in its day, and it was still an honest picture, which Hillegass, however, was representing—or which some entrepreneur was marketing by means of Hillegass, and also through Lavinia Randall Whitman, in her more rarefied econiche—as Rembrandt.

The known history of the Flinck, for what it was worth, had begun on November 11, 1905, in Amsterdam, when it was sold (by Fred. Muller) from the de Bloch Collection of Vienna (No. 16). Knowing this much, Fred could find out who had bought it, and for how much, if he wanted to. By 1939, the same picture was recorded in the collection of the late Dr. C. J. K. van Aalst, of Hoevelaken. He'd maybe try to follow it forward from there later. But for now, he'd let Clay know that the thing being marketed as Rembrandt was not Rembrandt, so to hell with it.

Fred made copies of what he needed and put the books back. He'd identified two pictures in half an hour. They were old pictures, falsely attributed by the merchandiser, who in each case, as far as the Hillegass approach indicated, was inflating the real market value by millions of dollars. The "Velázquez" was a not-very-interesting antique, worth about five thousand dollars for its age; the Rembrandt portrait that turned out to be a Flinck might be worth eighty grand if the Flinck attribution held up.

If Lavinia Randall Whitman was acting as the agent for a mine that was for sale, and these were the diamonds it was salted with, no prospective buyer with any sense would need to look down the shaft. "Or take the shaft," Fred said aloud, noticing he'd accidentally picked up a copy of *Greek Erotica* from Duckworth. He had to search the carrels to find out where he'd been working, so he could put the volume back where it was supposed to be.

But still, how could one not be curious? There were eighty-eight paintings unaccounted for.

The last task was to check the *International Registry of Stolen Works of Art* and its supplements. The presence of Hillegass near a picture made it especially important to ensure that the painting being offered was not hot. But the *Registry* mentioned neither of the pictures. So the works were real, if not what they were advertised as; and they had not been reported stolen. "Two down and eighty-eight to go," Fred said, resolving to eat lunch before he chased the two he'd found into the more recent past. If he could get far enough, he might be able to identify their present owner. Clay's anxiety to learn more should not be dismissed: a cache of ninety paintings had to contain *something* good. Hell, the Flinck was a good painting; it just wasn't what Hillegass and Whitman had pretended. In fact, as a Flinck, it was perfect for Clayton Reed.

"Clay's right," Fred said to himself. "We may as well find these paintings, drive up to the guy's house in a van, and dicker with him straight out."

Fred went upstairs carrying his sheaf of Xerox pages and fed money into the pay phone in the library's cold foyer, which overlooked the merciful snow covering the poured cement outside. Clay was not in his room, which meant that a good deal of spelling had to be parlayed over the line. But it was necessary that Clay have accurate information as quickly as Fred could get it to him. Fred dictated, and spelled where necessary, "Say nothing to our

94

friend. Do nothing till I call. I am following a trail. Meanwhile, the Rembrandt is a Flinck. The Velázquez is a fraud. Fred."

The smell of hamburgers hung in the vestibule, as if someone from Bartley's had come with an aerosol can and sprayed it. He'd eat, but he'd call Molly first.

"Did you guess it?" Terry asked on picking up the phone, even before Fred had identified himself. Her riddle must be pending in many simultaneous venues.

"Because," Fred started. Terry's humor was not usually complex, being of the knock-knock mentality, depending on rudimentary word association. Knob. Knob who? Doorknob. Get it, Fred? Door? Knob?

"Three strikes and you're out?" Fred hazarded. Though it meant nothing to him, it could be Terry's answer.

"I don't get it," Terry said.

"I'm wrong," Fred said. "I'll keep studying the problem. Get your mom, will you?"

"You were going to call me right back," Molly said when she came on the line.

"I was? Sorry, I got sidetracked," Fred said. "I'm at the library, the Fogg, in Cambridge."

"I hope you spent the day looking for Ernie's picture."

"Listen, Molly—first, how straight can you be with Ophelia? It's a long story, and I'm talking in kind of the middle of the world here, but can you make sure she absolutely drops a matter I was looking at for her until I can sit down with her? And give me her fax number at home so I can send her something."

Frankie Wong at his desk was staring at Fred through the glass entrance doors, over his newspaper.

"If I can scare her, I can hold her," Molly said.

"Her contact is dead."

"That should scare her," Molly said. Then, "Fred—Jesus! You're serious? What's going on? What has my sister gotten into?"

"It was the people that guy ran with," Fred said. "I don't reckon his danger spills over. If I thought it did, I wouldn't fool

95

around. But—well, it's pretty awful, Molly. Nothing's moving in the world, besides emergency vehicles, and she's way the hell out there. Good place for her right now. I'll get to Arlington somehow and fill you in."

"You coming now?"

"No, I'm chasing a thing for Clay—actually, a collection—and as long as I'm here, I'll give Bookrajian's miracle slay-scene picture a poke, just to say I did."

"If it'll get you here sooner, I'll tell you who it's by," Molly said.

12

He's Mr. April, nineteen eighty-seven," Molly announced. "What?" Fred exclaimed.

"Not that I let on to that damned Bookrajian, but as soon as I saw the *Herald*, I knew I'd seen the picture. I'm good at faces. You know those funeral-home calendars my mother won't stop giving me? And that I save for the benefit of my future biographers?"

"Is that why you save them?" Two students, a male and a female, carrying armloads of books, shoved past Fred and created a flurry of cold air when they plunged into the brilliant sunlight of the afternoon.

"It's by Guido Reni," Molly said. "Or at least he painted one so much like it, that they're brothers or cousins. I have it for you. April nineteen eighty-seven. The painting's in the Louvre, so you'll find a thousand reproductions of it. Now you know what to look for. How will you get to Arlington? Nothing's running."

"I'll call you in an hour," Fred promised, and he went back to the stacks. If she was right, Molly had caught the prize. And if she was right, a hundred other people in the area who'd been in the Louvre last summer were calling Bookrajian by now. Unless Fred played this right, some officious researcher was going to track the Mem Drive painting much too far, too fast.

Forty minutes later, Fred telephoned Homicide's extension from the sidewalk in front of Bartley's. He was told curtly, "Book-rajian's out."

"I've got info for him on the Mem Drive murder."

"Tell me," Fred was ordered. "Bookrajian's off the case."

"He's what?"

"Personal time. Talk to Detective Cipriani. Can you come by the station? Or—hold on, I'll get her. Dolores?"

Fred hung up. He wasn't married to the Cambridge cops. But he was hot, and there was still hope that he was onto something. He didn't want Homicide messing this up. It was true, the painting from 1001 was close enough to Reni to pass—like the Flinck and the wannabe Velázquez. It had to be part of the same group—and so far only Fred could put the two killings, and/or the two places, together. A blind corporation owned the apartment? A mysterious client was hiding behind Lavinia Randall Whitman? A butcher worked each side of the river.

When he found the rest of the collection, he didn't want to have to look at those pictures through a grove of legs in uniform. Bookrajian, he could work with. Fred called the officer's home number and on the first ring raised a distracted and subdued Bookrajian.

"It's Fred," Fred told him. "I've made progress." He listened to an empty space on the other end of the line.

"I'll come by if you're not too far from here," Fred said.

"I'm out of it," Bookrajian answered. Fred waited. "Hell, come on over," Bookrajian went on finally. "I might as well keep busy."

The Bookrajians had the top floor of a three-decker off Magazine Street, near the river, down from Central Square, Bookrajian told him. The bright sun made a skin of ice that shot back glare from spots melted and frozen again on the abandoned streets. Fred walked it in twenty minutes since traffic was not a factor. Many of the principal streets were still little better than one-way tracks between snowbanks and abandoned vehicles. For all the cold and the discomfort, Fred's fellow pedestrians moved with the pleasure of people who had been unexpectedly reprieved.

Bookrajian's building was wooden, square, and gray. It stood between two others just like it except for the color, across the street from others of the same kind: structures slapped together for working-class families late in the nineteenth century, when families were regarded as an urban asset, to be encouraged.

Fred poked the buzzer and waited for Bookrajian to come downstairs and let him in. Perhaps he'd changed his clothes, but he was dressed as Fred had last seen him, in white shirt and wilted black suit, no tie, street shoes. Bookrajian's face was strained, as if he had been drinking heavily, or indulging in similar excess.

"Just so you know," Bookrajian told Fred in the hallway, after he let him in, "I'm on administrative leave, starting this morning when I got to my desk. Just so you know. Come on upstairs."

Fred followed him past bicycles and unclaimed circulars that lined the landings and the stairs. The place seemed shabby and rent-controlled, although rent control in Cambridge had been repealed for several years. But inside, the Bookrajians' apartment was different. Fred sensed a determined female effort to impose something pretty upon what had clearly been for too long a bachelor apartment.

"Blanche Maybelle," Ernie said, introducing his wife as she crossed the living room to take Fred's hand. She was a tall woman, maybe five-nine, the intimate shape of whose body Fred knew accidentally, concealed though it was by the denim jumper she was wearing, which mitigated the breasts Fred happened to know Michelin would characterize as at least "worth a detour." Her blond hair was pulled back into a careless ponytail, and she looked as if she had not stopped crying since Fred talked to her two nights ago. The hand trembled when Fred took it and told her, "Hi, Blanche Maybelle. We talked on the phone."

"I'm going in the bedroom, Ernie," she said, turning away.

"It's OK if you want to be here," Bookrajian said. "We're just talking about—"

"I don't want to talk about whatever. I'll watch TV in the bedroom."

She went away as Bookrajian slumped into a large chair covered with fake black leather. Once again he had done and said the wrong thing. This room was carpeted in baby blue, its walls painted pinkish and lined with shelves made of chipboard, which were filled with trophies and wedding presents: punch bowls and pedestal coffee mugs with gold trim, and clock radios with decorative sculpted appendages. The room had been a den until Bookrajian brought Blanche Maybelle home. Bookrajian gestured toward a collection of corpulent armchairs facing the chair he sat on, near a large entertainment center in fake veneer, in the midst of which a TV presented pictures with no sound. The pictures were of doctors, nurses, and patients talking passionately to one another. As Fred sat, Bookrajian looked around the room, shrugged, and offered, "You want anything? Beer? Coke? Coffee?"

Fred said, "I'm going to go straight through this since I'm hoping to get to Arlington after." Bookrajian brightened and leaned forward as Fred started talking. "On that painting. I have more than you need. In fact, you don't need much."

"I'm taking notes," Bookrajian said, grinning lopsidedly and tapping the side of his head with a forefinger.

Fred said, "The painting looks like the work of Guido Reni, an Italian who lived from 1575 to 1642. I say 'looks like.' You want to accentuate that. Maybe the picture was painted by the guy, but the odds are not. They did make multiple versions of their own pictures sometimes, and Reni did several of this subject. But it could also be by someone who worked in Reni's studio, with Reni adding a touch here and there, but again, the odds are not. Or it could be a copy based on a Reni, done by someone who never met the guy. There your odds are better. In financial terms (and here's where the scholar's opinion can make a big difference to someone), a signed, sealed, and delivered Guido Reni—admittedly bigger, and very different in subject—recently sold at auction in New York for well over half a million."

"Holy shit!" Bookrajian exclaimed.

"It's called *Liberality and Modesty*," Fred said. "But don't let the title fool you; it's a big picture full of naked Romans, very theatrical. Whereas if the painting rates only a 'circle of' or 'studio of' or 'attributed to' Guido Reni, the value drops like a stone. The best you could hope for—well, a *Lucretia* that was billed openly as a copy did make nine thousand at auction. But with Lucretia you've got the chick factor, which connoisseurs like, and the naked-female-breasts factor. The people go for breasts."

"Oh, for Christ's sake," Bookrajian said, his face suddenly white. He started shuddering. Fred stopped, amazed.

"Sorry," Bookrajian said after a few moments. "Go on, Fred."

"If the department wants to commission a real study, there are similar pictures in the collections of the Louvre in Paris, and the Detroit Art Museum, and the National Gallery in London. A couple of others are mentioned as having been in the collection of the Dresden Museum before the war, and two more are said to exist in Bologna, though the boys are real leery about those.

"But we both know all this is way off base anyhow, since from Homicide's point of view it doesn't matter a damn whether the thing is real or dubious. Real as in *by* Guido Reni. If it's real it's worth, say, a hundred and fifty K; if it's not, which it's not (between you and me), make it ten K. But the killing issue's going to be the miracles, don't you agree?"

"Miracles," Bookrajian said. Were this not his own house, he would spit. "Talking about real, this Father Ernesto, how did he get the fucking thing to bleed tears?"

Fred said, "Just out of curiosity, I can't help wondering . . ."

"Thanks for the info," Bookrajian said absently, cutting him off. "If it looks like we need it, I'll tell someone to call you. You've been a big help. If I don't seem grateful, it's just—well—listen, Fred, how are you getting home?"

"I thought you might get someone to drive me," Fred said. "There any chance of that? An emergency ride home?"

Bookrajian grimaced painfully and stood.

"I don't buy miracles," he said. "I was in the seminary too long." He crossed toward Fred, reached the entertainment center, and switched off the TV picture, showing dogs comparing dog foods. He stooped lower and opened a drawer. "Take this and put it on the roof of your car." He pulled out one of those revolving-ball lights that attach magnetically to a car's roof. The cord to connect it to the lighter trailed umbilically from it. He handed it to Fred.

"Being off the force temporarily, won't you need this?" Fred asked.

"I got more."

Fred took the light and, standing, dropped it into the pocket of his parka, which he had not removed. He in his parka and Bookrajian wearing a suit jacket in his own home, they looked like transients or burglars, people who had no business being in a house. For the first time since they'd met, Fred reached his hand out to shake Bookrajian's. The man was suffering. Whatever he'd done to mess things up with his employers, whatever was going wrong, the man could use some fellowship.

"I'll get this back to you," Fred said, patting his pocket. What was he supposed to do, put it on his head like a beanie? The ex-cop pro tem was distracted by his troubles, not thinking things through. Bookrajian walked him to the door. "You need any more help with that painting," Fred offered, "call me."

"It's not going to make a difference. But I do appreciate it," Bookrajian said absently. "I do." The telephone rang once and stopped. Bookrajian stood at his door, trembling, and Fred left as he was saying, "Excuse me, Fred, I've got to . . ."

102

"The poor guy looks like the boys in the back room have been beating him with hoses for a week," Fred told Molly. He'd arrived at her place in Arlington, ebullient and triumphant, just after they finished supper, having hitchhiked to within a mile of the house on a series of snowplows. When he got in, the kids were fighting in the living room with a couple of friends, over a game of Monopoly that was deteriorating into pandemonium. Molly was banging around the kitchen making muffins for the morning. She'd hung the old Hovey and Roper calendar next to the fridge, with April exposed, so that she could refer back and forth between it and the front page of the *Herald*, itself attached to the fridge with magnetic ladybugs.

"Am I right?" Molly asked.

"I got the name of the Guido Reni expert," Fred said. "I think you are absolutely on target. If it's not Reni, you could make a good case for it anyway. I can't say which it is myself, but I now know who to ask: a scholar in New York who claims Lyndon Larouche is his big inspiration. I had not known Lyndon Larouche was also an art historian."

"So call him," Molly said.

"Only as a last resort. I hope he's in Mongolia. If he is familiar with the Mem Drive picture, and knows the name of the owner, which I'd love him to tell me—though likely he would not—I couldn't keep him from doing his civic duty if he felt like it, and running to the cops. And I think there may be other paintings involved."

"Ah," said Molly. "We are not pure."

"Not till we know more. I couldn't read Bookrajian."

"Bookrajian did seem a man with a secret sorrow," Molly said. "The son of a bitch was so sweet to me yesterday morning, I didn't know if he was coming or going. What's he done, did he say?"

"Administrative leave usually means a cop's under an internal corruption or disciplinary investigation. Maybe Bookrajian's suspected of taking bribes or shooting too quickly or too often. He didn't say, and I didn't ask. Is there meatloaf left? Any more of those mashed potatoes?"

"Sorry, Fred. We were hungry. He's not in this much trouble over the photo leak, is he?"

"I do not know the Bookrajian story," Fred said. "As first runner-up, I'm thinking baked beans on toast. Do we have beans?"

"Toast will be a struggle: we're out of bread. Beans we have. Muffins in half an hour."

Fred said, "I'm going to wash, then fill you in and get your advice on how to deal with the Ophelia question."

"I made her promise to keep out of it. Another dead man," Molly said, her face white.

"Yes," Fred said. "And it was nasty."

13

"That murder at the Hotel Brittannee," Molly said. "It was on the evening news, but they didn't say who the man was. I hate that you were there, Fred, but God! Is Ophelia safe?"

Fred, over beans and cranberry muffins, had laid out the Hillegass situation more broadly.

"As long as you got her promise to keep out of it, I don't see why we should be worried for her," Fred continued. "I just don't know how far she'll trust my judgment or follow my advice. She should have asked me before she started buying paintings, or went to Hillegass."

They had to sit in the kitchen since the living room had been coopted by the kids, and they couldn't get comfortable in Molly's bedroom for the same reason. Molly had made herself a cup of tea to keep Fred company, and she was taking her time with it. She'd turned the outside light on, so the white backyard shone in and gave them the illusion of bucolic space.

Molly said, "I can't believe she has that kind of money. You know one of Ophelia's motives had to be to buy something that would make Clayton Reed look sick. She thinks he's a snob."

"He is."

"She resents it."

"Many do."

"She didn't want him to know what she was planning. She figures you have to be loyal to him. Then, when she had to let you in on it, she was embarrassed in case she'd been a fool, which of course she had been, since she's Ophelia; but maybe she hasn't lost any money. If she has time, she can revise the story to accommodate the facts. You sent her that fax?" Fred nodded and put more water on. "Let me call her. Stick around, Fred, I may need you to talk to her."

Fred sat at the ready while Molly telephoned her sister. Judging from Molly's side of the conversation, Ophelia, alone, was climbing the walls. She was not only between marriages, she was between significant others. Fred couldn't tell where Molly's subtle and wide-ranging themes were tending until they suddenly focused in on how touched she was that Ophelia had trusted her enough to go to Fred for a second opinion.

"I don't just mean that it was the obvious smart thing to do," Molly said, "before you put down so much money; but trusting Fred to be the one. Hold on, I think that's him coming in now. He told me he was going to hitchhike. I know he wants to talk to you. Honey, it's Pheely on the phone."

Fred took over. "Ophelia, listen, the main thing is—" Molly started shaking her head in a warning that Fred interpreted to mean, Stick to the modified limited hangout, as the old Nixon White House would describe it. "They don't have his name in the news yet," Fred veered. Molly nodded: Trust Ophelia only with what you have to give her. "But Hillegass was murdered in his hotel."

"Someone killed him for that picture," Ophelia concluded quickly. "Which you said was worthless? They stole it?"

"I can't say. Nothing's been published. Supposing he made notes, someone may ask you about it, if and when they look into the contacts Hillegass made with people in the area."

"I wanted him for my show," Ophelia said. "But he didn't want

106

to do it. Once we got to talking, the idea of my buying paintings came up. That was to *keep* him talking, frankly. He would have been perfect on my show. I don't know why he refused."

"He was on parole," Fred told her. "Speak no ill of the dead and all, but he was under court order not to set foot outside New Jersey, and not to deal in art."

"So he was a criminal?" Ophelia mused. "So that's why he was killed. I'd have paid twice as much if I'd known he was breaking parole. Three times as much if I'd known he'd be killed. It's a great story! Who's handling it?"

"Let's keep our heads down about this," Fred warned.

"I can't pass it up. 'Talk-show hostess's brush with death'? It's a natural. I'll ask my publicist what would be the best way—"

"Hold on," Fred interrupted, covering the mouthpiece while he told Molly, "She wants to hand this to her publicist."

It took Molly ten minutes to talk her down.

Fred did not get hold of Clayton until almost eleven, by which time he was stretched out in Molly's bed, skimming a lengthy biography of John Sloan that Molly had taken out of her library for him a week back, before all this began. Molly, next to him, had a better deal. She was reading Edith Wharton and simultaneously watching Eddie Murphy on the bedroom TV, which she had not allowed the kids to commandeer to replace the big one downstairs they had busted.

"What a day it has been," Clay exclaimed. "I am exhausted, and I brought nothing to read. That woman—all day long I have been courting her. What are these cryptic and ominous messages you have been sending me? You may speak freely. No one knows I am at the Four Seasons."

"Briefly, Hillegass was killed in his hotel room last night. No sign of paintings or of anything relating to his occupation. It's murder, though. My guess is it relates to the killing in Cambridge. How or why, I don't know. Has Lavinia Whitman let anything slip?"

"I do not believe she knows who owns the paintings," Clay

said. "Hillegass killed?—it sounds like an awful brouhaha! What are these paintings? Is this organized crime? But I note that Hillegass was murdered *after* Mrs. Whitman warned us she would have words with her client! Because she claimed an exclusive agency! Ominous, Fred, would you not agree?"

"Clay, let's not throw logic out the window just because we hope it will land where we mislaid our sense of humor."

"There is nothing I would not put beyond Lavinia Randall Whitman. I have been with her all day. She reads Danielle Steel! She quotes Danielle Steel. She can't wait for the next one! Fred, what on earth is Danielle Steel?"

"An author. The hotel newspaper shop will have one of her books," Fred said, "if you have nothing to read. To finish up with Hillegass: he was strangled and castrated. I assume he had a falling-out with an old buddy. It did not look like Lavinia's style."

"You have not spent the day with her," Clay said. "But never mind. Since I received your message, I have been suffering over your claim that the Velázquez is not right. What is it, what was it, what should it be, and how can you be so certain?"

Clay had his priorities. He could not stand to renounce his Velázquez even before he'd heard its title and description. The imaginary Rembrandt he could bear to lose, if it meant he might have a chance to buy the Flinck cheap. He made Fred promise to bring him everything he had concerning the two pictures, and debriefed him suspiciously. Clay did not willingly bow to the opinions of experts unless he himself approved them. He regarded scholars as slightly less trustworthy than dealers since frequently they were not even guided by the profit motive.

"So," Clay concluded their conversation, "I shall stay close to Lavinia Randall Whitman, inserting myself within her confidence. Meanwhile, on the basis of a wild surmise, you think the Memorial Drive painting may give us access? Suppose we discuss our various plans of attack?"

• • •

Not having given in to sleep until well after midnight, Molly and Fred started breakfast late. The kids were still in bed. Fred had dressed, while Molly lounged in her blue bathrobe. They carried coffee into the blue and white living room and settled in amid kicked-over Monopoly.

"The received wisdom is," Fred remarked, lounging onto the couch and interrupting himself by looking for the metal token he'd sat on (the shoe), "if you sleep on a problem or a quandary, you'll arise with a clear mind and a solution provided by your unconscious."

Molly sat next to him. The floor was covered with play money and bombed real estate. "I feel like Juno gazing down from Olympus after the sack of Troy," she said. "What solution have you arrived at, and to which quandary?"

"My subconscious failed." Fred took a sip of coffee from the cup Molly had given him, emblazoned with the wake-up motto, Death before Dismemberment!

"What Mom does," Molly said, "is close her eyes and let the Bible or the Yellow Pages fall open, and wherever her finger drops, there's her answer. Then she spends days fitting the answer to the problem, but she swears it works."

"Aside from the whodunnit and the whereizzit, which I resolve to table for today because my brain is overloaded, Fred said, "I keep foundering on that question of logic that nobody else seems to worry about. It boils down to using one thing to measure something of an entirely different kind. An eye for an eye I understand; I don't like it, but it makes sense. But an eye for a house?"

Molly took a wary sip of her coffee. They'd made love earlier, and she didn't want that to devolve into the subject of murder. She didn't open her mouth except to let coffee into it. Fred went on, "Bad example. There are two things in my way. One is placing a money value on a painting; it's like saying this much cheese is or is not worth this amount of salt water. Or Baltic Avenue is worth so many dollars in play money, which Terry damned near killed William over last night, resulting in this chaos." Fred gestured around him at the living room, which Terry, sent to bed, had been condemned to set right this morning before she did anything else.

"Another thing," Fred continued, "because I think it's basically the same question—this business of miracles, cures that attach to that painting from Mem Drive. You put any object against another kind of object, and I'm lost. Put it against an imaginary entity, and I am gone forever."

Molly said, "Tell you something that happened at lunch with a bunch of my fellows and coworkers, back in the old days before the blizzard, when I had a job I could get to. It was a nice day, so we sat in the park between the library and the high school, with our sandwiches. We were about eight people. A couple of kids joined us. Somebody finished the Pepsi he was drinking, held up the can, and said, 'Brad Pitt drank this Coke. I'll sell it to the highest bidder.' Then he auctioned it off. More people gathered around, and the bidding went on until a colleague bought it for three seventy-five, three dollars and seventy cents more than the nickel you'd redeem the same can for across the street."

"How does this help me?" Fred asked.

"I'm not finished. The guy who bought it took it back to his desk and kept it there, like in a shrine or a museum, because now it's worth something, right? I've been tempted—it's been sitting there since last October—I've been tempted while he's in the john to replace it with a genuine Coke can and see what happens. But I don't have the guts. The thing's become a relic of Brad Pitt, and it's a miracle also, being a Coke can even though it's painted like a Pepsi can. I can't bring myself to cheapen the miracle by substituting the real thing."

"You haven't helped," Fred said.

"I'm joining. A story's no good unless you invest in it. You're not going to shave?"

"Not until they straighten out that business in the Middle East."

Sam got up late and did not bother getting dressed since he'd slept in his black jeans and Georgetown sweatshirt. He insisted on having coffee, which he doctored with as much cream and sugar as it would accept. Terry would not get out of bed, revolting at the injustice that awaited her once she came down, of having to sort and put away last night's wrecked game.

"It isn't fair," Terry shouted whenever she thought she heard a human noise.

"Let's take a sled shopping," Fred suggested to Sam. Molly and the kids had run out of staples while Fred was gone.

"Did you find out who killed the guy that was killed?" Sam asked when they got going. Yesterday's blaze of sun had disappeared into a haze of gloom. Traffic was still forbidden. Sam wore a Russian Army surplus greatcoat he'd got in trade from one of Walter and Dee's kids—a boy who was closer to the trends since he lived in the heart of Cambridge fashion. Sam's leather combat boots were untied and slippery. He would not button his coat or wear gloves.

"I do not have a clue," Fred said. "I have an idea about the painting only because of your mom."

The town they walked through this late morning was dim and quiet, as if it had given up all activity in favor of talk shows about the weather.

"Did you fix our TV?" Sam asked.

"It's beyond me," Fred said. They'd be better off without it.

The sled, a blue plastic disk like a contact lens on a rope, yawned and fribbled across pits and ruts in the street in back of Sam, who insisted he would handle it both ways. Sam said, "I know his head was cut off, but how did they do it? A Samurai sword? Did you notice a sword?"

Fred said, "I don't know which is worse, seeing it or not seeing it and thinking about it. If it was done in the bathroom, there wasn't room to swing a sword. Nobody told me what weapon was used."

"It would be bad, watching your head get cut off," Sam said.

"He wasn't alive by the time they did it."

"How come? How come you think that?"

"I didn't see any blood."

"Good." Sam shrugged that burden off. It had been worrying him. It wasn't the idea of death he minded, but that of the slow death by decapitation of a conscious person.

14

Before they went into the grocery store, Fred grabbed the day's papers from the CVS next door and scanned the headlines. Hillegass had missed his chance at fifteen minutes of fame. He didn't have a prayer. How could he compete with miracles, the big story in the daily papers? Their headlines made the weekly tabloids' look lame: there would not be a "miracle head" story on their supermarket racks for many days. The *Globe* and *Herald* tried to look serious about it, but you could hear the slobber of satisfied gloating between the lines.

Fred tucked the day's papers into the bags along with noodles, canned beans, corned-beef hash, rice, bread, peanut butter, cheese, SnapJaks for Terry, Frosti-Glos for Terry (a new glow-in-the-dark breakfast cereal that Fred couldn't believe the FDA had signed off on; it wouldn't be good for Terry, but it might cheer her up), grape jelly and orange marmalade, a turkey, hamburger, frozen french fries, potatoes, toilet paper, Jell-O, coffee, and sugar. Molly had made a list that they had left behind.

The sled was overburdened, and Sam struggled with it. Everything wanted to fall off. They laced the bags together by their handles, using Fred's belt, and Fred walked behind the load, watching for stragglers.

It was necessary to begin work on a snow fort before lunch. Terry watched from her window, still unwilling to admit to her guilt by cleaning up the mess downstairs. Not until Sam, Molly, and Fred were eating grilled-cheese-and-onion sandwiches in the kitchen did they hear furtive sounds of urban renewal from the living room. Then Terry strode into the kitchen, pajamaed and redolent of challenge, striving to trick her mother into the injustice of forbidding her to eat. Sam saved Molly from the crisis by sneering at his sister, "We heard you the whole time, Terry."

"And we kept you a sandwich," Molly added.

Terry attacked her meal and accepted with better grace than did Sam Molly's edict that both children must go outdoors until teatime. Molly would determine when that was.

It was almost three o'clock before Fred settled down to see what the papers had to report about Hillegass. He and Molly had the run of the living room, where Molly lay on the couch reading his John Sloan biography. "It's like a lot of couples," she complained. "I can't take Edith Wharton unless Eddie Murphy comes along. Doesn't it feel sinful to have this long paid vacation, especially with the children thrown to the wolves!"

Fred had taken to an armchair with the papers, which had laid into the miracle-picture story as if they'd been fasting for the last forty days and forty nights. "Crikeys," Fred said. He himself had as many facts as the papers did: enough for six lines. The rest was pomp, opinion, and vainglory. A whole op-ed page headlined THE MEANING OF MIRACLES umbrellaed articles by a pop shrink, an academic shrink, a priestly voice from the Catholic right, a nunly voice from the ex-Catholic left, and an unclassifiable froth of nonsense from a self-induced somewhat-Hindu rejoice-in-your-own-potential mystic improbably named Heekram Mranjit. Fred spent five minutes trying to figure out how this might be a code for or anagram of the name of the real author, Dave Barry. And that was only the opinion page.

Worse, because sadder, were the seven people the two papers had lined up between them to testify how they had been miraculously cured of something, at some time, or knew someone who had been and had since died of a different complaint.

"A lot of soft-core crazies out there," Fred remarked, flipping pages. The focus of the papers was the picture involved at the scene of the Mem Drive slaying. The only reference to Hillegass mentioned that the "dead man's" identity would not be released until the police located his family. Fred suspected there was no family, unless Hillegass had salted away a secret numbered wife in a vault in Switzerland. "Do you suppose I could get my car as far as Worcester, with Bookrajian's light on top?"

"I'd wait," Molly said. "*Temperamental* is too positive a word for your car, Fred. You want to corner people and ask them about Gigante?"

"Not really. I want to find that girl. The one who lived in that apartment held for her by a dummy offshore corporation. If I don't do something, I'm afraid Clayton will. Clayton's like everyone else. The big snow works like a full moon."

"Is he in love?"

Fred chuckled. "Not likely. But he'll shadow-box with Lavinia Randall Whitman at the Four Seasons until the thaw.

"About Father Ernesto: a priest can't just be on the loose," Molly said after a few minutes, thumping down the fat blue and gray book about the painter. "He has to be part of a corporate pecking order, with a line of superiors going back to the Pope. How come nobody says, 'Aren't we missing one of our boys?' Didn't Bookrajian give you a hint?"

"Bookrajian's out of it," Fred reminded her, tossing the papers onto the floor. The window to Molly's left overlooked the children's snow fort, from which Sam and Terry were throwing snowballs at his car. "As far as he's concerned, I am out of it as well," Fred added.

Molly said, "I'm calling Dee. Check out the scuttlebutt. You want anything from the kitchen?" She got up from the couch, brushing imaginary crumbs from the thick red knitted sweater she was wearing—a man's large size that Fred had never asked her about. It had been in her possession already when he turned up.

Fred shook his head. Aside from Molly's place on the couch, and the continuation of this lazy afternoon, he couldn't think of a thing he wanted. Molly came out of the kitchen with a cup of tea and the last muffin, saying, "Dee won't be home for a bit. She had to work, getting all those cars towed." She put her cup on the table next to Fred, stooped, and picked up the papers Fred had dropped. "You mind trading me for the couch?"

Fred lay on the couch and dozed.

"Miracle, miracle, miracle," Molly exploded after about five minutes, waking him. "All these experts and opinionists forget their dictionaries." Fred heard her get up and go into the kitchen. She kept her dictionaries next to the cookbooks.

"Here you go," Molly said. "A miracle, Fred, is 'an event that appears unexplainable by the laws of nature and so is held to be supernatural in origin, or an act of God.' I quote the *American Heritage Dictionary*, which also defines 'God.' Once you get sappy and talk 'miracle of birth' like this idiot—who is Heekram Mranjit? If you call birth a miracle, nothing means anything. I'd like Heekram to try a purple bunch of heads and elbows blasting through his vagina, demanding lunch. Miracle, hell—that's nature. A miracle is something you can't explain that isn't accompanied by an episiotomy. A painting that weeps blood, OK, that's a miracle. There's a mystery to it."

Fred coughed. "That's part of what I didn't go into with Bookrajian," he said. "There's not much mystery. It's an old trick; the Egyptians did it. If you don't mind my taking a miracle away."

"I am no friend of the unexplained," Molly said. "What's the trick?"

"I noticed that the back of the canvas was singed," Fred said, "when we looked at it in the apartment that morning, Bookrajian and I. The picture had been treated clumsily. For instance, someone had mended a tear with silver duct tape. They'd dropped the picture, or put the car jack through it while sticking it in the trunk so as to make tracks out of town."

"And the Betsy Wetsy aspect?" Molly goaded. "Where do the 'real tears' come from?"

"Put colored wax in the corners of the eyes, where it's red flesh anyway. Then, when the crowd is primed, apply heat, ideally to the back. The wax melts, and voilà! Real tears of sympathetic agony."

"Where does the heat come from?"

"Ask Father Ernesto. Could be a light bulb, or candles. Could be an iron. Just enough to make the wax melt and run. Then Father Ernesto takes up his collection and leaves town before the miracle cures, if any, backfire. He picks up his shill, the blond girl, who happens to be cured of her lameness, in fact by now she's running like hell, from under a bridge at the edge of town, and they move on together to Portsmouth or Biddeford, or wherever the next set of faithful may be gathered with their troubles and money."

The phone rang. Molly, looking at her watch, said, "That's Dee. Walter said she'd be home by four." She sat at the end of the couch, shoving Fred's legs aside, to take the call.

"Nothing on my mind except scandal and scuttlebutt," Molly told the telephone. She nodded at Fred, mouthed "Dee," and settled back to have a good time. "Dee? Give me the inside scoop on Dirty Ernie Bookrajian." Fred picked up the Sloan book and dabbled in a section called "Renewal and Decline" while he listened to Molly's peeps and exclamations of encouragement, coaxing and rewarding Dee for information tendered. Dee loved a story, and she took her time laying out the foundations. Fred went to put water on to heat. Being in the kitchen, he did not hear when the pitch of Molly's conversation changed. But when he came back into the living room, Molly was saying, "That's awful," listening, then saying again, "How awful." It was intimate bad news, compounded by worry. Fred looked a question toward

Molly, interrupting a "But that's terrible"; she shrugged him off impatiently. "It's OK," she whispered to him. "It's so awful," she exclaimed into the phone. "The poor thing. God, the poor thing. Him, too. No wonder . . . no wonder . . . *I'll* say."

Molly went on like that until she hung up. "Those poor people! Oh, those poor people," she said again, plunging into the kitchen. "And you—you said Bookrajian must be on the take or some damned thing!"

"What's happened?"

"No one knows about it, so don't say anything, Fred. Book- rajian's wife just learned she's pregnant. Wait a minute: that's the good news, except it makes the bad news worse, all those hor- mones tearing through the system of a vigorous young woman. She's got breast cancer, too. Both breasts."

"That's bad."

"You're goddamned right it's bad," Molly said. "It's terminal." She started crying in that way Fred never could get right, because it did not distinguish between fury and pity: Molly's *lacrimae rerum*. "They've been married not even a year," Molly mourned.

"There are things . . . ," Fred started lamely, leaving room for her to pick it up and help him with a suggestion offering the Bookrajians a way out. The branches of Molly's pear tree clawed against the window. It was almost dark. Last time he'd put his head outside, it had looked and smelled like snow coming.

"Like surgery?" Molly blazed at him. "An abortion? Hysterec- tomy? Plenty of people will offer her more pain, more loss. But nothing's going to stop the hormones. Everything in her body is screaming at those cells, 'Divide. Divide. Divide and conquer.' "

118

15

Bad news had found Bookrajian in his trap, then spread out to find Fred, attracted by the bait in Molly's trap. The bait was Molly herself, who was devastated by the bad news belonging to a woman she did not know, and to a man she disliked. Fred offered what comfort he could, but there wasn't any. Then he went outside to send the kids in for the tea Molly was making them, and to dig out his car. The snow had packed under its own weight and crusted from sun-glare; and now more snow was brewing.

"That poor son of a bitch," Fred said, digging. "Ex-seminarian, works years on a cop's salary, already too old to get lucky easily—and all of a sudden, bingo! God opens the sky, drops Blanche Maybelle Stardust before him, and says, 'Increase and multiply.' Then zap!"

They'd put Bookrajian on leave, personal leave, because the poor sap had to be half off his head with fear and worry.

The clearing of car and driveway made for a forty-minute job because he extended it to reach the garage doors so Molly could get out when she wanted to, once the driving ban was lifted. The kitchen screen door slammed out back. Molly came around the garage on the far side and looked up at the sky. "You going some-where? Won't you be pulled over?"

Fred took the ball light out of the pocket of his parka and held it up. "My passport," he said. "I'll come back later, or I'll call."

Molly struggled, wanting to ask him to stay, maybe, or at least where he was going.

"Thought I'd better get moving," Fred explained. "I'll call you."

"They've got one week to decide," Molly said. "The choice is, do nothing, or try a double-dip mastectomy and hysterectomy, with chemotherapy and/or radiation. The odds are close to zero either way." She shivered in that man's red sweater she kept, hugging herself around the chest. Fred leaned the shovel against the garage door, dropped the ball light back in his pocket, and put his arms around the awkward bundle she was making of her upper body.

Fred placed himself in the middle of a group going into 1001 for cocktails. It was a mixed bag of people about his age who, from their talk, lived within walking distance but would qualify to live here if they cared to. Fred reeled his name off at the desk like the others: "Heekram Mranjit." Heekram should go unremarked at a party among Pulitzers in apartment 612. "I read all your books," a woman told him in the elevator. "Indeed," Fred answered, with cold disbelief. He let the group disembark on the sixth floor and rode to the seventh alone.

The door of 710 was not sealed or even posted with a warning. They'd had four days. Whatever they wanted to do here had been done; whatever they wanted to have had been taken. He took his time getting through the lock. Once inside, he looked for signs of an alarm system, but the owners were evidently satisfied with the effect of the uniform at the desk in the lobby.

The place was Fred's. He could sleep here if he wanted to. It was familiar, though staler than it had been, and the indulgent feel of panic was gone. The kitchen fan no longer buzzed. The odor of the burned hands was gone, replaced by something lemony. Fred turned on a few lights, recalling the layout of the place: entranceway, kitchen ahead leading to the bedroom, with the bathroom off that corridor; or, turning right, the hallway with closets, and the big living room from which the body had been removed.

The blinds were drawn across the wall of sliding windows: the sunlight must have bothered some technician. Fred opened the blinds, and white night stared in. The painting was gone. It had been crazy even to hope it might still be here. The prosecution would depend on hauling it out at trial, in order to elicit the courtroom gasps that would nail the poor bastard who was accused of the killing. The china dogs now guarded nothing but a fireplace with dry flowers in it.

"Three people I want," Fred said. "The girl; the dead man; and whoever killed him, which may be several people."

To take the body down, the technicians had sawn through the nails holding the wrists. The man working the Sawzall had done the job so skillfully there wasn't so much as a nick in the blond wood mantel—just the ends of the nails for Maintenance to deal with. Fred listened to the air and feel of the place in which no other signs remained of all that stage set. The air and the feel told him nothing. There'd been too many people, all looking, counting, taking pictures, dusting for fingerprints, then, finally, cleaning.

"Fred wandered the apartment. Plenty of blood in the bathroom," Bookrajian had said. There wasn't anymore. It looked like a motel bathroom; some shivering Irish or Mexican girl had scrubbed it.

Fred took his time, looking at everything. The sheets in the linen closet—indeed, all the linen—came from Wamsutta. Sheets and towels matched. The bed, a king-size, filled most of the bedroom. Fred's grim face in the wall of mirror, with its week of beard, shadowed whatever ghosts of dalliance and preening might lie behind it. There was nothing under the bed, not even dust. The whole place was so clean it seemed derelict. The bed's headboard shelves contained a row of books Fred would look at later. The bureau, in some dark wood, was empty: whatever had been in it at the time of the killing, if anything, had been taken for evidence. The big Jane Peterson flowers—zinnias—leaned against the wall of mirror. Fred carried the picture into the living room and faced it against the wall next to the long white couch on which he would sleep if he decided to sleep here. The painting had been bought on Newbury Street, yes: from Dmitri Signet. Signet's paper label was stuck to the foamcore backing.

Jane Peterson had been, in her day, a solid painter. The early pictures, when she was still looking hard at Europe and her teachers, were rambunctious, lively, daring, and passionate. They tended to be small. Likely she had been poor; anyway, it was not easy to carry big pictures around the world. The larger, late pieces, after she lost it, she sometimes tried to dress with clumsy humor. By this point, she had added size and productivity to her other crimes.

The possible Guido Reni had belonged to someone, been someone's taste or passion or speculation: the girl's, or the dead man's, or the killer's. It did not fit with anything here.

The remaining art should provide some clues about the room's inhabitant. According to their labels, the posters on the wall all came from local shops: the Harvard Coop, Renjeau in Wellesley. In two instances they had been "Framed by loving hands at Kwik-Frame" of Porter Square, in Cambridge. It was impossible to identify any human character here; the place was as bare of personality as a hotel room, all the furnishings decreed by a decorator. The big lamps, new "antiques," came from Paine Furniture in Boston. What was not new was anonymous. Only the Peterson had a personality at all, and that was crass and safe and sadly boring.

Fred went back to look at the books, concluding that it was a collection assembled by the same decorator, who, seeing a shelf, had been obliged to fill it. Of seventeen books, three were by

Danielle Steel, Lavinia Randall Whitman's favorite author: over eighty-five million sold, boasted one jacket's flap copy.

"I never thought people actually read them," Fred mused. He let the reddest, *Zoya*, fall open, following Molly's mother's prescription, and dropped his finger on a passage:

> *Everything about him bespoke nobility and distinction.* ["Sounds like Clayton," Fred said.] *There were many in Paris like him now. Counts and princes and dukes and just men of good families, driving taxis and sweeping streets and waiting on tables.* ["Sounds less like Clayton," Fred said.]
> *"Nothing has happened to her, Captain," he said, and Clayton breathed a sigh of relief. . . .*

"Clayton! There's a character in *Zoya* called Clayton!" Fred chortled.

The rest of the books, like the Steels, the decorator might as well have lifted from a rented summer house. None was inscribed with a name, or held any interest in itself, except the one Fred saved for last, which stood out, being completely out of place here aside from its bright blue color, jazzy against the red of *Zoya*: a serious-looking medical study called *Trypanosomiasis*. It stuck out like an erratic boulder, but it didn't bring Fred any closer to the owner of the maybe-Reni, or the not-so-Velázquez, or the non-Rembrandt.

After two hours of close looking, Fred had nothing. The cabinets in the kitchen were empty, dusted and cleaned. Not even the dead lived here. Fred lifted the bedroom phone and found that it was dead, too, then figured the reason: it had been disconnected from an answering machine clipped into the jack. That had been carried off by some functionary in case there was something on its tape. Fred found the wall jack, plugged the phone in, and got a dial tone. There was no number label on the phone; still, a record existed of this number, assigned to someone or some entity that the phone company knew about, and therefore the investigation as well. It was presumably the blind corporation again.

Fred made himself a mug of hot water. The snow was starting again. He could stay or leave, but if he left, he might not be able to find a way back in. The body he had seen pinned to the mantel presented physical questions that he might as well try to resolve while he was here. The work done on the young man's body to get him from a clothed state of robust health to what had met Fred's eyes when he first walked in wanted a large, private, tiled room with good drains and a minimum of furniture, not a crowded small space with neighbors and lots of absorbent off-white surfaces.

Fred lay on the couch and gazed across the living room at the fireplace. He called back the image of the man's body. The corpse was not that large, and if the head had already been removed, that was twelve pounds less to lift. The mantelpiece was the proper height for the shoulders, to allow the arms to extend outward to the nailed wrists. But you'd have to hold the body, position the nail, and hammer it in.

But then there was the thing with the broomstick: the most patient martyr in history could not have stayed still for that. You'd have to rope the man, gag him, tie him down. There should have been bruises of restraint all over the body. From the logistics of the situation, Fred had been positing at least a pair of killers. However, the aesthetics of the scene looked like one man's work. It was consistently outrageous, right down to the ribbon. The tableau argued for one person's showing off to himself, and to the world. "So," Fred asked himself, "if I'm one person, how do I nail him up? Assume the man has already been killed and decapitated. A headless dead body does not cooperate. The absence of blood in this room suggests that the butchering was completed elsewhere, and the body emptied of fluids, before it entered the living room. The hands—they were charred, too, on their way through the kitchen. Does Gigante have fingerprints on file? He must, or the killer"—there, Fred was using the singular—"the killer, singular, suspects he does.

124

"So. Pull that big chair over to the fireplace, lay a tarp across the beige leaf pattern on the white ground—a tarp, or a shower curtain. Yes, the shower curtain from the bathroom is missing. Haul the body up—I've already dragged the body from the bathroom, on the shower curtain—get curtain and body onto the back of the chair, and wrestle the body into place, using my knee to hold it—but the chair takes the weight, and leaves both my hands free. I center the body nicely, stick the painting in place, revise and check my work.

"Whoever did this knows bones. The sentimental icon of Christ crucified shows the nails through his palms. That doesn't work; the body's weight pulls the nail past the tendons governing the fingers, or rips between the knuckles. With all that weight, to hold a hundred and fifty pounds, you want to anchor through a wrist. Otherwise the condemned man pulls loose and falls onto his mom."

Yes, Fred decided. One person could do it if he was not interrupted, was reasonably fit, and did not mind having an intense relationship with a corpse.

He got up and started prowling again. Where was the rest of the broom? No doubt in the same locked evidence room as the painting, and the contents of the bureau, if any, and the answering machine, and the rest of it. Had the dead man been a tenant or a guest? Where had the nails come from? Were there more? Did there just happen to be a hammer here, heavy enough to do the job? Or a nail gun?

Fred found himself once more in the bedroom, where he stood at the foot of the bed gazing at the stripped mattress. He looked into the mirror and asked it, "Who is the blond girl? While I'm at it, why is Roger Clemens like a TV set?"

He sat on the side of the bed, picked up the phone, and was about to call Molly before his own good sense, or Clayton's paranoia, told him, "Don't be a fool. The line's active. They tap whoever uses it. If you excite the line, you get company."

No, he'd drive back. With so few other vehicles on the road, he could be in Arlington in half an hour.

"Heekram Mranjit," he told the old man at the desk.

The guard looked quizzically at him and said, "I thought you'd all walked into the Square for dinner."

"I got detoured," Fred said. He put his fingers against his lips and gave a mystic leer.

16

S aturday," Molly gloated, first noticing that Fred was in her
bed, then elbowing him awake early. "Ain't it grand? No work
today."

Fred took his time showering and dressing. He found Molly in
the kitchen, at the table, reading the paper over a steaming mug.
"Paper so soon?" Fred asked. It was only seven-thirty.

"I'm recycling an old one," Molly said. "Can't drink coffee
without a paper. Make us toast. Somebody finished the muffins."

"That was you. Two days ago."

"Look, in the classified ads," Molly said, "here's one. What's
the date on this paper? Last October? Are they serious? Is it a
joke? Inner Peace Pilgrimage to Betania, Venezuela. See it? Right
next to the five-hundred-dollar reward for Lost Cat in Newton-
Watertown, all black with tuxedo chest, white snout, declawed,
white dot at end of tail, neutered. . . ."

"Haven't seen it," Fred said. He sat down with his coffee and
looked across the table at the page that Molly had turned to face
him. True, under "Inner Peace Pilgrimage" you were given a chance

to visit "Maria Esperanza, Mystic-Healer. Many see Bl. Virgin. Adore Eucharistic miracle, bleeding Host. CCs accepted."

"We missed our chance. The trip was last December," Fred said. "Party's over."

"What kind of pet cat's worth five hundred dollars?" Molly asked. "Venezuela," she went on. "In the Third World, you expect all those believers. But if people in Boston will pay the fare to adore a bleeding host a million miles away, you have to wonder where the Third World stops. I got so tied up in poor Blanche Bookrajian's troubles, I forgot to ask Dee about the local miracle. Did you get anywhere last night? I didn't even ask where you were going."

"Had a look at that apartment on Mem Drive. The 'slay scene.' I'm driving into Boston later. I don't trust Clayton on his own. Did he call?" Molly shook her head. "You want to come into Boston with me? Bookrajian's whirling light works like a charm."

"Your heater gives me pause," Molly said. "Your car and your no heat and your beard all at once, I don't know. . . ."

They headed into the wild at ten-thirty, Bookrajian's light on Molly's car, and Molly driving. "Officer, I am a public official," Molly practiced saying. "I am a reference librarian in good standing at the Cambridge Public Library. Die, bitch! *Sic semper tyrannis,* and *amor vincit undique.* Also, make my day."

She'd arranged for Sam to spend the day with Arjun, and Terry, with friends who lived next door to Arjun—twin boys who needed a third for Monopoly. "Is that wise?" Fred asked. "Do Mark and Alan know Terry thinks Monopoly is a contact sport?"

"Better they learn it in their own house, not mine," Molly said. She kept to the quiet main arteries, on many of which the three inches of new snow from last night had not yet been plowed. At some supermarkets and mini-malls they saw considerable activity of dump trucks receiving chunks of older snow heaps from bucket loaders. But the only thing that would make more than a dent in this was two weeks of June weather. The sky today was dark, but it would not snow more. Fred fell into a vacant musing, gazing out at the beleaguered landscape, being a passenger.

"I'm going to Mountjoy Street, I presume," Molly interrupted. Fred snatched himself into gear and looked around. He'd been so intent on his goal that he had not mentioned it to Molly.

"Newbury Street," he said. "Sorry. And I'd better describe your part."

Newbury Street, though crowded, was a disaster in terms of high-end commerce. The big bucks were either in a different environment or at home waiting for this environment to change. The rabble on the street was after coffee or placemats or one book.

Dmitri Signet almost tackled his greeter, a pretty young woman in an ensemble, practically hurling her to the floor in his rush to get past her and welcome human adults into his gallery. He recognized Fred vaguely, not sure from what context, but quickly chose Molly as the more likely customer of the pair.

Signet's current show hardly deserved its title, "Selections from the Gallery Collection." Collection, indeed! At least half the stuff was on consignment, having been bought in at local auctions where local dealers, who had bought the pieces at other local auctions, then cleaned and framed and shopped them, had failed to dump them.

Signet was a young man so Russian in origin as to look almost Japanese. He wore a dark-green suit, a white shirt, a broad tie covered with eagles, and as much jewelry as he could get away with in New England. His hair was long, as if he yearned to conduct an orchestra and fling his locks during the crescendos. He'd lost a week's rent, and he was surrounded by a very dull bunch of goods, most of it turn-of-the-century landscape with some water in it, though he'd also hung a few seascapes with a bit of land. Molly let herself be drawn to a George Howell Gay, in which an encarnadined receding wave reflected the full moon.

"One of my own favorites," Signet approved, hovering at Molly's shoulder as if she had been bereaved, and smelling better than the occasion required. The picture measured two by three feet, in a heavy bobbled frame. Worth maybe eight hundred dollars at auction, it represented a lot of salt water and atmosphere for the fifteen thousand dollars Signet's tag demanded. No wonder the sea was drawn back in a blush! Signet believed in the long con. But then again, you got inflation from pressure on both sides. Someone had posted a notice in the paper offering to pay five hundred dollars for the return of a lost cat.

"The value of your coin depends on whether you have another," Fred said.

"What?" Molly and Dmitri Signet both asked.

"A saying," Fred said. He introduced himself to Dmitri Signet, explaining his relationship to Clayton Reed. Signet's eyes lit up: Reed's was a name he knew. He kept himself from rubbing his hands together.

"For special customers, I have—," he began, then interrupted himself before he started his "Come into the back room" routine. "Tell me what Mr. Reed is looking for? It would be an honor . . ."

"All this snow," Fred said, gesturing toward Newbury Street.

"Of course, naturally," Dmitri Signet said in confusion. "I know exactly what you mean." Molly moved along the wall and hesitated at the place where Fred was standing, before a pair of watercolors, rainy Paris street-scene sketches that looked like Prendergast but turned out to be by the Bostonian William Emile Schumacher.

"I'll take these," Fred said. Signet wanted five thousand dollars for the pair, which were mounted together in a single mat. "If we can come together on the price," Fred added.

Signet looked sick. He knew the things were nice, but he also knew nobody recognized the painter, and in any case there wasn't enough of his work around to make a market. Schumacher had never quite decided who he was. He'd gone Postimpressionist and almost abstract by the time of the Armory Show; these water-colors were earlier than that, dated 1910.

Signet came forward, glanced at the label, and started back with a Hollywood double take. " 'Come together on the price'!" he exclaimed. "I'm giving them away now."

What he was doing, in fact, was feeling out the market. "No

offense," Fred said. "We'll pass, then. I'm actually here to keep my friend company." He strolled off to inspect the other offerings on the wall.

Molly began, "Big bunch of flowers in a bowl. Fred says the artist must be Jane Peterson. You had it, oh, I don't know how long ago."

"I get a lot of Peterson," Dmitri Signet said. He gravitated back toward Molly. "I love her work. She is so vibrant, so . . . Only Rotenberg can touch the later works. The verve and zest, the—"

"Zinnias," Fred interrupted. "That's what you said, wasn't it? Zinnias."

"The thing is," Molly picked up, "I just redid my drapes, and then I remembered that painting. Do you still have it?"

Dmitri Signet grimaced unhappily, hating to disappoint a live one. "We have no Peterson at all now, although they do come in from time to time. Get the Peterson file, Carolyn, dear, would you?" Carolyn crouched before a file cabinet behind her desk, getting as much coverage as she could from a skirt that had not been designed with coverage as its primary aim. "A Peterson still life is never on the wall very long," Signet confided.

Carolyn rose and brought Signet a manila folder half an inch thick. He withdrew to his desk, sat behind it, and leafed through the file, holding it in such a way that only he could see its contents. He pulled out three four-by-five transparencies and one small Polaroid photograph and laid them on the desk. "Take a peek at these four we've sold to give me an idea of what sort of piece you have in mind."

"It's not a 'sort of' thing, it's an *exact* thing I have in mind," Molly said. "I'll know it when I see it." She took the transparencies and held them up one by one to the desk light. Fred, leaning close beside her, looked with her, over her shoulder.

"This one," Molly said when Fred pinched her. "I remember the beaten copper bowl."

"Glorious textures," Signet affirmed, accepting the transparency Molly handed him and peering through it. "I sold this, what?

two years ago. Perhaps I can find one like it." He swept the pictures together and put them into the folder. "I will ask around."

Molly, facing Dmitri and smiling, settled into one of the two chrome-and-glass chairs that such places use to make clients feel welcome without, however, wanting to stay long. The comfortable chairs were out back, reserved for clients who had proved their worth. Fred wandered around looking at the walls. Carolyn sat in her place next to the door and did whatever the upmarket equivalent was of chewing gum. Well-wrapped people hustled along the street and sidewalk, carrying paper bags containing coffee and croissants.

Molly said, "I don't want a painting *like* that one, I want *that* painting. Can you get it for me?"

"Once a client incorporates such a work into his or her life," Signet demurred, "it becomes *family*, almost. . . ." Fred listened, ready to hop in if Molly faltered, but she did fine, projecting precisely that acquisitive petulance which makes them cringe with hope on streets like Newbury. She'd wanted to change to something that looked rich, she said, but Fred had insisted that the blue jeans and big red sweater were perfect. "Can you try?" she now pleaded. "Call them, ask them if maybe they'll sell it to me? I mean, obviously, let *you* sell it to me, with your usual whatchamacallit, commission?"

Signet began a spoken paragraph in which the word *confidential* occurred six times. Molly swung a booted foot, rattled her purse, and refused to listen. "Yes, but why not ask them?" she persisted when Signet ran out of breath.

"What did you do, dump it in an auction?" Fred challenged, breaking in. "There's no way he'll get it back in that case," he told Molly.

"No, that's not the problem," Signet said.

Molly began a verbal sonata on the theme of Peterson's "symphony of color." "Therefore it must be this painting or *new* new drapes," Molly finished. "And I've already chosen my drapes." She sat, at her unreasonable ease, until Signet agreed to try.

Once Signet had made a note of Molly's number, he attempted to retrieve the sale of the Schumachers. He began hinting that should they be destined for an important collection, the price structure, though already far from aggressive, might bear reexamination.

"I'll think about it," Fred said. "No hurry. When you call Mrs. Riley with the good news on the Peterson, that will be time enough."

They took an underground lunch that was arguably Greek. The cafeteria was crowded with people not buying art or suits or antique armoires or Tibetan masks. They didn't want to carry anything; they'd walk, pop into a shop when they wanted to get warm, then pick up a video to take home.

Fred ate a pickled eggplant. "If I could use Bookrajian, I'd make him drop a court order on Signet and compel him to reveal who bought that painting. Nobody's thought of it, or asked about it at Signet's, or we would have seen them jump when we goosed them with that painting."

"He's going to try to sell me the picture," Molly said. She ate a pickled eggplant. "I feel it in my—well, where you pinched me, you dirty man."

The plan was for Molly to idle on Mountjoy Street while Fred nipped in to check the mail. But Molly found a space, disengaged the light, put it between the seats, and stuck with Fred.

"Haven't been inside Clayton's for a while," Molly said. "It's more than three months since he had me for tea and those things he claims are crumpets."

They jumped and slid over the frozen troughs that rendered the steep sidewalk an obstacle course. Last night's snow had left a misleading skrim of softness across the rugged weathering of the real cover, which citizens had beaten into a conundrum of gullies by trying to get around without shoveling. Beacon Hill was like an uninhabitable moon reserved for rich people who refused to pay for service.

"You going to make me tea?" Molly challenged as they reached the stoop to Clayton's town house.

"If you'll settle for chamomile. Unless I slide down to Charles Street and get us a box of real."

"First put me inside so I can get my feet warm," Molly demanded. "Then forage for genuine tea and cake."

Fred opened the door, and he and Molly found themselves among coats, boots, and fresh snow. Clay's voice came warningly from down the hall, through the open doorway to what he called his parlor. "That you, Fred?" Clay, in his blue suit with the wide gray stripe, stepped into the hall, holding a teacup from which a barely fragrant steam rose. "Ah, Lady Molly," Clay said. He came toward them, blinking and holding a finger to his lips.

"Dear dear, Fred," he whispered. "I regret the guest room is no longer free. In order to control events, I must learn what they are. So help me, I have determined to nourish the viper in my bosom, under the guise of chivalry."

Molly stepped out of her coat and handed it to Fred. Short of knocking her out, there was no way Clay could prevent her from learning who was in his parlor. Clay, cornered, bowed slightly toward Molly and managed, "Won't you please come and meet my guest?"

17

In the yellow version of the pink and blue suits, Lavinia Randall Whitman sat, in a tizzy of lust, on a rosewood love seat in the shade of the Copley, staring in frank amazement at Clayton's walls. "But that's a Gauguin," she was stammering, reaching with a podgy, jeweled hand for the little sacking-covered panel on which three naked bathers, two of them mauve and one chrome-yellow, wrestled for the attention of a Tahitian member of the fox family: a recent acquisition of Clay's from a flea market in Bordeaux (where he had intended only to buy wine). After cleaning, the artist's monogram, PG, had indeed emerged from the undergrowth. When Lavinia spotted it, the Gauguin was lying (all several million dollars' worth of it, if you wanted to think in those terms) on Clay's coffee table, as if it were a *House and Garden* magazine. "And a Sargent," she murmured, noticing the watercolor portrait of the Comtesse Francesca d'Aulby, née Lunt, of Scituate, Massachusetts. That was a story Lavinia would give her eyeteeth to hear. Her gaze swept shuddering across the boat picture Clay had refused to lend to the MFA for its Bunker exhibition; plunged into the elegant pink riot of Manet's peonies; and faltered in questioning agony before the ragged and raging bosom of the Gericault *Madwoman* before skittering on to Hopper's huge *Truro Chimneys*, which hung between two windows overlooking Mountjoy Street. She'd put her chattering teacup down in order to get hold of the Gauguin, which she must now relinquish so as to accept Molly's hand, offered while Clay made the introduction.

"You'll have tea?" Clay asked Molly.

"You bet," Molly said.

Clayton admitted, "It is Lapsang souchong." He'd shopped for his guest.

"Dropped in for the mail," Fred said. "Didn't know you'd left the hotel, Clay."

Clay's paintings, reflected in Lavinia's eyes, looked merely like money. She buzzed in the avaricious impotence of a fat but wingless bee offered "all you can eat" in sixty seconds in the gardens of Versailles.

Clay, on his way to the kitchen, paused and said distinctly, using the voice that children understand is not intended to be understood by them, "We had a shock, Fred. A colleague of Lavinia's—a distant colleague—Burton Hillegass, was killed in his hotel room. I thought it prudent that Lavinia leave the Four Seasons. Fortunately, a few taxis are running."

Lavinia Randall Whitman shivered, then gained enough self-possession to drink Lapsang souchong. There was only one pot in use. Clay'd been drinking real tea, going so far as to allow himself a stimulant in the attempt to seduce his guest. Fred took his parka off and held it, watching Lavinia. The Gauguin was just the right size for her to slip under her blouse. All around them was flagrant proof of Clayton's lie about having the place redecorated. But almost any lie was Lavinia's home turf.

"Lavinia, there are problems with the Rembrandt," Fred began. "You want to tell us about it?"

"Never mind, Fred," Clay interjected. "The situation may not be of interest to Molly. Not that chair, perhaps? The Chippendale is stronger. The Sheraton will do perfectly for our guest—do you think so, Molly? Fred, before you sit, maybe you would help me carry the things from the kitchen?"

With this transparent plea for a secret conference, Clay marched into the kitchen, Fred behind him. "I cannot rest with her at large," he whispered hoarsely when they were alone. "Suppose her offer passes elsewhere? Given the happy coincidental stimulus of the death of her colleague, I thought, Why not keep her under my nose, as well as put her in my debt? A damsel in distress . . ."

". . . is worth two in the bush?" Fred finished.

"I do not follow. Never mind." Clay began splitting crumpets and arranging them in his toaster oven.

"You know all she wants is to see your collection," Fred said. "She's got her wish."

"No matter: I shall keep the upper hand. It is a matter of psychology. I placed her in my power, after breakfast, when I informed her that Mr. Hillegass had passed on. My plan—"

" 'Passed on'?" Fred murmured.

"A polite circumlocution," Clay assured him. "Did people not speak of the Rosenbergs as passing on?" He peered into the toaster oven.

"She had paintings in her bedroom," Fred said. "Did they come here with her?"

"They are not relevant. She has given me her word. She will arrange for them to be shipped to New York," Clay said, bustling the crumpets onto a plate, transferring the plate onto a tray, and setting a stoneware crock of marmalade beside it. Fred took the tray.

"From your end, have you managed to get closer to the cache of pictures?" Clay asked. "I did not dare bring the subject up again. She was adamant that I must first commit to the structure of the plan."

Fred carried the tray into Clay's parlor. Lavinia was no longer craning her neck to gawk. Her body language now announced she'd seen it all before. What was one more Copley? A nude female back, reclining, by Chase—so what? The man had female students, after all. She even managed not to blink when she noticed the Watteau sketch Fred had bought from a glass and china dealer who'd picked it out of a yard sale. It must be causing her considerable curiosity since she'd once tried to sell it to Clay, having somehow wangled a duplicate transparency from one of the experts he'd consulted.

In fact, the subject of conversation had undergone a drastic change. Lavinia and Molly, sitting across from each other, the brass tray emblazoned with Asian dragons between them, the Gauguin resting on it, seemed to be involved in a contest or litany.

"*Kaleidoscope,*" Molly said.

"*Fine Things,*" said Lavinia.

"*Wanderlust, Secrets, Family Album,*" Molly said.

"*Full Circle, Changes, Thurston House, Crossings,*" said Lavinia.

"*Now and Forever, Summer's End, Season of Passion, The Promise, Passion's Promise,*" said Lavinia.

"And my own personal favorite," Fred climaxed, catching on, "the red one with the double-headed eagle on the cover: *Zoya!* Over eighty-five million sold!"

"I would never have guessed you to be a devotee of Danielle Steel," Lavinia said.

Fred made a gesture of noncommittal response as Clay poured tea into Fred's and Molly's cups.

Fred asked Lavinia, "Are you aware that the so-called Rembrandt is a well-known work by another painter? And the Velázquez is about as bankable as a souvenir sliver of the One True Cross? There are other questions, too. . . ."

Lavinia Randall Whitman put down her cup and reached for a toasted crumpet. "It was lovely of you to get us crumpets, Clayton," she said. "And it is lovely to be among friends. Fred? Molly? May I burden you with a confidence? I have seen only a small sample of the collection. As for the two paintings Fred mentions, the Rembrandt and the Velázquez, as you know, reputable scholars will vouch on either side of many attributions. But never mind! My agreement was that if I had exclusive representation of the collection, I would make preliminary inquiries." She sighed and held the crumpet near her mouth. "My client gave me his word of honor. I relied on it." She sighed again and took a bite.

Clay coughed. "I am certain Fred meant no slight to your bona fides," he announced.

"Of course not," Lavinia purred. "Once I learned someone else had offered the Rembrandt, I telephoned my client and informed him that my position had become anomalous. My client is naive."

Molly exclaimed. "Speaking of which, Clay, may I use your phone? I left my daughter playing Monopoly with—" Fred motioned her to the telephone on the piano.

Lavinia continued coldly, "I breach no confidence when I say this, Clay. The owner of the collection enjoys what we might describe as a sudden fortune, which there may be present reason to convert to cash. For such a person, efficiency is paramount—and sometimes speed, as well as absolute discretion. . . ."

"You know J. F. Kennedy read a lot of James Bond?" Fred asked.

"I don't follow," Lavinia faltered.

"We are what we read," Fred said. "It's a saying. But go on."

Lavinia continued, "You asked about the Rembrandt."

"Flinck," Fred said. "It's by Govaert Flinck."

Lavinia said, "I do not blame my client. But at this moment, what with the weather, I'm too much in the dark. Clayton, I have heard you possess a magnificent Fitz Hugh Lane. . . ."

"There, you see?" Clay said. "We are all of us in the dark together."

"That's not a woman, that's a barricade," Molly exclaimed, moved by Lavinia's performance. "She's Bismarck and Marie Antoinette wrapped up into one fell swoop. She's a mixed metaphor on wheels, if ever I saw one. Now she's alone with Clayton? O frabjous day! Callooh! Callay! Our mittens we have found!"

She climbed into the car while Fred stood outside to jockey, push, or kibitz as she maneuvered out of the pit between snowbanks and iglooed vehicles. Fred took the note from Molly's windshield and stuck it under the wiper of the car behind them, digging under virgin snow to do it.

"What did it say?" Molly asked, once she'd got the car out and Fred in.

"Whatever they say in those notes. The Beacon Hill equivalent of an icepick in the tires. I didn't read it," Fred told her.

"I should get home," Molly said, heading down the hill and turning left on Charles. "You coming? Or where do you want to go? Bookrajian's light is good, but I wish we had a siren. We'd feel less lonesome on the road."

They found Terry and Sam watching TV in Molly's room, rolled up in Molly's unmade bed. That devolved into a supper of coleslaw, bacon, and french fries, followed by a long game of Hearts on the rug in the living room. Molly allowed the kids to stay up until midnight, since, why not? As they sorted themselves out at the top of the stairs, Sam said, "Oh, Fred, Aunt Pheely called. I forgot."

"What did she want?"

"She said, will you call her back? Don't be upset, Fred. I forgot. She didn't say like it was the end of the world or anything like that!"

"Call back tonight?" Fred pressed.

"If you want, I guess. I know: she said a man called her? About a painting?"

18

Ophelia's voice was sleepy, not happy, and surprised. "Ophelia Finger," she said. "What's up?"

"Ophelia, Fred. Sam just told me you called."

"I forgot," Sam shouted from upstairs. They'd come back down to the living room, Fred and Molly together, Molly having picked up Fred's alarm.

"It's OK, Sam," Molly yelled up. "Go to bed."

Ophelia complained, "Couldn't it wait?"

"Who called you? It's about the same picture? The Velázquez?"

"He didn't leave his name. I was shoveling the walk. I like to stay in shape."

"What did he say?"

"Oh, Fred, must I wake up? He left a message and said he would call back. I wanted you to know."

"Fred, what's the matter?" Molly asked, leaning against him and pulling at his telephone arm.

"You're not listed, are you?" Fred asked.

"Of course not!"

"Get dressed. I'm coming for you. You're sleeping here."

"Fred, what's the matter with you?" Molly and Ophelia said in chorus.

"Hold on, Ophelia." Fred whispered quickly to Molly, "Some-one got her number from Hillegass. Thank God for the snow." Molly's face blanched with understanding. "Here, talk to Molly," Fred told Ophelia. "Give me half an hour. Don't answer the phone again unless your machine gives you me or Molly. Don't let anyone in."

"Take my car," Molly whispered to him before she started in on Ophelia, "Now, honey, we don't want you to be frighened. . . ."

Ophelia was a quarter mile of field and woodland from her nearest neighbor. Her long drive had been well plowed. She had plenty of room, but not the time, for extensive gardens. Behind her prerevolutionary clapboard house was a small river big enough for canoes. Fred drove Molly's Colt up the driveway with the headlights off and looked the spread over before he left the car. A few lights burned upstairs and down. Fred walked around the house, making sure, before he poked the button for the pre-revolutionary chime by the big front door.

Ophelia, still speaking to Molly on a portable golden tele-phone, let him in. She was wearing a garment that the silkworms had spun directly onto her. It left so little to the imagination that the imagination immediately flailed about trying to find anything else to dwell on. Wind blew into the hallway until Fred closed the door. Ophelia shivered and let her long blond hair swing, casting random interjections into the mouthpiece. Her full breasts twitched against the cold. This was more naked than nudity: the combination of transparent nightdress, cold, and the fear Molly had put into her sister, maybe. Fred couldn't read it.

"Get rid of the beard," Ophelia ordered, breaking the connec-tion with a button. Barefoot, she led Fred down the prerevolu-tionary hallway toward the prerevolutionary den. Ophelia had the kind of body for which they made those five-part exercise garments that searched out every crevice.

"Find yourself a glass," Ophelia said, curling into a mahogany and leather couch in a room done up with gilded accessory eagles and antique inn signs with sheep on them, along with ancient boot jacks, cauldrons, and a questionable pillory from which philodendron trailed. "Can you imagine being stuck almost a week in a place like this?" Ophelia groaned. She reached for a glass that was already darkly charged, putting the phone down in its favor. "Fred, explain why I should leave my home."

She set her jaw while Fred paced. Ophelia could be more unreasonable than Nero when she put her mind to it; it was one secret of her success. She flipped a remote-control device and caused a picture to blossom on a large TV under the window: a late-night exercise program accompanied by Offenbach.

"I am going out of my tree locked up in here," Ophelia said.

Fred sat in an armchair next to Ophelia. He put his feet on a prerevolutionary coffee table. The one window in here was black with night, over the TV. He got up again and went over to pull its shade. Until further notice, he'd assume some murdering bastard had Ophelia's address, as well as a plan.

"A Spanish voice," Ophelia said.

"What?"

"You're going to ask me what he said, what he sounded like," Ophelia proclaimed impatiently, and she took a gulp of her drink. "I am going crazy out here. I am a person of action, Fred; what do you want me to do? Try to make sense. Molly couldn't, but that's Molly. Excuse my dishabille. You want me to put on a couch or something?"

"You're fine," Fred said. "It's just that the person who killed Hillegass—well, if that's how this new guy has your number; that's what's got me nervous. I don't want to take any chances. Have you still got the man's message on your machine?"

The machine was on a table between them. Ophelia twitched, stretched, poked some buttons, listened to a fast scramble, and

143

edited one out, a male voice, emphatically Hispanic. She played it through three times.

"You want some painting. The man is delay. I call again. May be tomorrow. Next day may be. This for Ofélia who is on the TV?"

"Some pass on; others are delayed," Fred mused. "Let's pull the tape and hold it, Pheely. We'll bring it with us. I don't want you found."

Ophelia stood, said, "Fred, I'll clothe this gorgeous body and throw some duds into a sack, and then let's go. Here's the plan. We want this guy, right? Well, I can use him. I gather he's at least a link in a murder case, if not the actual murderer. So I spend Sunday at Molly's. I have my calls forwarded to her number. 'Talk-Show Hostess Nabs Killer.' "

She started upstairs. The walls throughout the house had been stenciled with prerevolutionary designs in milk-paint colors. Fred followed her since she was still talking. "Fred, you didn't really believe, did you, that I was going to throw my money into old pictures? Melissa would kill me. I do no decor without her permission." She paraded along the upstairs corridor between hanging objects rejected by the Shakers as being too simple and functional, and turned into a bedroom. She did not stop talking. Fred stood in the hall and let her go on, accompanied by the swishing sounds of dressing and packing.

"No," Ophelia said. "I am always on the lookout for the next theme. Will it snow again?"

"Don't think so," Fred called.

"When Hillegass practically fell in my lap, I thought, He's got something we can use. My people love to hear what the rich and famous are buying." She poked her head into the hall. She'd put on a heavy blue sweater and jeans and was winding her hair into a red scarf.

"For the record, any big money I gamble goes on movies, where I know the difference between trash and box-office. Let me grab two more things." She disappeared again, then came back with a small black leather bag.

Downstairs, Ophelia eased into a voluminous coat of "natural blond female yearling Russian sable, but faux," she said. "Don't you love it? It's more expensive than the real, but who wants to wear something that eats fish?"

Fred watched her set alarms and timers. She checked that her prerevolutionary three-car garage was closed and primed with its separate alarm. Fred started Molly's car, and Ophelia leaned back in the passenger seat as Bookrajian's red light fled in swirls across the placid snowscape.

"Let's find out what's going on in Cambridge," Ophelia said.

Fred navigated the long drive and turned into the quiet solitude of Gibbet Road. "Molly's waiting up," he said.

"I told her we'd be late," Ophelia said. "Got a hunch about the Cambridge rumpus. Let's get there before it's old news."

"It's almost three in the morning," Fred pointed out.

"There's a demonstration in Central Square."

"Ophelia, it doesn't strike my fancy," Fred said. The road was vacant. Molly's heater worked, and the packed snow let them travel at forty miles an hour.

Ophelia said, "Molly claimed you'd be interested. It's at the police station. Candlelight vigil."

Fred eased onto the windy expanse of Route 2. One lane in each direction was cleaned to the surface, and the other passable. By Monday, traffic should be moving again. "What's it about?" Fred asked.

"The miracle murder picture. Miracles are my new idea: talking with the victims, before and after they get cured, or not. Great potential for TV. Then there's this priest nobody can find, what's his name?"

"Gigante."

"Right. Miracles. You forget how close we all are to the woodland mentality. At least my audience is. What do you say? You with me?"

"We're on our way," Fred said.

Ophelia elaborated as they drove. She'd been giving miracles a lot of thought, from the show-biz angle. "There's so much room for fraud," she gloated. "People love fraud!"

"You want to do a show exposing fraud?"

"Whatever—either exposing or going along with it, it doesn't matter. Like a counterfeit hundred-dollar bill. If it's good enough to pass, who cares? The real bill is a fraud anyway. All it is is, the government prints it and prints on it, 'Honey, believe this is money.' The counterfeiter does the same thing."

"Tell me how you and Hillegass got together," Fred said.

"I had his name from somewhere, and I called him. We started talking, and he asked would I be interested in blah blah blah and the rest of it. I said yes, maybe, he came up, and I thought, Here's a story or he's going to lead me to a story or something I can use. Most times it doesn't work that way, but you gotta give it a chance."

"You met with him?"

Ophelia hesitated. They reached the traffic circle at the edge of Cambridge, and Fred eased into it, spotting a slick of ice under the lights. The big new MBTA station at Alewife was lighted but abandoned, like a casino erected in a dry town.

"*Ecce homo,*" Fred prompted. "Also, *cherchez la femme.*"

"Just between us, I never met Hillegass because of the snow," Ophelia decided. "But if this goes anywhere and there's a story in it, and I'm a player, I may let on that Hillegass and I had a brief smoking relationship before the end, provided—Fred, would you call the man good-looking? I see a man with beautiful, tapered fingers as long as his hair, like Adrian Sellers. He sounded English. Was Hillegass English, or just cultivated? Fill me in."

"Remember, the police haven't released his name yet."

"I know how to keep my mouth shut," Ophelia said. They followed the river past 1001, where only a single penthouse window was lit. "That's where I'm going to live," Ophelia announced. "Bag all that grass. Next time I'm snowed in, at least I'll be snowed in *somewhere*." They moved on past the snowbound fake-nineteenth-century brick of Harvard. This part of the world was cold, quiet, and empty, giving up to human life only as they swung east on River Street and headed into Central Square. Fred's revolving light even ran into competition a few blocks down, where a fire engine idled and an ambulance crew argued with a man who demanded to lie in the street.

The cops weren't letting people within a hundred feet of the precinct station. They had a mumbling crowd snubbed up along the south side of River Street, at Green, behind manned barricades that Fred drove past. It looked to extend back several blocks toward MIT, a surprising number of people for this time of night, to judge by the crowd visible through the gaps between idling motorcycles and uniforms.

They left the car on Mass Ave, in a No Standing zone in front of the Purity Supreme, and walked down Pearl. Hundreds of people were gathered, many with candles shielded from the wind in paper cups. Some carried signs, and they were singing.

19

"O sacred head, surrounded / By crown of piercing thorn; / O bleeding head so wounded, / Reviled and put to scorn," the crowd sang at a Catholic-school pace set by the very sore feet of children wearing the shoes of older sisters and brothers, driven by armed nuns.

"Bach," Ophelia said. "His tune. The lyrics, I don't know who wrote those. Every Good Friday we had to sing it, back at the Madams of the Sacred H." She sang along, "Death's pallid hue comes o'er him, / The glow of life decays; / Yet angel hosts adore him / And tremble as they gaze."

"At least, praise God, they're not saying the rosary," Fred said. They pushed into the crowd, Ophelia leading. The gathered people, crammed into a straggle on Green Street between the G Spot and River Street, were elevated by the cold, and the adventure, into a cautious hilarity that was hard to read. It projected anger but was less focused than most anger.

Ophelia took the arm of a man covered in gray wool and asked him, "What's up?" He held his candle with both hands, as if afraid it would spill. He had a gray wife next to him who carried a home-made cardboard sign that read, RELEASE HIM TO US.

"Read the sign," the gray man told Ophelia grandly.

"The sacred head," the woman with the sign said, shivering. "They locked it up." She yelled across the crowd, "Render unto Caesar! Render unto Caesar!"

A rumble like a flushing tide on shingle started at the head of the gathering and sorted itself into choral speech: the opening strain of the first sorrowful mystery. "Here comes the rosary," Ophelia whispered loudly. "Must be a priest or leader up front." The crowd launched into the response to a Hail Mary. The people seemed patient and slightly ominous, but in a good-humored way, as if they had come out to watch Joan of Arc do her thing and she'd been held up by bureaucratic snags they knew were being taken care of. She'd burn when she was ready.

"The painting that does miracles?" Ophelia asked the man's gray wife.

"Silence! We pray the rosary," the group around them complained in hushed fury. The gray man nodded.

"I'm from the press," Ophelia announced in a frank, conspiratorial tone, looking around. "Did anyone here get healed? Any cured people?" She started passing out her card. The rosary rumbled around her, the throng parting as she forced her way through.

Ophelia maneuvered toward the front of the crowd, which continued its slow, bleating pulse, each decade of rosary followed by the same two stanzas of the slow song. "We want the leaders," Ophelia stage-whispered to Fred, like one wolf to another among sheep, confident the mutton would not understand her language. That the leaders were her goal did not prevent her from handing out her cards to any who would accept them. Many, holding placards and rosaries, and wearing gloves, had no way to hold cards, but Ophelia found their pockets. On either side of the gathering the garages and parking lots stood dark, though lights shone in a few three-deckers from which people stared between jerked curtains.

"You all from some parish?" Ophelia asked one man whose isolated, intent stance would have attracted immediate security attention in any airport.

"We are legion," the man answered. He would not take Ophelia's card but instead thrust one of his own on her. Fred read it under a garage-door light: JESUS SAVES. (ARE YOU?) *Revelations 2, v. 23.*

A little voice wailed, "I'm cold, and I have to pee." The child was on the far side of the street, buried beneath adults. They reached the front, where a dozen police officers, behind as many smoking and throbbing motorcycles, blocked the demonstration from broaching River Street. Up front, against the cops and, like them, facing the crowd, stood three bundled figures. The crowd was thicker here, and marginally warmer. Everyone was getting to the tail end of a "Glory be." The central figure raised a mittened hand to his or her lips and blew a whining note.

"Here it comes again," Fred warned. The crowd gasped in and started, "O sacred head surrounded, / By crown of piercing thorn." Half the cops sang along. "They're not going to talk to us until they get all the way around their rosary," Fred told Ophelia, looking at his watch. "That's going to be four-thirty, five. I have to tell you, I agree with that little girl. See what those leaflets are they're passing out."

Immediately on hearing his voice, nine singing people held out slips of paper the size and shape of bookmarks—heavy fake parchment, marbleized with fake sheep fat. One side, in Gothic lettering, read simply THE AGE OF MIRACLES. C C C. The other read, CCC: *Concerned Civilians for Christ. Contact: Brendan Rufus,* with a phone number on a Somerville exchange. While Ophelia struggled to start up a conversation with one of the leafleters, Fred elbowed to the front and tried a cop, one of the few who weren't singing.

"Friend of Ernie Bookrajian. What's this, Ernesto Gigante's people?"

The cop gleamed from his boots, holstered gun, motorcycle, and helmet. He blew a cloud of white steam. His motorcycle blew a cloud of white steam and roared, and shrugged. Fred tried the next nonsinging cop, further down the line, and achieved the same results. He had reached the person with the kazoo. The crowd finished singing, "And tremble as they gaze." It breathed in, ready to plunge into the next lap of the rosary.

"You Brendan Rufus?" Fred asked the bundle with the kazoo. It breathed white steam.

"I'm Brenda. He's Brendan. Call later," it said, gesturing toward a similar vertical bundle next to it, who breathed white steam and proclaimed, "The third Sorrowful Mystery: The Crowning of Jesus with Thorns. Our Father who art in Heaven . . ."

"We're busy. Call later," Brenda whispered. "Three–four o'clock in the afternoon. The number's on the thing."

"Gotcha," said Fred.

"Thy kingdom come, thy will be done," Brendan continued in white smoke.

Fred found Ophelia and told her, "I am now driving to Arlington."

Over fresh bagels Fred had picked up at an all-night place, Molly, absurdly chipper for so early on a Sunday morning, said, "From her youth, my sister Ophelia stood out for two—no, three—talents. She could blush on purpose. She could fart on command. And she could sleep through anything." Ophelia, demonstrating her prowess in the last category, was now asleep on the sofa in Molly's living room, under a pile of comforters.

Terry wandered into the kitchen after sniffing out the situation in the living room. She wore Ophelia's fur coat, which dragged along the floor.

"You look like the Princess of Uzbekistan," Fred told her.

"Thank you, Fred."

"How much grape jelly do you think that coat will hold?"

"I'm not putting jelly in Aunt Pheely's coat."

151

"Too bad."

"Besides, you never guessed my riddle." Terry sat at the table and started gnawing on a naked bagel. "It's been days, and you don't care."

"I haven't stopped thinking about it," Fred lied. "But it's a hard one, and your mother won't help me."

Terry shook her head. "Mom better *not* help you. I would inoculate her," she said fiercely, gnashing her plain bagel.

"OK, Fred," Molly said. "Let's see how good you are. You've had days. Why is Roger Clemens like a TV set?"

"Because he delivers on schedule?" Fred hazarded. "Also he works all winter? Also he has his bad days and his good days?"

"No, no, and also no," Terry crowed. "You are so cold you're stinking." She flounced out of the room, bagel and all.

"Eight o'clock isn't too early to call Dee, is it?" Fred asked.

"On a Sunday morning? Yes, but go ahead. Your cause is just, and you're bound to get at least Walter."

Fred dialed, looking out Molly's kitchen window. The morning was turning out gloomy. If there weren't so much of it already, you might look up at the sky, titillated by hope of weather, and think, Maybe it'll snow. Walter answered in his deep, courtly way. Fred chewed the fat with him before he asked for news of the ruckus in Central Square.

"Sounds like it petered out at dawn," Walter said. "The snow was on our side. "Dee's been on the horn with headquarters off and on. They thought they might need a rescue party. They just now let her off. You want to talk with her? She's pulling her thermal undies out of the dryer. We had them warming, just in case."

"Who's Brendan Rufus?" Fred asked once he had Dee.

"Brendan and Brenda," Dee said. "It's a set. You never know what's scurrying behind the plywood until something frightens them out. Brendan and Brenda Rufus see their big chance. Citizens for a Concerned—no, what is it? Concerned Citizens for Christ. Not to be confused with the Cambridge Civic Association,

152

which is CCA. Never heard of the Rufuses before last night. Everybody's an organization."

"You got somebody on the Rufus question?"

"Is the Pope Catholic? It's the first live wire we've found to pull. You gotta go easy in this state, but yes, you bet your ass somebody's on them, like you know what on you know what!"

"Can I ask some informed questions?" Fred asked. "Which you have no reason to care why I'm asking them?"

"Shoot."

"You any closer to identifying the John Doe from a thousand one?" Fred asked.

"My informed answer is: Nope."

"You have a cause of death?"

"Something weird there," Dee said. "They don't know. The lab people say the blood's all wrong. They're still testing. But I'll give you what I've heard: the removal of the head, and the nailing, that's post mortem."

"No surprise."

"The thing with the broomstick, which was broken, so it was sharp, I have to say—they're confused. That was done while the guy was alive. The way the organs reacted, the blood, the folks described it to Dolores Cipriani—that's who took over from Bookrajian—it's like the blood is gelatinous, not liquid. It's weird. And there wasn't enough of it outside the body. Some, yes, but not enough. He died of that operation, is one theory, and the other theory is that he died of whatever went wrong in the blood, which nobody has seen anything like it. They call it the virus from outer space, but they don't see any virus. He should have died much sooner than he did, is what everyone agrees on."

"A kind of miracle," Fred observed.

"Not one you'd pray for if you were the guy," Dee said.

"Nobody's happened to bump into the head?"

"The victim is still referred to at the station as the—you gotta excuse some black humor about the hobby horse, it's been a hard week back at the ranch—they're still calling him the headless horseman."

"And you've gone through One-double-oh-one knocking on doors and asking questions?"

"I guess so, since the people who live there, all those prize-winners, keep making their lawyers call the mayor's office to complain. Dolores has talked to a hundred lawyers, but she's no closer to whoever lived in that condo. One lawyer refers you to another lawyer, and before you know it, Dolores says, you've spent the whole day bouncing across the world by satellite, and you wind up where you started, talking to yourself on a bad line."

"Your sisters and brothers across the river," Fred said. "You heard any rumors about the murder at the Brittannee?"

"Guy named Hillegass. They matched his prints with central and ID'd him as an ex-con on parole. No sign what he was doing there. If you can help, they're frantic for leads," Dee said. "That's all I know, beyond he died real hard. You men, what's the matter with you?"

"Oh well," Fred said. "You talk to Bookrajian?"

"They can't decide how to go. They're like standing in the window of the fifteenth floor of the burning building. It's the most awful thing."

A chunky thump shook the house.

"Randy Fibonacci, practicing his curve. I'll get it," Molly said, standing and wiping her hands on the hips of her blue wrapper. "Things are getting closer to normal if we get the Sunday paper before lunch. Tell Dee I said hi."

"Molly says hi," Fred told Dee. They were finished.

Sam drifted into the kitchen rubbing his hair and wearing the same clothes he'd gone to bed in three nights running.

"Bagels," Fred told him.

"Who's on the couch?"

"Ophelia stayed over."

Sam went to the drawer next to the sink and took out the largest knife he could find, about the length of his forearm. He

154

started operating on a bagel, watching Fred to see if he'd be stopped or edited.

"There's bacon if you want," Fred volunteered.

Sam shook his head and shoved his bagel halves into the toaster. "She's in danger," he said.

"Could be."

"Because I forgot?"

"Not because of that. We're not certain she's in danger, but there's a distant, remote chance. I should tell you and Terry both, let Molly or me take it if someone calls, OK?"

"If it's all right with Mom."

Molly's Sunday routine started with her putting most of the paper in the recycling bag in the garage. Having gone around the outside of the house, she came into the kitchen through the back door, shivering, carrying the remainder of the paper. "The Bruins are in trouble," Molly remarked.

"Let me see," Sam demanded, disregarding his popping bagel. He and Molly wrestled the paper apart until Sam had the sports section.

"Trains are running. Buses are going to be on Sunday schedule tomorrow—but running. Things are getting back to normal. Did Walter mention the library?"

"Said he'd see you tomorrow."

"So we're having school?" Sam asked.

"Could be," Molly said.

"But maybe not," Sam said. "You never know."

20

Ophelia slept until almost three, deciding to waken only when Terry persuaded her with a handful of snow. The four of them—Fred, Molly, Terry, and Sam—had gone sledding, although the day was cold and gloomy, and they came back hungry and noisy. Terry, not wanting to be hushed on account of an aunt, took things into her own hands.

Ophelia leapt into action, a most satisfactory guest from the children's point of view. She was attired in the transparent gown, for one thing; and she was in high gear as soon as her feet hit the floor, replacing the tossed cushions, folding the comforters, and yelling for coffee.

"Beans and franks in twenty minutes," Molly called from the kitchen.

"Gotta get on the phone," Ophelia gasped, taking a mug of coffee from Sam and swaying into the kitchen, where she stood, like Venus, drinking it, sniffing the beans and making fast plans. Sam and Terry gaped at her outfit. "Thanks for the wakeup, Terry, you monster. I'll get you for that on your wedding night. All I need is more coffee and time on the phone. I'll use the one in the living room so I don't interrupt lunch," Ophelia said.

"She's naked!" Terry whispered after Ophelia left the kitchen. "Worse!"

"Never mind," Molly said.

Sam, blushing, said, "Terry, you're naked plenty of times."

"Maybe, but not like that!"

"Anyway, don't notice. Like the emperor's new clothes."

"Shirley, honey, any calls?" Ophelia's voice came from the next room.

"She's calling the TV station," Terry said. "Her secretary."

The invisible woman in the transparent gown, soundless as she listened to a voice nobody in the kitchen could hear, held the room's attention until Molly said, "Sam, find the mustard. Terry, get napkins. Fred, you want to throw beans on the plates?"

Ophelia appeared in the doorway holding a small white pad on which she'd been writing notes with a gold fountain pen. "You get any response from that parade?" Fred asked.

"Nobody we can use. Just dorks lonesome to be somebody. My people hate that on TV, dorks like themselves getting a lot of air time. Fred, I mislaid that triple C flier. You got one? You didn't talk to those Rufus people, did you?" Fred took a folded flier from his shirt pocket and reached it across the table to her. "The beans smell good, but I've gotta watch my figure," Ophelia said, taking the piece of paper. She walked it back to her new office in the living room. Terry and Sam helped watch her figure.

Fred said, "Reckon I'll kibitz on this call." He followed Ophelia into Molly's living room and read the morning paper while Ophelia performed on the redial button until, after seventeen minutes, she got through.

"Channel Nine News. Ophelia Finger," Ophelia announced, stretching things a bit. Fred listened to her side of the conversation for ten minutes, but she said very little until she hung up, furious, without giving any signal that she was about to do so.

"Get anything?" Fred asked.

"Forget Mr. and Mrs. Potato Head," Ophelia said. She stretched out on the couch and glared at the ceiling. "Boy, are they talkers. Both on the phone the whole time, both extensions. Their trip to Fatima. Why they march. The age of miracles. Their trip to Lourdes. No, they don't know Gigante, never met him. Their trip to Guadeloupe. How miracles happen. Separation of Church and State. Their trip to that place in Yugoslavia that sounds like a gut-shot dog falling downstairs.

"They'd pay me to get on the show. They'd pay me to come to their home in Somerville and view their many souvenirs and relics. They can't wait to tell the world their secret."

"Which is?"

"Here's the problem from the show-biz angle: when a dork tells you a secret, all you remember about the secret is the dork. Mr. and Mrs. Potato Head. Doesn't matter what they say. It's dorks talking."

"Still, their secret might be useful."

"I'll trade their secret for another cup of coffee."

"Deal."

"God is love. And you can quote them." Ophelia got up and shouldered the bag she'd brought with her from Lincoln. "Fred, owe me the coffee. I'll wash, then check my messages by remote, then see if they'll do call forwarding on a Sunday."

When Fred got back into the kitchen, Sam was developing measles, diphtheria, and appendicitis. Molly was prodding and needling, teasing him with suspicious questions.

"He's scared there's going to be school tomorrow," Terry said.

"Silly me," Molly said. "Terry, get lost while I inoculate your brother. Sam, what's the homework situation?"

"She wants seven book reports," Sam admitted. "I was gonna do them."

"They were due before the snow saved you?" Molly asked. Sam nodded. "Then you let the whole week sail by and still did nothing? Even after you were saved?"

158

"I forgot," Sam mumbled.

"I now declare you miraculously cured of all that ails you, including being a lazy poop. I am going upstairs to lie around and read, and chat with my sister if she wants to. Fred, do you feel like doing book reports with Sam?"

"We've got till midnight," Fred said. "It's five o'clock now. That's one report an hour. Get your paper and pencil and the books you're doing the reports on."

"What books shall I use?" Sam asked.

"We're not very far advanced in this project, are we? What books are you expected to use?"

"Whatever we want, as long as they're more than a hundred and fifty pages. She gave us a list, but it was a long time ago. Before Christmas."

They were deep into an intense skim-reading of *Wars of the Planet Vuldar*, the third book in the pile Fred, Terry, and Sam had thrown together, when Ophelia stuck her head into the kitchen. She was dressed, as last night, in jeans and a heavy sweater. "Business office is closed until tomorrow," she said. "But he called again."

"Sam," Fred said. "Stick with the planet Vuldar. What did he say?"

"He will like to meet me," Ophelia said, giving the words a Hispanic flavor. "He will wait for me tomorrow evening at South Station, in Boston. If I cannot come, he is calling again tomorrow night may be."

"What time? Sam! Vuldar!"

"Five o'clock. What do you think?" Ophelia asked.

"He's giving us time. Let's talk tomorrow."

On Monday morning a great wail arose from the house in Arlington. Ophelia slept through the children's wrestling, conniving, malingering, dressing, and eating of breakfast. There'd be no school bus, but the kids could walk. Molly planned to drive her car to work, with Fred's light on it, while Fred—Fred would figure things out as they came. He wasn't going near Mountjoy Street until the coast was clear. His patience would snap like fine porcelain if he had to submit to another tea with Clay and Lavinia Whitman.

"It's not fair," Terry shouted about something, while Fred got them into their coats and kicked them out. He walked Molly to the car and told her to take care. He looked up at a cold, overcast sky. All around, the snow had begun to settle under its own weight; gray birds poked around the sky, between one bare tree and another, looking for luck or pity or an even break. In the top of an ash tree down the block, crows worked to dismantle a squirrel's nest.

Inside again, Fred tiptoed past Molly's sleeping sister and sat in the kitchen over a fresh cup of coffee, to think about the pros and cons of the proposed encounter at South Station. The question was how to use Ophelia, and whether to use Ophelia. She was determined to go ahead.

"Here's the thing," Fred said aloud to himself. "I want to find out what's going on. That is just ordinary plain cussed curiosity. It's also ninety paintings I might never see unless I run them down, and I want to understand what they are even though the only ones I know anything about are real, real iffy. I've got Pandora's box sitting at my feet, and I've got a hammer handy, and the moral of that is, obviously, why not use the hammer?"

Fred poked into the refrigerator and found the remains of last night's beans. He himself had shaken them from the can and interfered with them, trying to provoke them to attain a goal of chili, though Molly told him he couldn't get there from where he was starting. He added mustard and put them, cold, on toast.

"Shades of the Middle West begin to close about the growling boy," Fred said, chewing and adding sugar to his coffee in case it might assist the beans. "Here's the thing. I've been assuming the two murders are related. It's true there's an ugly similarity between them, given the excessive cruelty. But beyond that, and

160

the fact of the associated paintings by putative Old Masters, why connect the murders? The style of presentation's not the same when you get right down to it. The murder scene in Cambridge is ritualistic, perversely sexual, capitalizing on lengthy torment. The ribbon bow on the poor guy's penis is, as it were, the killer thumbing his nose at everyone. The coagulated-blood aspect is weird: notable, and unique to Cambridge.

"These are not good beans. So, the two scenes are not the same, even though mutilation figures in each. Still, my instinct says they are connected. But to go on with the differences: nothing slowed down or mysteriously coagulated old Hillegass's blood. He'd lost enough into his mattress that he was almost white."

Venus said from the doorway, "Fred, the beard has got to go. Who are you talking to?"

"Myself," Fred said.

"Don't let me interrupt you," Ophelia said, making for the coffee. She poured a cup and stood at the sink, looking out the window.

"Here's the thing," Fred said. "The Hillegass killing is efficient. Its cruelty is goal-oriented, the work of a technician who has the power to feel and sees the value of causing suffering and terror, or he wouldn't bother. If it's one man, as I think it is, he's strong and good at what he does. Hillegass would not sit still to be strangled, or to have his genitals hacked off."

"Jeekers, Fred," Ophelia objected. Fred held up his hand to stop her.

"The assailant is in control. He takes his victim by surprise, strangles him until he's lost consciousness, then brings him back with the pain of the surgery; lets the horror of that dawn on his man while the shock's still anesthetizing him from the big pain that's coming; asks his questions while the subject hopes he may still be able to change the outcome. (The TV's going all the time in case Hillegass yelps or talks too loud, the killer squatting next to his head, where it's dry, holding the necktie tight again, whispering

161

questions.) Hillegass thinks, I'll give him what he wants, then he'll run for a doctor.

"Everything about it says efficient, superior strength directed toward menace, intimidation, and death. The killer, on a different day, might have the imagination to be humane."

Fred looked at the scene as he'd re-created it, considered it, found nothing missing, and nodded. "Then the visitor finishes him off, takes what he wants, and leaves. No frills, no time wasted, no wild geese to chase. And no grandstanding. No—what was the term those experts in the paper used? yes—no overkill."

"Jesus," Ophelia said. "Fred, this is awful."

"Let me just follow this where it's going," Fred said, shoving the last corner of embeaned toast around his paper plate. "Although the maybe-Reni fits with the pieces Hillegass was offering, when we come back and compare his murder to the baroque panoply in Cambridge, the feel on Mem Drive is that we are in the hands of a high IQ that hasn't a clue as to what it's doing. He doesn't know what his message is, the Cambridge guy, but he'll work on the goddamned medium until he's got it perfect. That stage set took hours of work after the killing. Sure, your sex kook and your religion kook are often one and the same kook, but despite the fact that the picture he left looks like it's about sex and religion, I don't believe it. The head of Jesus, the crucifixion, the pink ribbon—I don't believe it, and I don't think the killer does, either. It's got that Salvador Dalí feel of the smartest kid in eighth grade jeering at the teachers who make the mistake of admiring him for his technique.

"Here's the thing," Fred went on. "The murder at the Brittannee is honest. The scene in Cambridge does not tell us why the dead guy died. The medium and the message are disconnected, as if the killer can't feel what he's done. He's playing. He can't feel it. The Cambridge killer is also a liar."

21

Ophelia breathed in noisily, turning to face him. Her face was alive with interest. Her body in its transparent thing—really! Molly should invite her sister to put some clothes on. Fred held up his hand. "One more minute, Pheely. I'm following a cold trail into the dark recesses of my jumbled head. Let me get where I'm going, then I'm with you. It's a coincidence that both murders include mutilation. Is it also a coincidence that both are connected to paintings?

"In any case, I have decided that the killings were not done by the same person. I know it, but even so I don't want to volunteer any information to the boys in blue, in either Boston or Cambridge, for fear they'll follow it across the river and get in the way of that collection of paintings."

"Speaking of riddles," Ophelia interrupted, sitting across the kitchen table, "why is Roger Clemens like a toaster?"

"He's like a TV set."

"Toaster," Ophelia was sure. "I'm supposed to use the riddle on my show."

"If someone doesn't give us the answer soon, this riddle is going to become the symbol of the Great Snow," Fred said. "Get your call forwarding in place and then let's talk about this afternoon."

"You think the guy's a crazy, don't you?" Ophelia asked, shivering as she fiddled with her hair.

"Your guy, no. What do I know? But no, I don't think your guy is crazy. The one in Cambridge, absolutely."

Not long before ten, Fred telephoned Dmitri Signet's gallery on Newbury Street and activated the recording. They were closed on Mondays, but during their regular hours they were showing choice works from the gallery's collection. Please leave a message. Fred did so, reminding Dmitri Signet that Mrs. Riley wanted news about that Peterson painting of zinnias.

"Dolores Cipriani," the telephone told Fred when he responded to a ring at ten o'clock. The name rang a bell, but not much of one.

"We'd like for you to come in," the voice of Dolores Cipriani continued.

"Tell me who you are and where and why you want me."

"What were you doing in Central Square Sunday morning?" Oh, Dolores Cipriani. She was Bookrajian's replacement, according to Dee.

Fred said, "I bought bagels."

"We don't like civilians messing in. You identify yourself as a friend of Ernie Bookrajian?"

" 'Friend' is pushing it, Officer."

"You willing to come in? We'll send a prowl car."

"Come in for what?"

"Say hello."

"I'll pass," Fred said. Cipriani had no argument except bluff and moral authority and exhaustion and irritation at being clueless in a high-profile crime.

"What are you doing for Bookrajian?" Cipriani asked.

"I pass again," Fred told her.

"You step your foot wrong in this town, I can have you put away," Dolores Cipriani claimed. "Why can't we sit down somewhere?"

"Tell you what," Fred offered, "if I'm in Cambridge, I'll call you. That fair enough? I'm on another call." He hung up.

At ten-thirty Ophelia came down from the shower, wearing Molly's red sweater over her jeans. She set up shop at the kitchen table, beginning a series of phone calls circling most of the known world that was not asleep. Fred fiddled in the living room with a pile of Molly's old *National Geographic*s. The house was strange with just this couple of Gypsies in it, himself and Ophelia. Ophelia, in the kitchen, was simultaneously doing real-estate and book deals, talking with her publicist, and discussing the merits of potential guests for her show.

"No, Shirley, I decided to nix the miracle angle. I want to reach a better class of people. To hell with the supernatural. Paranormal is as far as I go. You talk aliens, at least you get the Mensa types. Not that I will touch aliens. That craze already peaked. Its cycle isn't due for eight more years."

Fred eased into the kitchen and started constructing a grilled-cheese sandwich. He glanced at Ophelia, who, the phone at her ear, answered by shaking her head and pointing at the figure everyone had to watch, while her conversation with Shirley continued. "To hell with this. Get me a suite at the—whatever you think. Meantime, if Brenda Rufus calls again, tell them the show's sponsors are Buddhists, we can't promote the competition."

Fred flipped his sandwich. Ophelia hung up the telephone. "According to Brenda Rufus, there's a new rash of miracles, all cures the victims got off that newspaper picture of the sacred head. One guy with a limp who's miraculously not limping, he used to have one leg shorter than the other one, now it's longer than the other one; and another, a girl who was supposed to have a Caesarean section, nothing else was going to work, but the girl put that front page under her pillow, and next thing you know, she wakes up giving birth through what we in the TV business like to call normal channels. The only real news is more fucking snow."

"How much?"

"Six to twelve inches, more or less, unless the storm stays east. I'm off miracles. It was a stupid idea." Fred sat down with his sandwich, reached behind him to the fridge, found pickles, and put the jar on the table. "Oh, and Clay Reed called an hour ago on call waiting. Said he'd turned up, and I quote, 'an intriguing snippet.' He called me Lady Molly. Where does that guy come from, Jane Austen? 'Lady Molly'? 'Snippet'?"

Ophelia pulled the pickles toward her and probed into the jar with long fingers armed with golden nails.

"He asked would I have you call him when the instrument was free. Straight out of Jane Austen. My lord, the instrument is free."

Fred finished his lunch and stretched before he took up the instrument. "Clay? Fred."

"One moment," Clay said. Fred heard an indistinct female mumbling and whispering, followed by Clayton's voice saying, "If you would, your Beef Stroganoff for this evening? Perfect, Maria. Yes, for two. I shall manage the noodles," then, "I am with you, Fred."

"You called."

"Yes. Taking advantage of Lavinia's adjournment to the shower, I have picked up an interesting snippet. She is still bathing. I may speak freely. She loves and appreciates money as if it were something real. I had never thought of money that way. Finite, yes, but real?"

"More snow is threatened," Fred said. "Does Lavinia Randall Whitman want to step through the window of opportunity into a train? Who knows when the next opportunity may be?"

"Fred, have you heard of Carlos Gato?"

"The name sounds familiar—but then it's a familiar-sounding name. An alias? Who is he when he's at home?"

"He is dead. His airplane was destroyed a year ago. He and the pilot and some others rained into the jungle."

Ophelia ate the last pickle, drank the juice from the jar, and took herself into the living room, where she started fiddling noisily with the TV set and swearing at it.

"He was Colombian," Clay said. "One of the leading figures in the drug movement. I have learned that Hillegass operated for a time as Carlos Gato's agent. Before he died, apparently, Carlos put a notable portion of his fortune into paintings."

"Interesting. All those greenbacks, you have to do something with them. Art's portable. Who's your source?"

"For all we know, the paintings Carlos owned rained down with him. He was leaving his native land. But no one is sure, and people are looking. Fred, I talked with that disgraceful Newboldt who diddled me once. It is from him I have this information, which I shall keep from Lavinia. He told me that the drug lord's native taste was not far different from—Fred, are you familiar with Louis Ferré's collection in Ponce, Puerto Rico?"

"Can't say I am."

"Imagine a brothel erected in an Italian church of the baroque, with the aim of appealing to the sensibilities of gentlemen from the Middle East—are you following, Fred?"

"If you mean huge pictures about breasts and knives, large black fruit, and little angel children with knowing looks and big pink knowing buttocks, yes."

"One thinks also," Clay went on, "of the Ferdinand Marcos collection, and of many of the works that came to the Worcester Museum. The strongman turned collector—but every cobbler to his last. I should be forbearing, knowing what difficulties I myself would face in undertaking a new career, for example in cocaine trafficking or tyranny."

"Thousands of rich people buy art stupidly," Fred pointed out. "Probably half of them hire expensive experts to help them waste their money."

"People such as Hillegass," Clay said.

"But since Hillegass was *selling*," Fred said, "one wonders whether what he was offering was his to sell."

Clay said, "Now that the drug lord has passed on. Suppose—just suppose the collection is again available. Perhaps the only way we can know is by investing. I cannot guess who Lavinia's contact is, but it is not the owner. Lavinia has not seen even the list of what is in this collection."

"Who gets the sixty thousand dollars?" Fred asked.

"Perhaps I shall ask Lavinia."

"Clay," Fred said, "have you forgotten that Lavinia is not to be trusted?"

"No, no, of course not," Clay said absently.

"I have something else working that might get us closer, Clay. If Lavinia's gone cold on this thing, she has her reasons. Don't get her started again. The two pictures we know of from this list, they're both duds," Fred reminded him.

22

F red reached Molly at the library before she went to lunch. "Do me a favor on the Internet, will you? See what they have on a Colombian drug lord named Carlos Gato. Died about a year ago, blown up in his plane. Could be that's the collection Ophelia's Velázquez comes from. Big money. Dirty money."

"That's going to be pages."

"What I want to know is, where are the pictures now?"

"I'll do what I can. You and Pheely not eating each other alive?"

"Not yet."

"Because you're not the easiest person in the world to get along with, Fred."

"I need a nightgown like that one she wears."

"Fred, if you and my sister are talking with murderers this afternoon, watch out for her."

"If we were going to be talking about murder, we wouldn't do it. We're talking art. We'll say hello, find out what the guy has to say, then ease him down slowly once I get a line on him. I want Ophelia out of this, but in a way that doesn't get anyone excited."

"Watch out for my sister, is what I'm asking."

The main concourse of South Station was extremely crowded. The ban on passenger vehicles still being in force, and with more snow threatening, the usual struggle of the rush-hour crowd was drowned out by a panicked sense of bored emergency. At South Station, there was no longer anything fun about this continuing natural deviance from the normal.

Fred and Ophelia had come into town through the beginnings of this latest snowstorm, using bus and subway. The trip had been crowded, noisy, and irritating. Ophelia stood out in her blond fake fur, so Fred kept an eye on her bag. When they walked through South Station's Summer Street entrance, Fred caught Teddy's eye and sensed the man falling in behind them. Not knowing where he'd have to go, they hadn't been sure how Teddy should dress. It was important to settle on exactly the right point along the stretch between derelict and white tie, either of which Teddy could carry off. Ophelia remained oblivious to the tall black man in the blue suit and light trenchcoat behind them, ready to provide whatever backup might be needed.

They passed up the thousand and one ways to buy coffee and yogurt and picked up food at the McDonald's counter to earn them a table upstairs. At Fred's insistence, they were a half hour early, and Teddy had been there longer so as to have time to look the place over before they got there and to be there when their man made contact.

Fred chose a table near the stairs and started eating french fries. Ophelia looked around them, toying with a straw. "For lots of people, this experience must be common," she said.

"McDonald's?"

"The skull-and-dagger stuff."

Teddy came up the stairs carrying a tray with fries, a Big Mac, and an orange soda. He did a slow circuit of the balcony before settling tables several away from theirs, where he sat, arranged his tray, and pulled a newspaper from his coat pocket. He cracked it open and laid it in front of him. He and Fred had decided he would look like a bank officer.

No one, perhaps not even Teddy himself, knew his last name, or what he might do in the world once he put himself together and started doing it. In the meantime, he was more or less running the place in Charlestown where Fred, who owned an interest in the building, maintained, at least nominally, a room. Charlestown gave him an address for his driver's license and a place for the very few things he wanted to keep.

"Now what we do is wait," Fred told Ophelia. "You don't want your hamburger?"

"Of course not. It's a prop."

Fred ate the prop. Three people stopped at their table to initiate false alarms, recognizing Ophelia—as their man would—from her show. They all wanted to converse. She and Fred developed a routine of bitter argument that discouraged interruption. At five after five, Ophelia said, "He's not coming," just as a small, square man in a blue blazer dropped his short dark coat across the back of the empty chair at their table and sat down. White shirt, blue tie, gray slacks, clean-shaven, short black hair, Young Republican, went the quick inventory. That red and gold shield on the blazer pocket was vacant heraldry.

"Who is these man?" the blazer asked Ophelia. The Hispanic tinge was still in the voice, but less pronounced than it had been on the tape.

"He works for me," Ophelia said. "Driver, bodyguard, like that."

The short haircut dipped in acknowledgment. "So you are interest in these picture," the short man told Ophelia.

"What shall I call you?" Ophelia asked.

"I like 'Rico.' I go by that."

"Mr. Rico?"

"Rico. Front name. Like Ofélia."

"Rico, what's the deal?" Ophelia asked. "I'm busy."

"Is simple. These painting. No tax. No tax is nice." Rico

opened his face into a boyish smile. Fred stared around the room. The opening moves were Ophelia's; he was the muscle.

"Is worth a lot of money, these painting," Rico proceeded. "Thirty-five millions of dollar."

"You like a fry?" Fred asked, offering the carton. Rico refused without looking at him, shaking his head.

"Thirty-five million," Ophelia speculated smoothly. Lavinia Randall Whitman had floated the figure forty-five million equally smoothly, but she'd been in the Four Seasons, and working in a Lapsang souchong environment. Rico, having to make his presentation at McDonald's, was down ten million.

Ophelia said, "I hadn't realized there were a lot of paintings. The money's no problem if I like the paintings. That other man mentioned only one."

"The other man. He is delay. He is also confuse," Rico said, smiling. "So now he is out of this."

A garbled loudspeaker announced a train heading for New Haven and New York, six hours late. "I did not like the other man," Ophelia observed when the competition stopped.

Teddy, at his table, turned a page of his newspaper and took a sip of his drink. In the concourse, a ragged heave of passengers converged on track 9. Fred ate a fry, then cleaned his fingernails with a corner of cardboard that he tore out of the container.

"When can I see the paintings you are selling?" Ophelia asked. "What are they? I buy only the best. But for the best, I pay top dollar."

"Then you are going to love these what I have."

A fat man with a pink, determined face hesitated near the table, recognizing Ophelia and asking himself if he dared break into the conversation. Ophelia said sharply, "Fred! Dork!" Fred rose and escorted the protesting man a short distance away. "Give me your card, I'll have her send you a signed photo," Fred promised.

When he got back to their table, Ophelia was running her

finger down a typed list that lay between her and Rico. "Amazing," she crowed. "Giovanni Paolo Cavagna, Lavinia Zappi Fontana, Gianantonio Guardi's *Madonna with the Sleeping Infant*." She had trouble with the names, but she lurched speedily across them anyway, as if they were merely bad potholes, and she in a rented car. "And look, here's Giovanni Battista Pittoni's *Sacrifice of Polyxena by Neoptolemy at the Grave of Achilles*! I can't believe it!"

She started leafing through what looked to be five or six pages, exclaiming once in a while and pointing with a golden fingernail at an entry. She made it sound like a birthday party. People from neighboring tables glanced up and over.

"Here's a mistake, Rico. They say Rembrandt van Ryan where they mean Rembrandt. Van Ryan is the man in the picture he painted. A portrait. Lotta portraits in this group, but I like portraits. Here's a *Shipwreck* picture by R. Wykins. I'm glad it's not all Italians, not that I have anything—oh, here it is! The very last on the list, *Three Men at a Table* by Velázquez. This is terrific, Rico. I had no idea."

Ophelia suddenly folded the papers and stuffed them into her bag. Rico, taken aback, reached for them. Fred took his arm and held it. "Those aren't for you," Rico objected. Fred held his arm and made everything look calm. Rico was strong, plenty strong enough to do to Hillegass what someone had done to Hillegass, if he was also smart and quick.

"The papers, that stay with me," Rico demanded.

"Oh, honey, you have copies," Ophelia said, tapping him on the arm. "It's too much for an afternoon. I have to think. I'm not that fast." She stood up as suddenly as she had filched Rico's list. Fred's hand was still on his arm. Teddy turned a page of his paper, took a sip of his drink.

"I can say definitely I might be interested," Ophelia promised. "Tell my man when you can bring the paintings for me to look at them, how you want the money if I decide to buy, and what your best price is. I don't haggle. I'm running late. Glad to meet you, Rico. Keep in touch. You are much nicer than that other fella. Please, don't get up."

Ophelia gave a mighty swish of her fake fur and, swinging the leather bag that held both Rico's list and her nightgown, descended into the lobby. Fred, still holding Rico's wrist in a friendly, absent-minded way, used his other hand behind his back to signal to Teddy that he should stick with Ophelia. If Rico had friends with him, Fred wanted Ophelia clear to go where she was going.

"Some lady, ain't she?" Fred asked, with a crooked Old Democrat grin. "Drives me crazy, that lady. But I'll tell you, buddy, she makes up her mind to do a thing, she does it. No point getting in her way, she'll run right over you. Can I get you something? Coffee?"

"You want to let go my arm?" Rico said. "Or you want me to break you face?"

"Sorry," Fred said, noticing his hand on Rico's arm and removing it.

Rico adjusted his clothing. "She's too fast. You tell her, she want to see these picture, your lady, she pay me fifty thousand dollar. Then we talk. Is a good price, thirty-five millions. You tell her." Rico stood up and brushed off the arm of his jacket.

"Fifty thousand just to see the pictures?"

"Fifty thousand, I tell you where they are. Fifty thousand, I tell you how to see them, how she buy them. Is all. She meet me with the money."

"I don't know if she's gonna like this," Fred said. "These pictures in Boston?"

"I do not talk to the driver. I call her. I talk to her, not you. Driver!" Rico turned, saying, "You sit, please, driver." He walked down the stairs.

The plan had called for Teddy to follow the contact, Rico, when Fred left with Ophelia. Ophelia, improvising, insubordinate with triumph because she had finessed the list of paintings, had forced Fred to change his tactics, and send Teddy with her. He couldn't follow Rico himself, since he'd been seen.

Still, they had something. They had the list.

Fred finished Teddy's drink before he set out, walking, for the Hotel Pilgrim, where Shirley had decided Ophelia ought to stay. On Beacon Street, overlooking the Arctic wonderland that slopped out across what had once been Boston's Public Garden, the hotel was so low-key that most people did not know it existed. Nothing in front betrayed the fact that it was a hotel; you pretty much had to tell them who knew you while standing on the stoop and letting the flakes filter down the back of your neck. Fred stood in the tired-lemon foyer filled with chintz-covered armchairs set just too far apart, thinking to himself, It looks like a rest home for the widows of ministers: a place swept clear and burnished, devoid of all reference to religion, but you know it's going to get you just the same.

"I shall inquire, sir," said an Iranian premed student passing as Reception. He hinted into a telephone, "Mr. Fred Taylor asks if we have a guest named Mrs. Finger—Ophelia." He paused, listened, leered at Fred with elevator eyes, and said, "I will give him the message." He hung up, scratched the side of his face, and commented, "It is beginning to snow. Is this a joke?"

"What's her room number?" Fred asked.

"Five-oh-three. Top floor. She expects you."

"Wasn't I great?" Ophelia asked, throbbing, in a vertical takeoff position in the corridor in front of her open door. She had half the floor, three rooms overlooking the Garden: bedroom, living room–kitchenette, and opulent bath that could sleep three. "Did that man kill Mr. Hillegass?"

"He didn't say. Let's see the list."

Ophelia, for her adventure, had chosen a dark-green suit that must have remarkable powers of deflation to travel in the black bag. She looked tough and elegant. She led Fred into her tired-saffron suite with chintz and poured Scotch whisky into a glass, handing it to him neat. "We are drinking Scotch," she announced. "Glen Tweedie, from the Isle of Malt. I've never felt so stupid in my life," she added, handing the list over. "Who are these people?"

Fred took a good slug of the whisky and sat in a padded saffron chair. It was generations down the copy chain. Most of the heading on the first page had been blanked out, leaving only the final sentence: "A Collection of Old Masters from the Fifteenth to the Eighteenth Centuries, with emphasis on the Italian, Flemish, Dutch, German, and Spanish Schools."

Ophelia plumped down next to him, looking over his shoulder. Fred started slowly down the list, turning the pages slowly. He took his time until he got to the end. "Tell you the truth, Ophelia, I'm surprised. I expected to find a Guido Reni *Ecce Homo*. A head of Christ—you know, the miracle picture? But there's nothing like that. The miracle picture is not here."

Ophelia sipped Scotch. "I may be ignorant, but who *are* all these people? Thirty-five million bucks, don't you get van Gogh?"

Fred reached for a nearby phone. "It's snowing hard, and I want to get to Molly's before the public-transportation system fails. I don't know what I'm going to do about Rico. I wish he didn't think you were interested. That was not the plan, if you recall. You sit tight here, will you? Until I get you clear? As far as the list goes, I'll call Clay and you listen, then I won't have to go through the paintings twice."

Clayton picked up his instrument on the fifth ring.

"Clay, if she's in there with you, don't say anything until I'm finished." Fred waited. So did Clay. "I have that catalog of paintings. No, don't ask anything. Ninety pictures, yes, which I was offered today for thirty-five million dollars. You note the ten-million-dollar difference? No, don't say anything. She's in the room with you, and she's not dumb. Clay, let's not forget she's the enemy. One thing's consistent: the man I got the list from also wants a sum up front—though he says fifty thousand. I don't know how to reach him, but he'll call again. We're closer to the

paintings than Lavinia is, that much I do know. Around ten million dollars closer.

"Let me say first that of the ninety entries, only half a dozen
names are interesting—like the Rembrandt, which we know is a
dud. But the catalog mostly reads like a *Who's Who* of who's he? I
mean, Clay, Giovanni Paolo Cavagna?"

"Who?"

"Exactly."

"I want to see it. I demand to see it."

"So you shall, but not tonight. And it's not worth reading to you,
I promise. It's mostly holy pictures. It's a snare and a delusion."

"Let me just, let me—"

"Careful, Clay."

"Suppose I speak the initials?"

"Of course not. She's right there. Clay, she's smarter than we
are. You want to hear about the Cranach, I know. Lucas the
Elder. He's down twice: number thirty-two is a portrait of Johann
Friedrich of Saxony, and the next entry is *Hercules in the House
of Omphale*."

"Good heavens!" Clay said. "The second one—"

"Is also going to prove to be a dud," Fred said. "If it were any
good, the money they want for the group would be peanuts. The
only pictures that are going to turn out to be what they claim to
be are the Alessandro Allori and that ilk. I've gotta run. Remember, the lady eating the other end of your Beef Stroganoff tried to
cheat you out of ten million dollars. Don't let on, OK? This call is
about something else. A family matter—wedding shower, something like that."

Fred hung up. "So you get the picture," he told Ophelia, and
polished off his drink. "They're mostly the art-history equivalent
of dorks, to use your term."

23

Molly's front stairs already boasted five inches of fast powder by the time Fred put his large prints into the approach to her house. It had blown up a whirlwind blizzard that had made the bus sway as it plunged through drifts. It was so cold, Fred noticed, walking from the bus stop to Molly's, something between one and two miles, that the new snow refused to marry itself to the old. It wanted to be the year's first storm, and to make its own rules.

Molly had put her car in the driveway behind Fred's, next to the sidewalk, facing out. Fred, on Molly's top step, looked himself over, reconsidered, and then trudged down again into the roaring blur, to the sidewalk and up the driveway. He opened the garage door and went in, shaking the snow off before continuing into the kitchen. He left his parka and boots in the garage.

It was after eight o'clock. Terry and Sam sat at the table doing homework, their resentment as adamant as Molly's looming stance next to the sink.

"No hope of school tomorrow," Fred announced.

"Someone named Teddy telephoned and left a message for you: 'She's clean,' " Molly said. "Whatever that's about."

"Your sister, safe as houses. Safer. Safe as hotels. Is that lentil soup?"

"Mine were the best," Sam said, looking up from his math book. "I'm getting a certificate."

"For those reports?"

"And the governor might write me a letter for reading so many books."

"Well, I got detention for three days," Terry said. "And Mom's being a . . ."

"Yes?" Molly asked dangerously.

"They're not going to have school tomorrow," Terry said. "So I don't see why . . ."

Molly proclaimed, "You will finish your work and show it to me before you do anything else. Both of you. From now on. Fred, bring your soup into the living room when it's hot."

"Thanks for fixing the TV," Sam said.

"Your aunt did it." Fred took soup from the larger pot and started heating it in a small saucepan while Molly went into the next room. Sam's pencil scratched at his yellow paper. His task was math; Terry's was harder to deduce. She had nothing but blank lined paper in front of her. She watched Fred working at the sink and stove. He'd started washing the supper dishes while waiting for his soup to heat. A sandblasting of snow scoured the cold window. "What's the detention about?" Fred asked.

"I was supposed to write a composition five whole pages long and it wasn't fair, and it still isn't fair."

"What's the paper about? The balance of payments? Gödel's theorem?"

"It's just a story. About anything," Sam said.

"It's not fair. If *they* don't even know what it's about, how am *I* supposed to?"

"How about a bear that gets loose and all the people she eats?" Fred suggested.

" 'She'?" Terry asked, interested.

"No: better. A dinosaur," Sam said. "A Tyrannosaurus Rex."

179

"That's maybe a page," Terry complained.

"Five pages—just have it eat one person per page. Tell about each person's house, their family, their pets, what they were doing when they got eaten, and make something else happen, like a flood," Fred said.

"Also adjectives," Sam said. "They love that. Anytime you want an adjective, just ask me. Like *shitty* is an adjective. Or *stink*."

Fred left them to it, carrying his soup in to join Molly, alone in the living room with her book. "I realize the question was open-ended," Fred started. "But did you turn up anything on Carlos Gato?"

Molly put down her book. "The name's Castillo. I would have phoned you, but I didn't know where you were until Ophelia called and filled me in. You're both crazy. I don't want her hurt. Carlos Castillo, also known as Carlos Gato. That's Charlie Cats: because in his heyday he liked feeding his rivals to his pet jaguars. I don't like you and Ophelia being anywhere near it, but what do I have to say about it? She's all excited, playing on the fringes of reality, where she belongs."

"I made her promise to stay in that hotel until I give her the green light," Fred said. "Once they know she's not interested, they'll bug off. Did you get more?"

"According to *El Tiempo* and the Caracol radio network in Bogotá, Castillo was running with a million-dollar bounty on his head—he's one of the Medellín boys—when his plane blew apart. By then the government had already arrested his mother, his sister, and his wife, Estrella. His brothers were already dead. There are aunts in the picture, too, also arrested."

"What did they want the women for?"

"Same thing Castillo was wanted for, is the claim, but they're obviously hostages: 'Illicit enrichment and managing front companies that launder money earned by Carlos Castillo, known as Carlos Gato, in illegal cocaine sales.' After Castillo was out of the picture, the stories stopped, but at the time of this government sweep of the women, it was reported that his mother might be released since she was in her seventies."

"Children?"

"The sons are all dead, naturally. That's how it works. The daughter, though, she's interesting. She was said to be a student at a college in New England. You've got to ask yourself if she had a condo at One-double-zero-one Mem Drive."

"You do. Name?"

"I couldn't find one. Since women aren't news, I'm not going to be able to find out anything more about the female members of the family in Colombia. But anything Carlos owned in that country is gone."

"She wouldn't use her name—her father's or her mother's name—here," Fred said. "The daughter wouldn't. These people have got seventeen governments to watch out for, as well as all their business friends."

Fred studied the blizzard falling through streetlights in front of Molly's house, on the far side of the window beyond the couch. The houses across the street could be made out only by inference, based on the blur of their window lights.

Molly said, "One possibility is that Castillo faked the plane crash. Or not the plane crash itself, really, but being on the plane. With a million dollars on his head, people were looking for him seriously. While the pieces of somebody who won a free plane trip to glory are settling out of the sky, suppose Castillo is on a slow boat from Bogotá to anywhere else in the world he wants to go, and now he's interested in very, very quietly liquidating some assets. Maybe some of those assets were in the form of paintings he was keeping in the condo on Mem Drive?"

"Meanwhile, the government of Colombia keeps wifey and Mama and the rest of the women out of his hair," Fred finished. "He's out of the trap. All he needs now is money. So if the paintings were his, or *are* his . . . But there's nothing to connect Castillo with this list of paintings except what could as easily be false clues: a repeated Spanish accent, blind corporations, and a hint whose provenance is Alexander Newboldt, to the effect that Hillegass once functioned as Gato's agent. How Lavinia gets into the mix, I can't imagine. But she's hooked up with someone."

"Fred?" Molly said.

"I'm sorry. What?" From her tone it sounded as if Molly had been trying to get his attention for the last ten minutes.

"Fred," Terry's voice called from the kitchen, "give me a Latin word that means 'queen.' "

"Do your work, Terry," Molly yelled.

"This is her work. It's for her story," Sam shouted.

"*Regina*," Molly called back. "R-E-G-I-N-A. Never mind, Sam. It's not that funny. Listen, Fred. I've been thinking. About that murder in Cambridge: tell me everything. Everything you saw there the first time. Everything you found the second time. Everything you thought, and everything Dee and Bookrajian said. Also, whatever you didn't notice that I would have noticed."

"That's a tall order."

Molly folded her legs under her and crossed her arms. "It's what I want," she said.

"Ophelia probably told you that I have that list of paintings to study. If I can get a fix on just a few of them, I'll be able to triangulate onto the present owner, see what the story is, and then decide if it's a story Clay and I want to know, or whether we should turn it over to someone else. Admittedly, it's mostly junk, even what it claims to be, but Rubens is on the list, and Jan Brueghel the Elder, and Gerard Ter Borch. Each item deserves at least a cursory look. Then, once I decide, I'll see if Boston Homicide is interested in Mr. Rico."

"Therefore you will spend tomorrow in the library, while both you and my sister prolong your flirtation with mortal danger," Molly said. "So that's the Rico who telephoned while the kids and I were eating supper. Thinking I was Ophelia, he explained that he wants fifty thousand dollars in blank countersigned American Express traveler's checks. He doesn't like the hundreds some

182

people are making, he said. He'll call tomorrow or the next day and tell me where to deliver the money. Me, Ophelia, he says. Not my driver. Tell me about it, Fred."

"That's separate from the Cambridge thing."

"I'll hear them both."

When Molly devoted her undivided attention to a matter, she would not rest until she had everything. She made Fred lay out for her the lines he saw converging toward Hillegass.

"So," she said at last, "we assume Hillegass had at least two of these pictures in his room? And someone we might as well call Rico walked out into the snow with them under his arm, once Hillegass had been 'delayed'?"

Fred said, "The supposed Velázquez is about three feet square. Add a frame to that, and you are going to be noticed in the lobby of the Hotel Brittannee. The Flinck, alias Rembrandt, is not as big, but those Dutch pictures they like to put in big frames, especially if the picture ain't so great. So Hillegass didn't have the pictures. And I'm sure Lavinia Randall Whitman hasn't seen them either. Correction: with her I'm not sure of anything. Her first story was that the paintings were in Switzerland."

"And possibly only Rico, and Lavinia's connection, could tell us more?"

"Right."

Molly went into the kitchen and came back five minutes later with a cup of tea. Fred put the list down as she entered, and said, "I don't know which is my favorite, Erasmus Quellinus or Theodor van Thulden. Seems to me that ever since Bookrajian woke us up that night, everything I look at leads to something else I've never heard of."

"I'm ready for the Cambridge story," Molly decided. As if he were laying the whole thing out for the prosecution, deconstructing it as a story and rebuilding it as a chain of evidence that just *looked* like a story, Fred took Molly through the condominium at 1001: the first visit and the elaborate dumb show that had been left for them, crowned with the single headless corpse;

the second visit, when Fred had roamed at will through a space from which the inquiring detectives had removed everything they thought might be helpful, leaving behind only the linens from Wamsutta and the yard-sale books, which Fred, showing off now, described as best he could remember them.

"Go back and get me the one that stood out," Molly demanded. "The one you say didn't fit."

"Holy Mackerel," Fred said. "Molly, will you look at the weather?"

"Use my car. It's got a heater, and plenty of gas."

"If I get stuck in Cambridge, I'll have to stay with Walter and Dee. You want to call and warn them?"

"Don't get stuck in Cambridge; bring me that book. Who's the author?"

"For God's sake, I don't remember the name of the author any more than I do the name of the book. I remember only that the title sounds like a 'gut-shot dog falling downstairs,' to quote Ophelia."

"But it's the name of a disease."

"With spermy-looking things on the cover, crawling all over the world, like Sherwin-Williams paint. I remember the picture."

"Yes, and according to the newspaper reports, Carlos Gato's daughter was thought to be a student. In New England. That book's a textbook."

On his way upstairs to change his socks and put on a sweater, Fred was waylaid by Terry in the kitchen, where he was leaving his dishes. Sam was no longer present. "You want to hear my story?" she asked.

"How about when I come back? When it's finished? So I don't worry how it comes out?"

"It's already two pages," Terry said.

"What's the title?"

"I won't tell you."

"Fair enough."

The door to Sam's room was closed. It would be an idea to take Sam with him, for the adventure. But Fred would have to talk his way into the building, and after that break into the apartment again, and much as Sam might enjoy that, Fred wouldn't. It was Molly's errand, but she wouldn't appreciate his getting her son in trouble.

Fred, making what noise and flurry he could, skidded up to the front of 1001 and jumped out, leaving Molly's lights on, Bookrajian's light flashing, and the engine running. He made sure he was seen from the desk, the drama of his arrival mixing into the storm, which quadrupled his own effort. He made an entrance, rushing into the lobby, telling the desk, "Trouble in Four-sixteen, I'll take care of it, watch my car, will you?" and flopping his wallet open as he ran to the elevator, which cooperated by opening immediately and closing him in for the ride up.

Inside 710, the ambience had changed again. Preparations for repainting had begun, to the extent that buckets and ladders had been assembled on a plastic sheet in the kitchen area. A set of folded tarpaulins was piled next to them. Rollers, brushes, and the rest of it—everything but the paint—were in a cardboard box nearby, which also held three or four white paper painter's hats that said JIFFY in scarlet letters.

Fred took a quick look at the living room, where everything had been heaped in the center and covered with more tarpaulins, leaving the walls bare for preparation. The two places in the mantelpiece where, last time he'd been here, he'd seen the ends of the two cut nails now showed only small round patches filled with spackle.

"They found a way to get the points out," Fred said to himself. "Or, no, the smarter thing, the easy thing, would be to take a nail set, drive the points in further, and leave clean holes to fill."

He nipped into the bedroom, found the book Molly wanted, and was out of the apartment in sixty seconds.

"False alarm," he told the old man at the desk.

"There's nobody home in Four-sixteen," the uniform said. "Nobody answers."

"I found that out."

"They're not supposed to have a private alarm company we don't have registered," the guard said, truculent. "Who you with?"

"That's between you and them," Fred said. "Take it up with them when they come back, is my advice. Don't call Jiffy Alarmco. It's between you and the tenant."

"You want to leave me your card?" the uniform asked, getting up slowly. The lobby's being made of glass, the falling snow and the streetlights and the river coated with reflecting dangerous slush, and Bookrajian's light revolving on Molly's car, all made enough romance sweeping around the building to keep the guard awake for hours more.

"Good idea. Lemme get some from the car," Fred said. "Might be other tenants want to use us. Thanks."

24

Molly was asleep in her bed with the TV going, a large male talk-show host pontificating to two cringing female guests about how sensitive he'd become to women's issues.

"Ho, sweetie," Molly said, yawning. "Oh, Fred, it's you." She sat up. She was wearing a blue shirt of Fred's. "Turn off the machine, will you?" Fred complied. "God, it's late." When he choked off the light from the TV, the only brightness came in through the crackling window, whose curtains Molly didn't pull at night because she liked having the sky next to her while she slept: the sky on one side, she said, and Fred on the other.

"What do you mean, 'Ho, sweetie, oh, Fred, it's you'?" Fred asked.

"While we sleep, we are not responsible for what we say," Molly declared. She turned on her bedside lamp, made waking-up noises with her mouth, and finished by saying, "Let's see it."

Fred dropped two pounds of blue book on her lap. "Enjoy," he said. "Be the first on your block to own *Trypanosomiasis: A Veterinary Perspective*, by Lorne E. Steven. Pergamon Press, nineteen eighty-six." Molly hefted the book and looked at the cover. "May I come to bed?"

"Get warm first. Even from here I can feel the cold winds creeping off you. What are these pink bladders with tails on the cover, eating up the world?"

"Trypanosomes, the heroes of the book. But magnified."

"Somebody paid ninety dollars for this yard-sale book, as you call it," Molly said. "OK, let me have a look."

Fred went downstairs, opened a can of beer and fixed himself a fried-egg sandwich, and brought it upstairs to eat while he watched Molly searching through the volume, examining each page. "These poor repressed scientists," she commented. "It all comes out in their language. Listen to this: 'It is very likely that *T. vivax* caught the attention of investigators before the turn of the century because of its vivacious movements in wet preparations.' To save you the suspense, Fred, a trypanosome is an infectious parasitic bacterium carried by blood-eating beetles and flies, which infect cattle, among other things. You know the tsetse fly? The book cares about cattle, mostly. That's what it's about, and it's no yard-sale book."

"You'd be amazed by what turns up in yard sales."

"No, I would not. What's that, an egg sandwich? With mustard?"

"Want me to fix you one?"

"I'll just have a huge bite of yours."

Fred took off his clothes and, under the guise of feeding her, got into bed. Molly, chewing, kept turning pages. "The girl who lived in the condominium owned by the mysterious offshore corporation—students don't read Danielle Steel. Those are menopause books."

"I figured they were decoration. Big fat books, lots of coverage. How did Terry do with her romance?"

"It's even better than her riddle. Surefire box-office. 'Tyrannosaura Regina in the Lonely, Terrible, Extinct Volcano.' Hold on to your hats." She flipped pages. "So most of the books you found were decoration. The girl, if she *was* a student, took her textbooks with her. Except for this. Jesus: bats. You forget bats. Listen to this: 'The digestive tract of the vampire bat is adapted to the rapid digestion of blood which is its only source of sustenance and allows the ready passage of trypanosomes both into the circulation of the bat and,'—eegh! Let's stay where it's cold!"

"What does she eat?"

"What?"

"Terry's dinosaur."

"Practically everybody. A crew of a hundred people making a movie, a bus filled with explorer scouts, three missionaries. Only a tribe of cannibals is saved, and that's merely because Terry was afraid she'd get onto the sixth page. How do these specialists stay awake? 'The quantity of inoculum and the route of inoculation, e.g., intravenous, subcutaneous, intramuscular, injestion, or contamination of abraded or incised surface area . . .' "

"On the other hand, with all this going on in their bed, how do they sleep?" Fred asked. He'd finished the beer and was ready to try for sleep himself.

"See, she takes notes now and then," Molly said. "I find the indentation of the pencil or pen; it's broad, so I guess it's a pencil. It's as if she put a thin piece of paper on top of the page she was reading, usually just one or two words, but sometimes a sentence like, 'See mononuclear phagocyte system,' or 'But NB Nantulya argues the contrary,' or—I know, she used Post-it notes, so she could pull the notes out and leave the book a virgin. Here's another: 'Pigs can be injected with *T. evansi.*' Mr. Evans evidently has his own private trypanosome."

Fred closed his eyes and let her study, the quiet ticking of the pages making a calm, irregular counterpoint to the tumult that continued outside the house. Now and again Molly would shift her weight, causing the mattress to tilt while she tried to maneuver a page against the light so as to get shadows in the indented lines.

"Fred, look at this," Molly yelped, waking him.

"Ho, sweetie. Oh, Molly, it's you."

189

"Look. Look at this! No, be careful, don't touch it. It's evidence," Molly said. "I'm serious. This is pay dirt. Wake up, Fred. I'll read it to you. Don't touch the page, all we get is the faint indentation, 'Oh, Tina'—I'm pretty sure it's *Tina*—'Have mercy.' "

"It's a moving message, but I would find it even more moving if I were less flat-out tired."

"It gets better. I'll read you the paragraph where the note was written."

"Isn't there some reason to put this off till morning?" Fred said.

"He's talking about—it doesn't really matter—the way some horses react when they're infected by one kind of trypanosome. Listen: 'Lingard (eighteen ninety-three) quoted Steel as saying—' "

"Not Danielle Steel?" Fred said. "No, sorry, you said *eighteen* ninety-three. A different author."

" 'As saying,' " Molly continued, " 'that mares sometimes show evidence of "heat" and stallions exhibit "quite uncalled-for erections of the penis" and suggests that this may be due to irritation of the erection center in the cord, or the function of clots in the erectile tissue of the penis, or "there may be embolic plugging in the vessels." A prescient intimation of disseminated intravascular coagulation?' the author asks. Then it goes on about how the horses maintain a good appetite until they die."

Fred sat up. This thing had suddenly turned exceedingly academic. "What's that about coagulation?"

"I was noticing the erections," Molly said.

"Naturally."

"And the implication. What we've got here is evidence of two people, where five minutes ago we had nobody. We have a girl named Tina. If she's a student, and a student of veterinary medicine, she's at Tufts. That's way the hell out in Grafton. There's only one other place in the Boston area she could be: Slater University in Chelsea. But even if the book is Tina's, the notes were written by someone else, someone very sympathetic to the stallion's point of view."

"And the stallion's plight," Fred said. "Poor fool's wandering the world with a quite uncalled-for erection."

Molly marked the place, put the book on the floor next to her, and flipped out her light. She lay down, saying, "If you insist on straightening this out, ask at Tufts or Slater for a girl named Tina. Ask if a young male grad student is missing from a School of Veterinary Medicine, a guy who used to stick out at parties because he was headless as well as running around with a quite uncalled-for erection."

"I didn't mention, did I, that the dead guy, poor fellow, had a remarkable foreskin?" Fred said. "Though you might not notice both at the same time."

"I pay attention to neither, ever."

Fred woke at seven, after sleeping very little. He looked out the window onto a shock of virgin landscape to make them weep in Kuwait. The snow had stopped falling. You could not tell how much there was, so much lay in the backyards that joined each other below Molly's bedroom window. He dressed, scooped *Trypanosomiasis* off the floor next to a sleeping woman as well concealed under down padding as her backyard was, and went to wake Sam and Terry to tell them, "No school." They might as well enjoy what they were getting.

The kitchen floor was cold under his bare feet. It helped him waken. During his brief sleep, something had been needling Fred with an annoying itch, which he moved to alleviate while hot water trickled through the coffee grounds. He went to the book's tail end.

"Gotcha!" he murmured in triumph. "Ho, sweetie. *Ecce homo.* There's no place you can hide where I can't find you. Behold Steel, J. H., author of *Investigation into an Obscure and Fatal Disease among Transport Mules in British Burma*, eighteen eighty-five (Bombay?). The world is so full of a number of things, I'm sure we should all be as happy as Tyrannosaura Regina."

That settled, and with a mug of coffee as backup, Fred started leafing through the book, responding to the other subject he had noticed while Molly was reading. He was so utterly ignorant about the whole area treated by the study, and about its language, that skimming was slow going. What he was looking for was coagulation, but it seemed the aim of all these blood-sucking beasts was the reverse. The ticks, flies, mosquitoes, Chagas-bearing beetles, and bats were all intent on encouraging the blood of their hosts to keep on moving. Even the trypanosomes, if they were going to be at their vivacious best, wanted to maintain their preparations wet.

According to Dee's unscientific account, the blood of the headless man had been—how had she described it?—gelatin-ized? There must be a thousand and one ways to get blood to that state, but not while a man lived. If your blood wasn't frisky and liquid, how was it supposed to chuckle through the chambers of your heart? If sluggish and in a manner solidified . . . Here was an ugly thought. Like that poor horse, had the dying man—tricked into it by his mortal agony—and then perhaps his corpse as well, once managed to exhibit an erection? Was that what the ribbon had been doing, trying to do?—maintain the penis in that state? Was that what they were all supposed to see when they came into the living room, a tableau of blasphemy to offend everyone of any faith or lack thereof?

No, that was too much. That was imagination feeding on igno-rance: the baroque quandary. Faced with the proposition, not by faith alone, must one find refuge in the mere grotesque?

Was it the oddness of everything, the otherworldliness of the shift in normal expectations caused by the weather, that made Fred speculate, while he thought about making toast, about some strange and terrible new bacterium, straight out of Terry's lost volcano, that might do its job of colonizing by slowing down the heart's whole system?

"To hell with this," Fred said aloud, and he went outside to shovel snow. This was a cold, windblown fall that had left trees and wires bare, and for the most part swept off the roofs as it came down. It was all on the ground, ready for him, a new fifteen inches at least. Fred was the only person outside; everyone else had decided on hibernation, and why not? There'd be no bus service anywhere. Deliveries? Forget it.

"The poor bastard lived longer than he should have," Fred said, heaving snow off Molly's walk. It was so light that a big pile lifted easily. One lane had been plowed down the center of the street sometime before the snow stopped. The trough, a blade's width, had three more inches on top of it. Fred reached the end of the walkway and started on the sidewalk, working toward the driveway. He did not like the cars' being trapped that way. He must be able to move. Ophelia was in Boston, and Rico was presumably there, too. If Rico had killed Hillegass, he was making himself oddly available, but maybe he was sticking around for the fifty thousand he hoped to get by selling Ophelia the chance to see the emperor's new pictures. Clayton was snowed in on Mount-joy Street, with Lavinia Randall Whitman in the guest bedroom. The Tufts Grafton campus was unreachable for now. Meanwhile, Fred might as well go to Chelsea, near the airport, to see what he could learn about a headless veterinarian who Molly had deduced existed, while at the same time he neglected a headless list of paintings, any one of whose history, if he could smoke it out, should lead him to the power behind the game Rico was playing, for high stakes and on a field complicated by weather.

When Ernie Bookrajian and Blanche Maybelle looked out the windows of their third-floor walkup and saw this happening to their city, did it not look like Divine Grace transforming everything? The Lord of Snow had granted a general amnesty, stopping all schools and traffic, putting everything on hold—except for the dividing cells of blastula and sarcoma. Blanche Maybelle: you'd have to forgive her for whispering, "The ground's too soft now. I should have jumped two weeks ago, before we did the tests."

Fred cleaned both cars and opened the driveway as far as the garage. Had Molly shopped yesterday? He couldn't remember if the lentils for last night's soup had already been in the larder. Fred took the shovel down the block and started clearing the hydrant closest to Molly's house. He kept on for a while, working around the neighborhood.

25

When Fred stamped into the garage a little before eleven, Molly flung the door open from the kitchen, dressed for the road. "Fred, where the hell have you been?"

"Sorry," Fred said. "I have your keys in my pocket. It didn't occur to me that you'd go to work in this. The roads are really bad."

"It's not that. Come inside. For all I knew, you'd gone walking to Boston or something. I don't know how to deal with Signet."

"You talked to Dmitri Signet?" Fred was about to take off his boots, but he hesitated. A call from Signet meant something had moved.

"Come on in," Molly said. "A message. I kept getting Ophelia's calls, and it was driving me crazy, so yesterday I started to listen on the answering machine until I knew a call was for me, especially after that guy wanted his fifty thousand. Signet called an hour ago. I didn't know what to say, so I didn't pick up. If we're doing something together, tell me where you're going."

"I smell coffee," Fred said. "You're right. Is it hot?"

"Get some while I find the message."

195

Fred carried his mug into the living room, where Molly, her coat thrown onto the blue carpet, sat on the couch next to the machine on the end table. She wore jeans and the same oversized red sweater. She fiddled until she found Signet's voice: "Mrs. Riley, I have good news. The owner of the Peterson is interested. This is Dmitri Signet, from the Signet Galleries. At your earliest convenience, would you please telephone me at . . ."

"Interesting," Fred said.

"What do I say? Fred, the truth of it is, I have two children here to think about. Did you want me to go with you?"

"Emphatically and absolutely not. See what Signet has to say, stall on account of the weather, and I'll give you signals. I can listen in on the portable kitchen phone. Let him struggle to make the sale. What we want is to learn who controls the picture—which is the last thing Signet wants to tell us. Let's go real slow."

"Doesn't Signet know what happened at One thousand one?"

"All we know is what's on that tape. You ready to call? The kids still asleep?"

"I walked them to their friends' in case I had to go."

"Sorry."

On their separate instruments they listened to a number of rings. Was the presentable girl in the ensemble snowbound in Wellesley? Then came Signet's voice, "Signet Galleries."

"This is Mrs. Riley."

"Good to hear from you. The Peterson painting *Still Life of Zinnias in a Copper Bowl*—you inquired about it last Saturday?"

"Yes?" Molly asked vaguely.

"I spoke with the painting's owner."

"Yes?"

"I have good news, but complicated," Signet said. He coughed. "The owner is willing to sell, but not through me." He coughed again.

While Signet coughed, Fred mouthed the words to Molly, "Mention his commission. Then stall."

196

"But you should receive a commission!" Molly exclaimed. "That's only fair!"

"I am glad you see it that way," Signet said. "What the owner will ask for the picture, I can't say. That is out of my hands. As a commission I normally expect ten percent. If you like, two thousand five hundred dollars will cover me. I shall leave the rest to you."

Molly looked at Fred and raised her eyebrows. Fred signaled, Cut. "One moment, please," Molly said. "I have another call." They hung up.

Fred said, "Molly, I want you clear now. I can't see where this will go next. Tell him you don't want the picture yourself, but I do—on my own account, not Clay's."

"You're going to pay him?"

"If I have to. I'll get it back from somewhere."

When Molly reached Signet again, she said, "Sorry, we were cut off. Listen, I have to level with you. You remember the man with me? He wants the picture. It's for himself, and he doesn't want the guy he works for to know about it. That's confidential. But with this snow and all, I can't deal with the whole thing. I'm going to call and tell Fred what you said, and then he can take it from there. If he doesn't call you, he's not interested, OK? I've got to go now, there's something burning."

She hung up and asked Fred, "If Rico calls again, what do I say?"

"Leave him to the machine. I can't be in two places at once. If I put on my suit, will I look like a man able to write a check for twenty or thirty thousand bucks for those fucking zinnias?" Fred asked.

"You're not serious."

"Of course not, but I don't know what'll happen after I pay off Signet. I have to look well heeled for the next act. The question is, if I wear a suit, will I pass?"

"Wear the funeral coat, too. I take it you're going to shave off the seven-day wonder? I'll miss it, but the world will be grateful."

197

• • •

"They say Charlestown is coming up," Dmitri Signet observed at 3:17, as he studied Fred's check. It was complete with printed address on Chestnut Street, and the telephone number at the place, which someone was always on call to answer.

"It was," Fred said. He glanced around the gallery. It displayed exactly the same stuff as last time, though everything had been moved so it would seem fresh to jaded eyes flicking across it.

"I'm not familiar with Chestnut Street," Signet confided.

"We try not to be all that exclusive."

"What did you decide about the Schumacher?" Signet asked, slipping Fred's check into the top drawer of his desk. The young woman in the ensemble was not here today. As much of Newbury Street as could be seen through the front windows looked as if everyone else in town had heard about the impending plague of trypanosomes that was scheduled to descend this afternoon. Four hundred billion billion bacterial adventurers would decide who got Signet and who got Fred. "If price is a problem on the Schumacher . . . ," Signet probed.

"Clay's thinking about it," Fred assured him. "On the Peterson, that's separate, you understand. My own sideline. What next?"

"Will you excuse me while I make a phone call?"

"Sure."

Signet, standing behind his desk, squirmed. He didn't want to go into the back room to make the call and leave Fred alone; he didn't want to make the call in front of him; and he couldn't ask him to step out into the snow.

"I've got to run down to Vose and throw some of Clayton's money at them," Fred said. "It may be a few minutes."

"Take your time."

Fred went to the empty underground café where he and Molly had eaten an almost Greek lunch. He ordered coffee and telephoned Clayton. There was still the wild card of Lavinia, who had been under Clay's roof for days, enough time for them to

198

learn many of each other's patterns: familiarity might make him forget that he and Lavinia were not friends. Clay responded on the third ring, and then Fred had to let him talk. The swarthy man from behind the counter brought his coffee over and broke a dollar so Fred could continue to feed dimes into the pay phone while Clay exposed a bee that had got into his bonnet: a variant on the game of Monopoly. Each square reproduced a painting from either a public or a private collection.

"Lavinia and I spent hours on this, refining the idea. The game has potential, we feel. It is educational and harmless. We have chosen all the works we intend to use and laid out the board. To be truthful, we plan two versions, one on American painters, another on Europeans, though there again we might divide between the old and the new.

"Just to give you the idea, in the American version we begin with an unknown who frightens collectors, J. Frank Currier, in place of Baltic Avenue, and work up to Fitz Hugh Lane, at Board-walk and Park Place, since apparently Skinner's has developed the habit of selling Lane for three-and-a-half-million-dollars and upward . . ."

"Clay, this isn't how you think," Fred complained urgently. "Is this some ploy of hers to make you get your Lane out of storage and show—"

"I was not born yesterday. I know the risk, but we have been snowbound so long. My contribution to the joint effort makes for a great improvement on Monopoly. We factor in the imponder-ables of shifting taste; every time the characters get around the board, it's five years later, with consequent fluctuations in the market. Did I mention that when you land on a painting, you must either buy or sell it? And when the cards for Chance and Critical Taste are . . ."

"So you're all right," Fred concluded.

"Yes, yes. Actually—Fred, let us leave it at yes. Yes?"

"And you're not forgetting that Lavinia is not, in the larger sense, our friend?"

"Of course, of course. We end our selection with works painted before nineteen twenty. After that date, especially for living painters, the game needs a different model to follow, such as Parcheesi."

"Terry has a board game called Candy Land," Fred said. Ophelia had given it to her, as an interesting antique. "It's duller than polishing shoes." Fred hung up and sat at a table nursing his empty white china mug, which was still warm. He told the man behind the counter, "That guy has absolutely flipped his lid."

"All this snow, that's what it is. Everyone goes crazy," his host agreed. He wiped his hands down the orange sides of his white apron. "This snow. Nobody eats. I should close, but what am I gonna do all day, watch TV? Everyone in the snow goes crazy," he repeated.

"Or they fall in love," Fred said.

The man nodded. "Yes, love could do it. Snow or love."

Fred had given Dmitri Signet, and his blue suit and his William Morris–ripoff necktie, more than half an hour, which should have been plenty of time for him to do whatever he had to. He walked back down Newbury Street, slow in his street shoes. He'd had to wear them to go with the suit, leaving the half-treads in Molly's car, which had been parked who knew where by the valet for the Ritz Hotel, where Fred was ostensibly a guest. What with the street shoes and the funeral coat and a white silk scarf Ophelia had left behind, and the absence of a week's beard, Fred's disguise was complete—so long as you didn't look too closely at his socks, one of which did not match the other.

Dmitri Signet had a late-afternoon customer, a short man in a short dark coat who was examining the George Howell Gay moonscape that had caught Molly's eye. The painting had been shifted to the rear wall behind the desk, where it could be spotlighted and noticed from the street. Signet himself stood nervously next to the front door, which he opened for Fred, saying, "The owner sent his driver."

The short man turned and was Rico, right down to the excruciated Young Republican smile. He carried a dark cap in his right hand.

"These the party?" he asked Signet, glancing at Fred and then away.

"He'll take you," Signet told Fred. "It's out of my hands now."

"These way, sir," Rico said. "Please excuse. Is very bad, the road. I bring the car. You wait."

26

Fred stood tall and rich and sleek as Rico strode past him and out the door, putting on his hat at a cocky angle: a black chauffeur's cap to go with the short dark coat.

"You want to tell me the name of the owner?" Fred asked Signet, keeping his voice easy. Rico was either awfully smooth or damn near blind. If he couldn't recognize Fred in a change of clothes and a shave, he shouldn't try to play in the thirty-five-million-dollar league.

Dmitri Signet sat behind his desk and moved around some papers on its surface. "I'll let you introduce yourselves," he said.

A blue Mercedes drove past, Rico at the wheel in the blue blazer with the scarlet medallion that signified nothing. He pulled far enough ahead for Fred to read the plate. Fred said, "Do me a favor, Signet. Call Mrs. Riley. Tell her I'm on my way to see the zinnias. Also—got a pencil?—tell her the call number of that video was MD one-two-three-X-three. Got that?" Rico got out of the driver's seat and stood next to the back door on his side. "And I'll call you in a day or two, tell you how it came out, and what we want to do on the Schumacher," Fred said from the doorway.

"And oh, about the Peterson—I'd appreciate it if you didn't mention that to Clayton Reed."

He crossed the sidewalk and allowed Rico, his face completely servile and impassive, to close him into the warmth of the Mercedes's rear compartment. Glass separated the front and back seats. With nothing parked on either side, Rico had Newbury Street to himself, the MD plates doing for him what Bookrajian's light had for Fred. Rico drove with a nervous insolence that came from fronting for wealth and power. They moved along Newbury away from the Public Garden and the Ritz and toward Mass Ave.

The deep dark of late afternoon was mitigated by the reflection of lights on snow. Boston was almost a ghost town. Rico turned right on Mass Ave, which, if they followed it north across the river, would then take them west through Cambridge, then north and west through Arlington and into Lexington. The glass partition had a sliding panel to allow for communication between the driving classes and the driven, but given Rico's earlier-expressed opinion of the worth of drivers, there seemed little point in asking him what was going on. Fred would find out what he found out when he found it out.

They swung left on Commonwealth and headed toward Kenmore Square: Cambridge was not their destination. Then, leaving Fenway Park on their left, Rico bore left again on Beacon, which they followed for a while, among the ineffable banks and apartment complexes and medical buildings, until they turned off into the mazy intricacies of a residential area near Brooks Hospital, where you could get immediately lost on roads that were good for sledding, and half the cars had MD plates.

Rico pulled into the well-plowed driveway of a low brick house shadowed by evergreens, pushed a button under the dash, and slid the car under a rising garage door, coming to a stop in a clean, well-lighted place that remained lit when the door descended again. Rico was out before Fred, to open his door. "In the house, please," he said, with neither a flicker of recognition in his eyes nor the forced indifference of the person pretending not to know

you. We are as sheep that pass in the night, Fred mused as he followed Rico through the side door into the cold, protected air of a
clean cement path that ran between high bushes to the back door
of the brick house.

They entered a dismal kitchen that had not been reconsidered
since 1962. It was all dark-brown cabinets, brown fixtures, and
wallpaper with green diamond patterns. It smelled like a place
where they mostly ate takeout. "I take you coat," Rico said, spinning, and he hit Fred hard on the left side of the head.

Fred shrugged and was ready the instant two armed men came
in, both in the same uniform: gray slacks, blue blazers, smiles and
short haircuts. Fred stood tense but quiet. Those were assault
rifles, HK-53s, favored by many for being easy to handle in tight
places. Rico hit Fred again on the other side of the head, using his
gloved fist. Given the armed men and their placement, there was
not much for Fred to do other than get hit.

"Watch the dishes," one of the new men said, in Spanish.
True, the kitchen was too small for four men fighting. When Rico
swung at his face again, Fred took his right hand out of the air and
twisted it, squeezing the fist inside its glove until the knuckles
started popping. The two armed men wavered and came in closer
while Rico gasped, his left hand moving to help the right.

"Why don't we talk?" Fred suggested.

"First we suppose to hurt you," one of the armed men said.
"Then talk. If you shoot both, is OK," he told the other one as he
moved in back of Fred. There was a swish of sound, a swirl of the
scent of Dakkar Noir, and a jolt of pain that stopped everything.

Pain bubbled in the back of his head, and in his blinded eyes, and
in his back and shoulders. "Hit him again," came a voice—a thin,
high voice, an angel's voice, speaking in Spanish. "No, not the
head."

The blows were on his arms and back, so he must be lying on
his face. Yes, that was carpet against his mouth and rubbing the
bruised right side of his face: blows of a short pipe, it felt like, fol-

lowed by kicks and stamps on the legs and buttocks. The jolting pain helped clear his head and readied him to move.

"Hurt him, wake him, then I will talk to him," the Spanish angel said, quick Spanish to the Spanish lackeys. Light footsteps left the room.

Fred could not see because his eyes were closed, not because he was blinded. He cracked them open to a scene of feet in black shoes with a brown background. (Kick in the thigh on the right side.) They could have killed him if they'd wanted to; therefore they did not want to. More interesting, they could have hurt him enough to put him out of action, and they had not done so. (Kick in the gut on the left.) They knew what they were doing; therefore he was to be intimidated but not immobilized. (Kick in the ribs on the left side. "Wake up, Mister," in English.) Someone, the angel, had given the order, "Give him a number four," and they'd done so, supposing Hillegass had been ten on the scale of one to ten.

The carpet, brown, smelled like 1962. Fred was jerked upright by Rico and one of the armed pair, while the other stood in back with the weapon they certainly hoped not to fire in the house. He'd lost coat and jacket while he was out. The weapon was intimidation, like the beating; if they'd been serious, they should have taken care of him in the garage. Fred groaned for them.

The room they struggled him upright in was a living room or office, made uninhabitable by large bright paintings on the walls that vibrated with garish, even salacious, impressionism. Each had its florid, gilded, Madison Avenue fuck-me frame. These constituted the only windows since the windows themselves were covered with long brown drapes infected by floral creepers.

"Sit," Rico said, pushing Fred backward into a fat embrace of chair that wheezed under his weight and stank like leather. A string of blood ran down the left side of his face, starting next to the eye. In the part of the room he could see without moving his head, it was hard to get past the big pictures, each of which was lit by one of those brass overhung lights that make an instant shrine of any painting. The furniture was armchairs and a TV set and a desk with nothing on it under a Renoir bather with breasts that shouted to the world, "We are insured for six million bucks." They were fakes, hand-painted. All of these paintings.

"We are behind you," Rico warned.

Maybe the Redon was real. From here, since it was behind glass, and since Redon had done so many on that theme—the floating poetic head—Fred wasn't sure. But the Renoir was as fake as the lumpy Pissarro peasant chopping cabbages, and the Modigliani portrait of *Young Girl with Toothache and Neck Trouble* worse than what Fred was going to have if he survived.

An old woman came in and said in fast Spanish to the lackeys, "Stay there. If he moves, hit him. Don't shoot unless I tell you. I live here." She was five feet tall, a skinny thing in black, with her hair dyed black and cut severely at the bottoms of her ears—unless it was a wig?—as if she hoped to pass for thirteen.

The woman nodded at the gathering behind Fred, then looked him over before sitting down behind the desk. She moved as if her back hurt as much as Fred's did. "I talk. You be silent. You will lie. I say one thing: stay away from the girl," the old woman said. She nodded, and something whacked Fred on the left shoulder, but on the muscle, not the available bone. Pain without breaking things was the aim. The pain was real, flickering into and out of his skull, making a void open in there where he'd just been unconscious—For how long? he wondered.

"Stay away from her," the old woman said again. Her English was correct but heavily accented. She nodded again. The other shoulder jolted and exploded with a thump of trouble.

Fred scrambled to think, but pain and danger intervened. A hundred stupid things to say clustered on his tongue, all eager to make things worse. The pipe, if it was that, tapped the left side of his neck.

A phone rang on the woman's desk. She picked it up and said into it in Spanish, "I am busy." She listened a moment, told Fred in English, "You will not find her," nodded, and then, while they whacked at Fred some more, talked Spanish into the telephone again: "A man tries to find Christina. A smart boy, asking the man where I bought a painting that he saw in her apartment."

She'd stopped nodding, and so the pounding had stopped, too. His arms and back and shoulders were going to be very sore if this went on; maybe even out of commission for a while. Blood still trickled down the left side of his face. So far he could move if he needed to. He could get his hands on the woman, or kill one, maybe two of the men in time, but three? And after, he wouldn't be able to move well outdoors, if he got that far. He was ill heeled because of the street shoes he'd worn to make him look well heeled. There'd be more people here, upstairs.

"I don't know. Who cares?" The woman said into the telephone. "Who cares about Miguel? What was he doing there? Playing games with Christina! Why did you call? I tell you, I am busy."

Fred sat there choking on the three thousand stupid things he was not saying, many of which were questions. The woman listened to her telephone. Fred smarted and throbbed and listened blankly to the silence until it was replaced by his hostess speaking in Spanish again. "If she says they are fakes, again, who cares? It is all he bought. The fool. Carlos bought nothing but fakes. Millions of dollars, he wasted. But the option is real. The option he bought is all we sell. A piece of paper. Sell that. You say it is transferable? Transfer it. My people here may already have a buyer. The rest, who cares? Now, leave me in peace while I decide what to do with this man. No. No. Leave it. I say what my son would tell you, cut it off. Sell it. The apartment and everything in it, when it is safe. Everything here is worthless. I must have cash. Do what you are paid for."

She hung up. "Give me his identification," she demanded. One armed man moved in front of Fred in order to make his weapon visible while a hand burrowed under his bruised backside for the wallet, which—it was Rico's hand—which Rico carried across the room and put on the desk before he went behind Fred again. Correction: the Redon was a fake, too. It was too sappy. The forger could not read the artist's abiding subliminal horror. The woman was surrounded by fakes, and she knew it. If Hillegass had sold them to her . . .

The woman studied Fred's driver's license and leafed through his money, which should be thirty-six dollars. The license was all the ID Fred kept in the wallet. "We know where you live," she told Fred, putting the license to one side. "She is not here. The slut. If you come here again, you will be killed. If anyone you send comes here, you will be killed. If you look for Christina again, you will be killed."

"We should kill him," Rico's voice came from the back, in Spanish.

The woman shook her head, putting the money back into Fred's wallet. "Later," she said. "If we want. For now, it is a waste of trouble. Who knows, maybe all he wants is the painting of flowers, which we cannot go near again. Too bad for him. I cannot take chances with my granddaughter."

God, Fred thought. With all the rest of the crap they bought, suppose the Peterson's a fake? What's next, a fake T. Bailey?

The old woman stood and tossed the wallet on the floor and, for the first time, allowed passion to twist her features and her voice. "In my country, I would kill him now. However . . . Santo, leave him somewhere." She turned and left the way she had come in, and Fred heard her footsteps on a carpeted staircase before the three men began to hustle him out, gathering his wallet, jacket, and coat.

Rico—otherwise known as Santo—took his short dark driver's coat from where he'd dropped it on the kitchen table, put it on, and followed Fred and his escort outside and into the garage, the way they'd come. Fred did not say the stupid things that wanted to be said, or try the stupid things that wanted to be done. He moved slowly, on principle exaggerating his discomfort, but not enough to make them wary. These people knew what they were doing.

While the other two packed Fred into the backseat, Rico, now Santo, stood at the driver's door and said, "One of you ride with him."

"I'm not going way the fuck to Charlestown," one said, sitting next to Fred and slamming the door. He'd left his weapon in the garage, but he let Fred get a look at the small piece under his arm.

Santo turned the ignition over and watched his rearview mirror while the garage door rose. "Who say we goin' way the fuck to Charlestown?" Santo asked. "Take him somewhere, the lady said. We take him somewhere."

27

They shoved Fred out at Beacon Street and Park Drive, in a deep drift on a windy expanse of parkland where someone had made armies of snowmen. Last night's fall had smudged their contours. The blue Mercedes with MD plates screeched away, skidding. Fred started walking. He left his coat and jacket open so cold air could work on the battered meat. He was already getting stiff. The tramp that lay ahead would loosen him up. Since things were moving, he'd want to be able to move himself. It was a relief, after so long among blurred contours, to stumble finally upon something real: real people with visible weapons and rational motives. The paintings they had were fake, but at least their cruelty was authentic, and could be depended on.

His watch told him it was seven o'clock; the sky told him it was dark. The weather told him there was snow everywhere, with a hint of more on the way. Only the landscape lied, since it said Akron, Ohio, although downtown Boston lay not far ahead. Keeping his eyes alert for a passing taxi, or any other form of transportation he might flag, Fred walked the sprawl of wilderness insulating Boston University from the rest of the world. He made Kenmore Square. The dismayed expressions of students walking toward and past him under the lights reminded him to think about how he looked. Because his gloves had fallen victim to the rumpus, he had kept his hands in his coat pockets; now he took them out and used them to wash his face with snow, which kept coming off red, so he must have started cuts bleeding again. He held his handkerchief against the left side of his face and walked that way until, at the corner of Mass Ave, he found an idling taxi, heaved himself into the backseat, and asked the man to take him to the Ritz.

"Looks like you been mugged and rolled," the driver observed, letting the cab continue idling by the curb. He stared a challenge into his mirror. "What are you, staying at the Ritz, or having dinner there with Queen Hortensia?"

"Give it a rest," Fred told him. "They didn't take it all. Let's go." He leaned back in the seat and closed his eyes until he was looking into the dismayed face of the Ritz doorman.

He paid the taxi off, thrust past the doorman into the hotel's lobby, and walked through brocade furniture and the mirrors that the management had positioned to discourage less-than-beautiful people from using the lobby.

On one of the pay phones situated between the coatroom and the bar, he started working to get through to Arlington. He kept getting a ring. Molly or one of the kids was talking and did not want to interrupt the conversation by clicking in call waiting. Or more likely, messages were being left for Ophelia. After trying for half an hour, he let them give him bourbon, aspirin, and coffee at the bar. In ten minutes he started again and this time reached the ambivalent message Molly and Ophelia had worked out to do the trick for both numbers: Ophelia's voice saying, "We are anxious to return your call as soon as we can. Please leave your message."

"Molly, it's Fred," Fred told the machine. "I'm still in town, and I don't know where I'm heading next. Are you there? Has there been another call for—"

"Fred!" came Molly's voice. "What's happening?"

"Dmitri Signet gave you my message?"

"No. Where are you?"

"At the Ritz. That son of a bitch! I even used him to send the license number of the car, thinking fast, being cute, all for naught."

"Why didn't you call?"

"No access to a phone," Fred told her. "Not until now."

"But you found the people."

"Yes. Tell Ophelia it's too risky, she should stay away. They can't be played with. When Rico calls again, tell him, as Ophelia, that your horoscope says you can't invest in anything for the next twelve months. You don't want the pictures. Those people don't own the paintings anyway, not that she'd care. It could even be true they're all in Switzerland. The fake Velázquez was in Zurich, last we heard. All the Colombians ever had was an option."

"You're all right?"

"No complaints." The Ritz offered a simple yellow armchair to sit in while you telephoned. Fred sat in his. That meant he'd have to get up again. He'd buttoned the coat and wrapped Ophelia's scarf as best he could around the abraded exposed areas above the neck, but sitting here, he was going to look tired and hurt, maybe poor, like someone they should throw out of the place.

"I thought I might ask Teddy and some of the folks in Charlestown if they'd want to talk to these people with me, but that's hormones and not intellection. It'll pass. I don't know what I'm doing next."

"Then listen," Molly said. "I got to thinking after you left, and you know, civilization can't stop just because snow keeps us from getting from one place to another."

"Let me put a dime in this thing," Fred said. The lonesome counterman on Newbury Street had given him more dimes than he needed. Near him a young woman in a fur like Ophelia's, but cheaper because the real thing, plinked a dime into a neighboring telephone and started making plans that sounded like fun for someone.

"So anyway," Molly continued, "the kids being planted and all, and me dressed, I mushed all the way to the Arlington Library and wired into the Internet, which connects us to everything in the world that plugs in, and I spent three hours looking for Tina."

"I'll come to Arlington, and you can tell me what you learned. You got class lists and things from Slater University?"

"I went through the whole catalog and lots of in-house stuff. Here's an example of what a good research librarian can do when you give her her head and the Internet and some wild guesses that pay off and then lots of persistence. Say you want to locate a Professor of Surgery and Pharmacology from the Slater University School of Veterinary Medicine, a recent recipient of the Plotkin Prize for advances in treadmill and forceplate analysis in the biomechanics of gait abnormalities, author of *Anesthesiology and Behavioral Pharmacology of the Horse*: D.V.M., Ph.D., living at One-oh-oh-one Memorial Drive, Cambridge, Apartment Four-sixteen?"

"You are shitting me!" Fred said.

"Wife Deborah, nicknamed Debbie," Molly sailed on. "She's the daughter of Tanning Winkworth, which alone would earn them that address. Two children, Winkworth and Gloria, both married. No pets. Hobbies—"

"Jeekers," Fred said. "I'm impressed. But I happen to know nobody's home in Four-sixteen."

"How did you get ahead of me?" Molly asked, crestfallen. "But did you know that he saved Grecian Urn when she was in foal? He wrote the whole thing up for—"

"It's an accident, Molly, I don't even know how I happened to remember. When I was there before, pretending I had business, I told the desk I was wanted in Four-sixteen, and they told me nobody was home. Coincidence is a trick of the universe and means nothing. Good for you, for what you found, and I'll look at

213

it all when I get there. In the meantime . . . listen, Molly, this is crucial. Telephone Ophelia. Make her lie low. I'm going to do an errand on the way. When I get back, you can tell me everything. Don't worry if I'm late. The roads are impossible."

"How did you get his name?" Molly asked.

"Whose name?" Fred stood. Everything felt awful.

"The prizewinner in Four-sixteen—Lucas, Dr. Drew Lucas."

"I didn't," Fred said. "I thought I told you. But thanks. I'll call you. If Rico phones again, get rid of him."

"So listen. Here's my idea. Suppose that book you found was his? Wouldn't that fit? I've been calling but there's no answer."

"According to the clerk," Fred said, "Four-sixteen is not home."

Fred handed a ten to the parking fellow, and after Molly's Colt was whisked to him at the curb, he put the light back on top of the roof. That MD plate idea was better, more discreet.

The world had stopped trying to do much about its roads once each had a single usable lane. Apparently the money budgeted for Public Works had been exhausted, and the city councils of greater Boston had decided to wait for the spring thaw. A few patrol cars prowled, and downtown there was a taxi or two, but Fred did not spot a single plow between the Ritz and 1001 Memorial Drive, whose lot he pulled into with his lights off, sliding into a space the building's own private service had kept cleared for him.

The goddamned suit was a problem, and the funeral coat was completely out of character for what he had to do. For a man of his size, worked over with blunt instruments, moving at all within the confines of the Colt was hard. He got rid of the street shoes, ditched the wet socks, and put on the half-treads; but the rest of what he had was trouble, and the best he could do was remove the necktie, as well as the coat and jacket. He did what he could but knew he did not look the part. Still, if the person at the desk could read, he might be all right.

In blood-spattered white shirtsleeves and wearing the JIFFY

hat he'd filched from Tina's apartment on his last visit, Fred slouched into 1001 and faced the same guard he had dealt with on the last go-round. He stood at the desk for three strokes waiting for a yip of outraged recognition that did not materialize. It was as if Fred Taylor had disappeared along with the beard, and been replaced by costumes.

"I have the key," Fred told the uniform. "Can you believe, Grmfttrm tells me to drop everything, get my ass over here, and check, he's afraid he left the thing plugged in where we're working in Seven-ten."

"Nobody up there today," the desk said.

"I know. Place'll be full of smoke," Fred said. "Well, live and learn." He sauntered to the elevator with every muscle screaming at him, "Please, lie down, but not on me." He pushed the Up button and waited. After fifteen seconds, seeing the old man watching him suspiciously, he scratched his head, making the hat wobble to reinforce its message. A laughing couple walked in from outside, man and woman closing in on sixty, covered with cold brown cloth and gray hair and stamping snow off. They waved to the desk and joined Fred.

"It's going to snow," they said. "Perfectly lovely night."

Fred bobbed his JIFFY cap.

"Will you check our toilet when you're finished?" they asked.

"What number?"

The elevator doors opened, and the three of them stepped in and paused reverently before they committed themselves to a specific level of the unknown. The man of the couple pushed five. The woman said, "Five-thirteen. The thing is," she tittered and paused as the shaft sighed and gravity was defied, "the thing is, I don't know how to say this, but when you flush, it gulps, instead of whooshes. It's—it scares me. It's so eager."

The elevator stopped at the fifth floor. Fred tipped his cap. "Believe me when I tell you," he assured them.

"Five-thirteen. Smiffle," the man said. "When you're finished. We'll be there."

Fred stopped on six and made for the stairs down. "Jesus," he said. "Coincidence hell. Tina, have mercy! Molly's onto something. What the hell, as long as we're here let's take a peek into the life-style of a world-famous veterinarian."

Fred knocked, and stood at the door of 416 and listened to the empty apartment for five minutes. "Tina, have mercy," he said. Then he started working on the lock. It was basically the same as that on Tina's apartment, but with reservations and refinements. When it clicked and freed, Fred pushed against the short surprise of a chain lock, which, not wasting time in thought, he kicked through into dark stink, hooking the door closed behind him.

"Jiffy," he called into the darkness while his eyes worked to find a place in it. Someone was here after all. Someone dead.

"You've been a long time coming," a man's voice croaked.

The place was too dark, and he'd closed the door too soon. Fred's eyes were dazzled, as if he'd been smacked. The smell was the clearest thing, after the darkness; then the voice, which had come from the left. The smell was awful. It came from everywhere.

"Trouble with your lights?" Fred called cheerfully.

"Touch the lights and I shoot her," the voice croaked. "Leave."

Fred's eyes started to make sense of the layout. He'd been thrown off because it was what he expected, the same as Tina's place, only in reverse. From where he stood in the foyer, the bedrooms and bathrooms were to the right, with the kitchen also in that direction. The living room, therefore, was to the left, where the voice came from, and where a female waited to be shot when he turned on a light. What was the name Molly had given him? A movie director? Yes.

"Dr. Lucas?"

"I warned you," the voice called.

"I'm from Jiffy. We thought you were gone. The neighbors. They complained about the smell."

"There is no smell," Dr. Lucas said. "Tell them that. Now go. I am working."

Where the space around him had been black-dark, it was now dusky. Fred felt his way cautiously along the short corridor to the archway into the living room of 416. The wall of window overlooking the river was closed with both blind and curtain—must be, since there was no light in the room.

"Tina," Fred called. "Christina?"

One lamp at the far end of the couch came on—big white china lamp with oversized shade, white couch. A medium-sized man sat on it in a white dressing gown, leaning over so as to keep the muzzle of the pistol in the woman's mouth. She lay at his feet, a middle-sized woman in stained tan pants and a tweed jacket over a white shirt, her eyes bulged out and her face contorted by the metal that her mouth warmed as she breathed very quietly around it. Fred could not tell much about the face because it was mostly fear. The stained carpet was white. The woman's hands were tied in front of her with cord, the fingers rigid and swollen red. Her ankles were tied also, and her feet bare.

"Well?" the man said. He was balding. The hair on the sides of his head was too long, black going gray. His face was squarish and had been clean-shaven until a week ago, with eyebrows that were too much. He wore black shoes and corduroy pants under the dressing gown. The thing on the wall behind him was one of those pop-up strike-your-match-on-this reproductions museums sell to offset part of their overhead—this one from Monet's Custom House at Dieppe, the scene of the Allies' practice landing, where so many Canadians had been lost to German guns some forty years after Monet painted there.

"So I dropped in," Fred said. "To make sure. Tell you the truth, I figured no one was home. Thought I'd do everyone a favor, take care of the trouble before you got home from wherever."

"There is no trouble," Dr. Lucas said. He was trembling, uncomfortable hanging over that way, keeping the barrel of the gun in the woman's mouth. Her anguished eyes were both pleading and hopeless. Her bag, made of brown leather, lay on the floor near her feet. "I gave you a chance to leave. You did not take it. Now you face the consequences."

"OK," Fred said. "I'm going to sit down. I'm hurt." He walked a few slow steps and sat quietly in a white chair that could be the little brother or sister of the sofa. "Looks like you two were having an argument," he said. The man started trembling.

28

F red let a minute go by while the doctor calmed down, before asking, "Will she be quiet if you point that thing at me? See, I'm more of a threat than she is." Metal clattered against the woman's teeth, and she coughed, choking. "If she pukes, she could drown," Fred said, "which would not look good."

Dr. Lucas straightened and pointed the pistol at Fred. He could see what it was now, a Sig Sauer P220 .38. The doctor handled the thing like someone who'd read about it in a book. Still, he aimed it at Fred in a competent way, resting the weight of his arm on his thigh. His breathing was high and fast from long stress, days of it. The woman was not young, not to be taken for a student: closer to the doctor's age. Not Tina, the granddaughter. The granny had Tina salted away somewhere.

"That's better," Fred said. What name had Molly found for the doctor's wife? Donna? No. "Debbie?"

"Don't talk," the doctor warned the woman, whose eyes were saying "Yes" while the muzzle of the pistol threatened her mouth again, then swooped back to face Fred.

"It's been a terrible, terrible week," Fred told them. "Everyone's plans screwed up by all this snow. My name is Fred. Things are so close here where three people are likely to die soon, so intimate. One of us is Debbie. I'm Fred. Dr. Lucas, may I call you—what name do your friends use?"

"Drew," the woman managed.

"Quiet," the doctor ordered. "I will shoot. You know it, Deborah. Do you know it?" The woman—Debbie, Deborah— nodded. Her doctor husband, in the presence of the Miss Manners of death, had to be formal. She'd fouled herself numerous times, lying there. That was part of the smell, an informal aspect of death's ritual.

A minute slouched by. Two.

"I'm going to cross my legs," Fred warned. "Just to get comfortable. See, I've been hurt." He did that while Drew Lucas watched. Aside from their breathing, and a loud clock ticking on their mantelpiece, there was not the companionship of any sound. They listened to the clock.

"When life is over," Lucas said, then let that thought trickle away. His wife shook on the condo floor, at his feet. His words roamed the dusky room. There was no point rushing to resolve this, Fred thought, as long as his bladder held out. If it didn't hold out, he could follow Deborah's example.

"So I slightly alter my plan," Drew Lucas said. "Fred I kill first, to prevent interference. He's a wild card, which I tame. Then we proceed with the double suicide." Fred watched that one saunter by. A man who would hold his wife in this condition was serious. "Killing you will be murder," Lucas said, nodding. A telephone rang in the room somewhere, and kept ringing, eight times before it stopped. With each ring Deborah Lucas jerked, as if she were being kicked by a cruel hope with spurs. The clock ticked. Light gleamed from the glass of a framed photograph of a young man smiling, under the one lit lamp next to the doctor. It was too hot in here. The young man—boy—in the photo, had a suit coat on, and a tie.

"What brought you here?" Lucas asked.

"Just curious," Fred answered.

"I am not curious," Lucas said. "I put the question, but I am not curious. I am passing time."

Fred's chair was ten feet from the doctor's end of the couch. He could get that far and probably not be stopped by a bullet, even if he was hit, but Lucas had shown how fast he could move the gun to his wife's head.

"Jiffy," the doctor said, reading Fred's hat.

"We're painting that girl Tina's apartment, Seven-ten, where the man was killed."

Mrs. Lucas gulped. She had nothing to do but entertain mortal terror.

Lucas asked, "How many days has it been?"

"Oh well," Fred said.

"The phone rings, people knock on the door, they buzz me from the desk. I don't answer. I am invisible. I am at work. There are advantages to being an important man." He gave a bitter laugh of pitying self-congratulation.

"It's been snowing all week, Drew," Fred remarked. "Don't think I ever saw it this bad."

"One, two, three," the doctor said. "Six seconds at most to shoot three people." He thought a moment more and added, "Fred."

Fred inclined his head. His chair was too soft, and he too large for it. It was a strain to seem relaxed and keep the muscles ready to move decisively. After a while he said, "I'm going to uncross my legs. I've been hurt." He uncrossed his legs while the doctor stared, alert, and Mrs. Lucas lay rigid on the carpet. It was amazing that she was still alive. Lucas was wrestling with shame, and losing, and men don't like their wives to see that. Sometimes they'd rather put their wives out of that misery. Therefore, above the body of the wife he held hostage while she fouled herself, Dr. Lucas the prizewinner talked about double suicide.

"Drew, I'm a layman," Fred said. "I walked into something that's not my business. You can kill me, probably will kill me.

221

That's fair. But do you know what, sitting here, I can't get out of my mind?"

A silence stretched. The telephone rang eight times. "I'm not listed," Dr. Lucas said. "I'd turn the ringer off, but it reminds me I am still living." "I'm" not listed, he'd said, not "we." As far as he was concerned, his wife was already gone.

"Coagulation," Fred mused. "That's what I don't get. Can you, Drew, as a medical man, explain it?"

"You're here alone, Fred?" the doctor asked. "Just some random, who-knew-it-was-going-to-happen fluke of chance, like a three-foot snowstorm, right? That cancels my wife's plane and stops everything?"

"How did the man live so long and bleed so little?" Fred asked.

"She must not hear," Lucas said. "I'll shoot her." He trembled. "You first. Move toward us and I shoot you," Lucas added.

"I'm hurt. You can see that. Let me get this straight," Fred began. "The thing between you and the Mrs., whatever it is, that's between her and yourself. But I can't write my confession and make it stick unless—"

"Your *what*?" Lucas said. The gun wavered with his surprise and suspicion.

"About how I knocked off Miguel," Fred said. "The guy in Seven-ten? So I said, 'Well then, I'll talk to the doctor and get him to explain this thing that slows down the blood and all.' The rest of it I can fake, but that's out of my league."

"It's out of everyone's league," the doctor said, smirking. "I don't know what you're talking about."

"See, they don't want you accused of killing Miguel," Fred said. "That brings in Tina, and Tina's people don't want Tina involved. They beat the crap out of me. Then they fucking pay me. I take the fall. I say how I was jealous about Tina fucking with—"

Deborah Lucas groaned on the floor.

"Where is Christina?" Lucas asked.

"She's out of it," Fred told him. "Which is what the Colombians want. If you shoot me—don't get me wrong, Drew; you have the right to, but if you do, you mess the plan up in a big way. Do you want to hear the plan? Am I imposing? For a million dollars—"

"You drop out of the sky and tell me you are ready to . . . I want my wife out of here. Who is this Tina you're talking about? I want my wife protected."

"We'll drag her into the bathroom," Fred suggested.

"I may want to use the bathroom."

"The bedroom, then. Take her in there. Unless, is she going to scream or some damned thing?" Fred asked.

"Hold it," Lucas snarled. With a quick move he flicked the gun down and shoved it again into his wife's mouth, then dragged her by the hair, upward, until she was sitting sideways between his legs, her head tipped onto his left knee, the barrel of the gun snugged safe into her mouth.

"This is better," the doctor said. "Deborah, I wanted to spare you the shame of certain actions of mine that you might not comprehend."

"Tina's your student," Fred said. Lucas shook his head. The clock ticked. Mrs. Lucas gagged and coughed, then urinated. How long had they been like this, the two of them? The telephone rang again, eight times. The drapes covering the wall of window were an off-white tweedy Herculon-looking fabric, furry, probably boasting insulating properties. A bullet fired now might hit Fred, too, or go through Lucas's knee, as well as finishing Deborah Lucas's head.

"As I began to say," Lucas intoned, "before the fairy tale began: at the end of life, things lose their value. Fred, I don't know who you are, and I don't care. I don't ask. I see blood on you. I don't ask about the story you tried to tell, because I am not interested, whether it's true or false, or what it is. You believe, when you are in life, there is either mercy or logic in the way things are arranged."

"That old horse with the erection he couldn't explain," Fred said, "the old sick horse in the textbook. That's an example?" Mrs. Lucas sighed. Her husband's hand was steady on the trigger. "You should know this," Fred went on. "About the situation we are in: if you shoot her, I will be on you before you can get the muzzle of your weapon to a place that will hurt you enough even to land you in the hospital. You made a mistake when you took the gun off me, if your main wish is to kill yourself. That option is now closed. Given where the gun is now pointed, whether you shoot it or not, you can't swing it fast enough to put me out of action. Your choice is to kill her and see what happens to you after I take the gun away, or to try for me and see what happens. I'm in no hurry. You I will force to stay alive, if you make me act. You will lose everything *except* your life."

If there were people passing or talking in the hall, their noise did not penetrate to this room.

"One thing I might allow," Fred said. "If you cooperate, we can make this happen. It's not my business, but I don't want you to kill your wife. I might give you permission to blow your own brains out."

The three of them thought about this idea. "I'm going to cross my legs again," Fred said. "Don't be nervous." He crossed his legs.

"Another possibility," Fred said. "Maybe it has appeal. Do you want, very quietly, to drop the weapon behind the couch, then see what we can work out?"

Dr. Lucas showed nothing in his face. He'd been in apprehension and terror for more than a week, waiting for them to break down the door and arrest him for what he figured to be the crime of the century, but which was, once the florid decorations were stripped off it, going to prove just one more cheap love story.

Fred said, "Under all the window dressing the story is about an older man with thinning hair and hope, and an uncalled-for erection, who is discovered to be acting like a jerk. You couldn't get rid of the head, could you. On account of the snow? And the Mrs. coming back? The head's here somewhere. I smell it. I don't get how the painting of Jesus fit in, though," Fred said. "The painted head."

Dr. Lucas was apparently thinking of something else. Fred's observation pulled him back to the moment. "We will all die and it means nothing. It was a good experiment, a success: and it will be wasted. Funny. That boy believed I was God's punishment for what he'd done, running around with Christina and selling miracles like a carnival act. He thought I was God's agent. He begged for mercy."

"So he could talk," Fred said.

"Whisper," Lucas corrected him. "Very slowly. With the inhalation of my anesthetic, which I call Eleuthracil, everything becomes very slow." He let his voice drop and distort, like a stalled record. "Very, very slowly he begged for mercy. I kept hammering. There was no mercy. And there *is* no mercy. In all this universe, no logic and no mercy."

The woman slumped and sighed against his knee, and her eyes rolled, staring. She sensed something Fred could not see. He'd made up his mind.

"I must be strong, Deborah," Lucas advised her. "Please don't distract me."

The room was quiet. Fred was getting used to the smell, but that did not improve it. They were both expendable men, Hillegass and the fellow called Miguel, another in the blue-blazer crowd. When his head emerged out of the Lucas closet, it was going to have a short haircut and an expendable smile.

"It would be years before it could be marketed," Lucas said. There was no context for the statement.

"It isn't fair." Fred tried Terry's all-purpose line.

"And it will never be approved for use on human patients," Lucas continued.

"No," Fred agreed. "Although we see it works."

"It works. I could have done anything I wanted to him," Dr. Lucas said. "Open-heart surgery, anything."

"And yet he did not suffer," Fred said.

"No, no, he suffered." Lucas laughed. He laughed until his wife choked on the gun again. "No, he felt everything, though he was utterly immobilized, except that he could whisper. No, he suffered, I promise you. The beauty of it is . . ." His talk dwindled and halted. They listened to the clock tick and the head rot somewhere in the apartment, and the muzzle of the gun click like rosary beads against the teeth of the woman whose impending fate it was to be cruelly saved from having to witness her husband's shame.

"For a Plotkin Prize–winner," Fred said, "you are taking a long time to make up your mind." His beaten body surged with fatigue and despair, the most persuasive of all the viruses—correction: vices. "The girl's bodyguard had to die because he was sleeping with the girl who wouldn't sleep with you," Fred said. "There're so many old fools like you, Plotkin doesn't even try to award a prize in that category."

"My decision is made," Dr. Lucas said. "I will accept your offer and shoot myself." His body tensed. The room tensed. His wife quivered as if electrodes had been charged, and her head jolted back and forward. She was struggling to keep the muzzle between her teeth.

"Go easy," Fred said. "I'll tell you how I want you to do this. There's going to be one bullet fired, and you want it to go through your head clean, so you don't fuck up your suicide."

Lucas, using both hands, pried the muzzle out of his wife's mouth and raised the gun warily, vaguely in Fred's direction. Her mouth shaped a scream that she held on to.

"Too bad the world won't benefit from your discovery, but then . . . now, raise the gun as you have it in your right hand, putting the barrel against your temple—a little further back. I'm going to uncross my legs . . ."

Fred jumped. The bullet took him in the left shoulder before he could get to the hand holding the weapon and break its wrist. He heard the bones crack as the gun fell. With his good hand he

226

smacked Lucas in the face. How badly he'd been hit he could not tell, but he wasn't going to fool with this monster if there was a chance he was going to black out now. Lucas let out a great man's squeal of impotent frustration as Fred kicked him down, then stood on his broken wrist until he was sure he'd found the gun and wasn't going to black out.

29

"Sit down so you don't fall," the woman, Deborah—Mrs. Lucas—said from a bleeding mouth, her voice thick and wary. Fred tottered and let that take him onto the couch where the doctor had been sitting. Lucas himself, on the floor, groaned and scrambled until Fred kicked the wrist he'd broken and put him out. Fred's left sleeve was drenched in blood.

"They don't come up when they hear shooting?" Fred asked after some time had passed, a limbo during which the clock stopped ticking. But Fred was not going to lose consciousness or anything that mattered, just some blood. He fingered the wound. It was real, but surface: four inches of burned groove in the shoulder muscle. The doctor stirred when he spoke, or shortly after. Fred kicked his wrist again.

"They don't like to interfere," the woman said from the floor. She was answering his question, after a passage of time he could not judge. The bullet had gone somewhere, since it was not in him. The weapon didn't make sense here. Was it the dead man's? "And they keep outsiders from interfering, too. The people who live here, lots of them are famous for one thing or another, like my husband. People try to waste their time. We pay for privacy. It's one reason to live in a place like this. That and the view. Some people care about the zip code. You shot him! My God, did you shoot him?"

"*I'm* the one who's been shot. I'll get you loose in a minute," Fred said. "You all right?" She lay five feet away, where she'd rolled out of the tangle she'd been briefly involved in with her fallen prizewinning husband. She lay on her back, her feet toward Fred, her head as far as it could be from where she'd been.

She said, "I don't understand anything. Drew was supposed to be at our place in Vermont, working on the new deck. I thought that was where he was. We don't have a phone there. We like to really get away. I came back yesterday, from Dallas. It was the first train I could get, and then this! He's badly hurt. I assumed he was snowed in. Do something, he's hurt. That's his hobby, carpentry. It helps him unwind. I can't move. You can get to the phone, can't you? What do you want with us? Where's that gun?"

"I kicked it under the couch," Fred said. It was quiet and dim in here, and smelled very bad. Lucas stirred and Fred kicked his wrist.

"Don't hurt him," the woman pleaded. "I don't understand anything. What happened? When I came in, here was a stranger. Do something for him. He needs care."

"We'll find some," Fred said. "Let's get you untied first." He stood and was all right. He turned on the other lamp, so both ends of the couch matched, before he wavered across the room and found light switches to fill the room with brightness. Lucas lay still. Almost everything in the room was decorator-white. Fred, if he kept bleeding, would soon fix that.

"I'll get a knife," Fred said. He found the kitchen area, turned on lights and the exhaust fan, and found a green plastic trash bag on the counter by the sink, containing bloody clothes and too much knife. He left that where it was and settled on something smaller from a drawer.

In the living room again, he opened the curtains and raised the blind onto the gaudy battering of new snow falling, making a screen of reflecting crystals that closed the Lucases' window off from the extended view they were buying. They still had their zip code to enjoy. Then he cut cord, working with his teeth and right hand. The left he could call on if he had to.

"Let's talk before we start telephoning," Fred suggested as he began tying together the ankles of Deborah Lucas's husband, using his right hand and his teeth. The man's feet had landed in the area she'd fouled on what had become the off-white carpet. He had to force his head not to get cute and dodge away just because it was disagreeable. The doctor's uninjured left hand he tied to the belt of the pants under his bathrobe. The right hand was not going to make trouble. That done, Fred started working on the wife, moving almost in slow motion, unless he was misjudging. The clock ticked again, a good sign. He hadn't lost all that much blood.

Mrs. Lucas rolled across the room, getting as far as possible from the place she'd spent the last twenty-four hours or more.

"Sorry to be so awful," she apologized. "Poor Drew. I didn't know, didn't see what was happening to him." She began shaking so hard that Fred, in order to get her ankles loose without cutting her, had to sit with them on his lap and hold them still with his left forearm.

"Your husband killed a man upstairs, did he tell you? He needs a lawyer and all that. Let's sit you up and work on your hands."

They leaned her against the wall between the fireplace and a whatnot cabinet holding white plaster busts and blown-glass objects and, for those color accents, seven stone eggs in seven colors. Fred made her rest her hands in his lap while he sawed at the cord between her wrists, and the rest of her shook.

"I'm awful. I must change," she said. "I know we must get him taken care of, but I'm awful. I don't know you. You say he killed someone, but I don't know. That will be for his lawyers to decide. There's no reason you should know this, working with Jiffy, but my husband is an important man. He saved the life of Grecian

Urn when she was in foal. He had an appointment from the Queen of England."

The cords parted and the woman's hands fell free. Lucas had not tied them well. The whole business unraveled once the right knot was cut. The hands were swollen and stiff.

"The guy's important, but not smart," Fred said. "After he killed his man, he fooled around with so much decoration, trying to make it look like a drug hit or a cult revenge, that he lost any prayer of projecting a coherent story."

"When I can walk, as soon as I can walk, I'll wash. Next . . . ," Deborah Lucas began. "What time is it?"

"Nine-thirty? Ten?" Fred said.

"Morning or night?"

"Night. Tuesday night," Fred said. "The problem is, Mrs. Lucas, this whole apartment is, they will argue, evidence in a crime. Two crimes, if we count what he was doing to you."

"I don't care. Before I see the world, I must change. People in this building know me. They are not going to see me in this state," she said, pulling herself upright. "Your name is Fred?"

"What I suggest is," Fred said, "I happen to know an empty apartment three floors up. The lab people won't want us in the bathroom here. My guess is you don't want to see it anyway. It was—do you prefer 'Deborah' or 'Mrs. Lucas'?"

"Deborah's fine. Let's be informal. You mean the girl's apartment, don't you? My husband's awake. We're getting help for you, honey."

When she stood, Fred rose to stay with her. He started undoing the shirt that had been white, so as to rip a bandage out of it in case she could help him, but that could wait. "What we'll do," Fred said, "is we'll go up and borrow that apartment to clean up and telephone—that's a cellular phone you have over there? We'll take it. We can't waste time. You don't want . . . I'll get what you need from your bedroom."

"My suitcase is there. Take a shirt of my husband's so you won't attract attention in the hallways and elevator. I hang them

231

in the closet. He won't mind. Drew, we're leaving for a few minutes, then we'll take care of you. I'm all full of weewee."

Fred said, "While I'm in the bedroom, Mrs. Lucas . . ."

" 'Deborah,' please."

"While I'm in the bedroom, it would be a big mistake to, one, untie your husband, or, two, shoot him."

"He is a danger to himself until we get him into care. Didn't you see he tried to kill himself?"

Fred noticed more plastic bags in the bedroom closet, but nothing stood out as the specific cause of the charnel stench. That seemed to be under the bed. He located a red flannel shirt and a loose jacket he might get over it. He'd start shivering in a while and wouldn't be of much use to anyone unless he could be warm.

"We might as well use Drew's secret key to that girl's apartment," Deborah said when he dragged her black metal suitcase into the living room and laid it down. Lucas was staring and silent, his wife still standing where Fred had left her. "He keeps it with his secret papers, under the carpet—his secret Swiss bank account I don't know about and all that. As you said, he loves making everything so complicated, because he's smarter than everyone else. It entertains him. He may be smarter than everyone, but *I* snoop. Help me move these shelves."

They moved the whatnot cabinet. While Drew Lucas kicked and remained speechless, his wife turned back a flap of carpet and removed a large manila envelope, which she dropped into her bag after withdrawing a door key. From her suitcase she took a folded yellow robe that she put on over her clothes, as well as a pair of slippers. She picked up her purse, dropped the telephone into it, and told Fred, "Let's go. I must be awful. You mind carrying the suitcase?"

JIFFY had done nothing more to Tina's place. Fred persuaded Deborah to bandage his shoulder with a temporary patch, then squeezed into the doctor's shirt again and prowled. Deborah, still shaking but doing her best to retrieve some dignity, told him she needed twenty minutes alone. It was impossible to judge, from her demeanor, how much she knew of what had happened here. The living-room floor was covered with tarpaulins, most of them clear plastic, but some of them canvas drop cloths that could be reused. These were spattered with a variety of off-whites. The walls in this room were to be repainted in the same off-beige flat latex, whose worrying, lethal smell as it dried would replace the odor of burned hands. The china dogs from the mantel, like the other movables from in here, must be under the heap of covered furniture in the middle of the room.

"No one would fake Jane Peterson," Fred said. "It can't be." He was stiff and sore and preoccupied and hung up and responsible, and his shoulder flamed. The shoulder should be, as they called it, "looked at." He burrowed under the tarpaulin until he found the painting of zinnias; he pulled it out and looked it over. It was still a dumb picture. As a work of art, it fell within Ophelia's generic classification *Dork*. It was the real thing, though, dumb but honest: as dumb as Fred was, and maybe more honest. It was what he'd come for. He'd either sell it or hang it in the front room of the house in Charlestown: the place could use some color.

Fred listened a moment at the door of a bathroom loud with falling water. "Those bastards owe me," Fred said, and he wrapped the painting in a canvas drop cloth.

"I found it," he told the desk guard, carrying the large package past him. "Be right back," he promised.

Deborah Lucas was in the bedroom, talking on her telephone, sitting on Tina's bed and reflected in Tina's mirror: a middle-sized lady with wet brown hair going gray, in a gray dress, talking tough. She looked up when Fred entered, and said, "Hold on, the maintenance man just came in," then waited until Fred excused himself.

"Put the key back where it was," Fred told her when she joined him in the apartment's foyer. She'd made a parcel out of a plastic drop cloth, with her soiled clothes in it. "The rest of what's in that envelope, I never saw. It's not my business. But the key, they have to find that, is that a deal? Wipe it. We don't want them confused about fingerprints. No fingerprints is bad, but ours are worse."

"Alden has to be with him when they come," Deborah Lucas said, wiping the key with the hem of her gray skirt and wrapping it in a paper from her purse. "I'm going to say—fortunately, with this snow, Alden couldn't go out tonight. It's just good fortune. Alden, the lawyer, wants me to say I washed and changed in his apartment. It's better that we were not in the girl's apartment. I'll pay you. Do you mind?"

"Was I in the lawyer's apartment with you? If so, I'd better meet him."

"No, you claimed you were going somewhere to call the police," Deborah said. "If you do call them, I'll probably see you later, Mr. . . . Fred. God, this is awful. I don't know how awful it is. It's too awful to know."

"I take it the lawyer's in this building," Fred said. "You want me to stick with you until you get there?"

"I'll make it down a flight. Give me ten minutes, then call. Let's get out of here. I'll send you money."

Fred tossed his cap into the kitchen as they stepped into the hallway. She carried her clothing, and Fred the suitcase. "I should thank you," she said. "I mean, that's why I said money. A tip, Alden said."

"Send it to me at Jiffy," Fred suggested as they waited for the elevator. "I'll walk down. Or no, my tip—when you see a home-less person, give *him* the tip. That's better. Or her."

"Funny how you bump into a person you never heard of," she said, "and they're a little piece of a whole story you don't have time for. I often think that. Whatever the story is, I probably don't want to know it anyway."

Fred drove five minutes through heavy white weather and found a Japanese restaurant on Fresh Pond in whose foyer he could lean against the wall and, by investing a quarter, talk to the Cambridge

Police Department and worry them until they gave him Dolores Cipriani's home number. This was complex, and it needed speed. Fred was next to the coats; there weren't many of them, but they all smelled like wet dogs, on account of the snow outside. Cipriani's phone rang.

"Dolores Cipriani."

"Fred Taylor. We talked before. Credit this to Ernie Book-rajian, will you? I've got your killer on Mem Drive. No, hold on, I don't need to hear you, you need to listen to me, OK? I'm hurt. I've got to get patched. Are we recording, or do you have a pencil?"

"Both. Hurry, then."

"The guy's in Four-sixteen, same building on Mem Drive. Dr. Drew Lucas. With his wife and his lawyer. The victim, you'll learn, was attached to the group that killed Hillegass, in Boston, at the Hotel Brittannee. His name was Miguel. Don't interrupt. The mother of Carlos Gato, the Colombian—no, listen, I'm hurt and you don't have time—the group is heavily armed. Three men I saw, and there may be others. Semiautomatic assault weapons and sidearms. Fortnum Street in Brookline, number Thirty-seven, single-family. These people are serious trouble, don't underestimate them. You want FBI, Treasury, all that. You've got lots to do. Meanwhile, I'm going to get patched up. Call me if you have to at the number you have in Arlington, otherwise . . . you'll need me to make sense of this. I'll come in tomorrow, we'll do lunch."

He hung up and watched the young woman behind the bar pick her teeth with a MasterCard. She wore a black dress, Asian style. She could command him a pot of tea while he made more calls, and while Dolores Cipriani sent a squad car for him. Cipriani was at this moment reading back the pay-phone number he'd called from, getting someone to pinpoint its location.

He bought aspirins from the lady at the bar and ate them as he went out into the weather again, eased into the Colt, and started driving along Route 2. The snow was thick, but without much wind. It was just settling in. It and everyone knew this was how it was going to be from here on.

He should call Clay, but Clay was not secure. Lavinia, possibly from Clay's house, had called the Colombians' agent to complain that the two sample paintings from the list were duds. In any case, there was no rush to tell Clayton anything. It either was or might as well be true that the paintings in question, those ninety "Old Masters," were in a bank vault in Switzerland. The Colombians had foolishly bought an option to see them, but that was all they had. Lavinia Randall Whitman had undertaken to broker the option for them. At the same time, she had tried to infiltrate herself into the big sale the Colombians were trying to get out of, adding her own ten-million-dollar commission to the selling price being asked by the owner in Zurich (or Nairobi or Bangladesh). Her hope had been to get near enough to the action, with a willing mark in tow. If she failed, she would be out only a couple of phone calls. She'd be better off than her competition, Hillegass, who'd lost much more.

No, let Clayton and Lavinia enjoy their Monopoly for one more evening, enjoy their hot milk and cookies and step into their—perish the thought of a singular noun here—beds.

30

Molly made him come up to her bedroom and strip to prove to her he was alive. He wanted to sit in the kitchen and drink tea. After he was allowed to dress again, they found Terry and Sam huddled in the hallway outside Molly's door, worried and upset.

"Fred's fine," Molly told them. "He'll tell you everything tomorrow. Now get lost. It's snowing like crazy, and we're all going to be stuck together for months, like the Donner Party."

"We're going to have a Donner party?" Terry asked.

"Terry, I've told you a thousand times to take off your clothes and put on pajamas. Now do it!" She had Fred by the right arm. They'd put him in the big red sweater, which was warm. The lot of them being jammed in the upstairs hall, the kids now started making rebellious noises.

"One thing before Molly and I go downstairs," Fred said. "Terry, driving out of Cambridge through the snow and all, and trying to stay awake, I thought of an answer to your riddle. You'll think it's strange. But I've been working on it."

"Oh, God," Sam exploded with disgust. "Just when she was

forgetting about it." He stormed into his room and slammed the door.

"I did not forget about it. What did you guess, Fred?"

"Pretend you're me. I ask you the riddle, and you say, 'I don't know.' Ready?"

"You're not gonna guess."

"Why is Roger Clemens like a TV set?"

"I don't know," Terry answered. "I give up."

"Because I said them both," Fred said. "Get it? I said 'Roger Clemens,' and then I said—"

"Mom, I hate you!" Terry screamed, and she stormed into her room, slamming the door.

They sat in Molly's kitchen and drank tea while Molly bawled him out and asked questions, and while they waited for Dolores Cipriani to call, or any of the army of the law she might have passed this number to. "Tomorrow I make Ophelia un-forward her calls back to Lincoln," Molly said. "By the way, Rico says, 'OK for you, Ms. Finger, you miss you beeg chance in you life.' The life that girl leads! No wonder she runs through a new secretary every three months. The kids, when there's nothing on TV, sit around the answering machine listening to Ophelia's voicemail. But it's been quiet since midnight, which is when Brenda Rufus, from the CCC, called with six more miracles caused by the Holy Face on the front page of the *Herald*. Terry's never going to believe I didn't tell you the answer to that riddle."

"I feel bad," Fred said. "I never imagined it could be the right answer. All I thought was, I looked so terrible, and they were so apprehensive and excited, I'd reassure them that I'd been think-ing about them the whole time."

"And now, for your reward, she's mad at me," Molly said. "And her faith is undermined forever because I lied when I denied I'd given her secret to the enemy."

"Opponent."

"OK."

They listened to the snow falling. It made not a sound. Arlington was quiet. Shortly before three, Molly said, "She won't call now. If they want you, they'll look at their watches, and the weather, and decide to put it off until seven. What shall we do, go to bed or go outside and make snow angels?"

"To tell you the truth, I'm feeling sort of gloomy," Fred said.

"I did not notice," Molly told him. "Bed, then?"

"Also, I feel bad for Bookrajian. Both of them. The problem is, if I lie down and let sleep come, I'll sweat and scream," Fred said. "At times like this, some old ghosts get shaken loose and worry at me. You go on. I'll sit in the kitchen. Turn off the ringer upstairs so you won't listen for Dolores."

"You sure?" Molly rose from the table and bent her head next to his so he could whisper if there was something to whisper.

"Sure," Fred whispered.

After she'd gone, he extinguished the lights downstairs and stared out the windows, one after another, all around the ground floor. Molly's house was bigger than the world outside it, but even so, it was a mere skin away from a blathering profusion of meaningless beauty that was more snow blundering into the path he'd shoveled yesterday and covering the cars again. What kind of monster would speak of a house as a trap, even as a joke? Trouble would find you anywhere. Fred sat at the table in the dark kitchen and put his head down.

He looked at his watch when the phone rang at almost four, and allowed the rings to click in to Ophelia's message. He stood over the machine in the living room, which was still lit only by the snow outside and the light it carried from the streetlights. ". . . Please leave your message," Ophelia's recorded voice finished.

"This is for Ophelia Finger." A woman's voice. "You gave me your card? In the march? You don't know me. Then I got this number from Brendan Rufus? CCC? I want to report something.

239

Stop, Ernie!" Laughter. "I said I would, and I will. Stop it, Ernie. I'm going to. . . . They said I have cancer in both my breasts? And now, we got the new tests back? No, I'm going to finish! It's just a machine, who'd be awake? And the new tests say they don't. My breasts, I mean. The first tests were false positive. I'm all right. We're celebrating, in case we sound . . ." Hilarity. "It's bad for the baby, I know it is, all this champagne, but what the hell! I'm going to be bad for this baby for eighty more years! OK, OK, Ernie. I won't say who this is."

Fred was on his way to the kitchen when a furtive sound on the stairs made him tremble and break into a sweat.

"Fred?" came Terry's voice.

"It's all right," Fred said. "Go to sleep, Terry."

"I heard voices."

"A message for Ophelia."

"What did they want?"

"They had good news."

Terry came down the last steps and followed him toward the kitchen. He sat again where he had been. He should send her upstairs. She stood in the doorway, wearing her blue pajamas with cowboys all over them, on horseback, with guns and lariats.

"I need your honest opinion about whether this cereal is fake," Terry said.

Fred studied a moment before he admitted, "I'm lost."

"The Frosti-Glos you bought me. I keep them in my room, and every night I eat one. It's almost been a week. Are they working?"

Fred took his time looking at the child glowing against all the darkness in the world. "I guess so," he told her. "I can even make out the cowboys."

"Ha! Then Sam owes me five dollars."

Fred did not sleep, but he did dream, a brief but tedious dream with Clayton in it. It was summer, full of birds and leaves. He and

240

Clay were walking on Charles Street, caught up in a ragged parade of dorks who sang, not well, a scrap of music stolen from Bach's *Passion of Saint Matthew*.

"Great Heavens!" Clay muttered. "Listen to them! Is nothing sacred?"